LINEAR TACTICAL SERIES

PHOENIX

USA TODAY BESTSELLING AUTHOR
JANIE CROUCH

PHOENIX: LINEAR TACTICAL (Adventurer's Edition with Bonus
Epilogue)

*This book is dedicated to Megan
Aka: Trouble Twin*

*Names have been changed to protect the guilty, but everyone knows half
the material in this book is taken from our shenanigans.*

*It requires a special kind of stupid to do the stuff we do. I'm just glad
I've got a bestie who's as dumb as me.*

*Here's to all the adventures left to come.
We're just getting started, baby!*

Chapter 1

"Frankfurt Airport is paging Mr. Eugene Harrison. Please come to the international terminal security office located near baggage claim."

Riley Harrison tightened his well-worn backpack strap more securely over his shoulder as the announcement repeated itself.

He stopped and raised an eyebrow at his two traveling companions. They'd just gotten off a flight from Spain and were only at the Frankfurt Airport a couple hours before connecting to Sri Lanka.

"Something I need to know about? There a reason Frankfurt Airport security is paging me when I've only been in the terminal for five minutes?"

Riley had been in trouble with multiple governments numerous times over the course of his career as an adventure and extreme sport athlete. Ten years of traveling all over the world to participate in and film adventure events and stunts had not always made the governments happy. Especially when Riley had sometimes used his celebrity status—ten million YouTube followers strong—to try to effect some sort of change in the countries he traveled to.

Michelle McGinty, Riley's longtime producer, pointed a thumb in Damon's direction. "Dumbass over here had a different girl in his bed every night while we were in Spain. Wouldn't surprise me if one of them was married or an international spy."

Damon held up his hands. "Hey, having a good time isn't illegal in Europe." He frowned. "Wait, is it?"

Damon Sullivan could ride circles around people on a skateboard, was willing to BASE jump from heights most people considered reckless, and was the top-rated stunt hang glider in the world—way better than Riley could ever hope to be. But Damon wasn't ever going to be called a mental giant.

Michelle rolled her eyes. "No, not keeping it in your pants isn't illegal in Europe, sadly."

Damon looked decidedly relieved as he opened a bag of mixed nuts. The tall, slender man was always snacking on something. "At least they used your middle name."

Riley rolled his eyes. "I doubt my full name would cause any riots."

Maybe a few fans might have recognized his name if they'd paged him by Riley Harrison, but probably not even then.

Phoenix, on the other hand... Yeah, he was much more recognizable by that name. Phoenix was the person people turned out in droves for to watch perform all sorts of ridiculous stunts. And even more watched—and rewatched—him online.

But Eugene Harrison? Eugene wasn't even on his passport, so security wouldn't have known it. There were only a few people in the world who knew his middle name.

One of whom he was pretty desperate to see. Was always pretty desperate to see.

He tilted his head toward the baggage claim sign. "Let's go see what trouble we're in."

Riley picked up the pace. He was already familiar with Frankfurt Airport—hell, he was familiar with almost every major airport in the world—so he knew where they were headed.

The gate agent working the counter in front of the office gave them a brief nod, obviously expecting them. She opened the door to the small office. Riley bit back his disappointment at the sight of the two men behind the table.

"Damn, Wyatt, look at Boy Riley's crestfallen face," Gavin Zimmerman said. "I think he was legitimately hoping we were security."

Riley grinned and shook his head. "More like legitimately hoping you were Girl Riley. I'm not ashamed to admit it."

Both men came around the table and hugged Riley. Gavin Zimmerman and Wyatt Highfield were founding partners of Linear Tactical and Riley's good friends.

Linear Tactical was a survival and defense training company that operated out of Oak Creek, Wyoming. Groups —both civilian and law enforcement—came from all over the country to train there. Groups came because of the facilities and equipment Linear had available, but also to work with the former Green Berets who made up most of the company's employees, including these two men.

Linear Tactical taught everything from wilderness survival, to self-defense, to situational awareness, to weapons training. They were known as some of the best in the world.

But training wasn't the only thing they did. And Riley knew that's why Gavin and Wyatt were here.

The *other stuff* Linear Tactical did.

Michelle and Damon gave Gavin and Wyatt a wave from the door as the guys sat back down.

"I'm just glad to see you're not the morality police," Damon said.

Michelle narrowed her eyes at Damon. "You do know that the morality police is not an actual law enforcement unit, right?"

Riley raised an eyebrow at Gavin as Michelle and Damon bickered—per usual. "Speaking of law enforcement, Germany's a long way out of your jurisdiction, Sheriff."

Gavin shrugged. "Sheriff Nelson is temporarily back in the office to see how it goes with his health. I volunteered to help Wyatt, so I'm out of the sheriff's hair. Nelson doesn't need the temporary sheriff hanging around while he decides what he wants to do."

Wyatt's nod was solemn. They were obviously here for business.

Michelle picked up on that too. "How about if Einstein and I go grab a bite to eat? I have a feeling our plans are about to change anyway."

Riley nodded. "I'll catch up with you in a few minutes."

He turned back to Gavin and Wyatt once the door closed, and they all sat down around the small table. "You guys know I have a phone, right? You don't have to fly halfway around the world just to talk to me."

"But then we wouldn't get to see your pretty face." Wyatt grabbed his tablet and punched in a code. "How are you at sandboarding?"

The sport—which was basically snowboarding, but on sand—had been rising in popularity in recent years. It was always going to be limited because its geographic parameters, the need for sand and hills, meant it could only be pursued in certain locations.

Riley leaned back in his chair. "Not as good as I am at

snowboarding, but better than I am at, let's say, ballroom dancing. Why? What's going on?"

Gavin crossed his arms over his chest. "We know you have a couple of days off before Sri Lanka. We were hoping you'd consider doing an unscheduled stunt stop in Egypt."

Riley nodded. He already knew why the guys were here —not the specifics, but in general. And it had nothing to do with stunts.

Wyatt Highfield had been head of Linear Tactical's kidnapping and corporate security division for as long as Riley had known him. Whereas most of the Linear team lived at the home base in western Wyoming, teaching survival intelligence to civilians, Wyatt had been floating around for years, going wherever he was needed.

Wyatt was amazing at what he did. He'd gained the nickname *Scout* in the Special Forces for a reason. He was able to read and defuse ugly situations. It had made him invaluable in ransom negotiations. And if things turned south, Wyatt had an innate skill for handling things quickly and quietly. He never drew attention to himself. But he almost always got the job done—and kidnap victims home.

If Wyatt was here, the situation was dire, and they needed Riley's help. This wasn't the first time they'd met in a tiny office somewhere.

Because of his profession and notoriety, Riley sometimes had access to places others couldn't get into easily.

"Egypt." Riley sat back and bridged his fingers together. "I'm assuming you guys have developed some sort of sand fetish and have decided to stalk me, looking for a private sandboarding show."

Gavin chuckled. "Duh. That's a given. We can work out terms later." He tapped the electronic tablet again, then spun it so Riley could see the picture. "This is Andre Barton and his cousin Josh. Americans, both twenty-one. We believe both are currently being held by Sayed El Kadi—an international businessman, suspected terrorist, and local Egyptian tyrant—at his big-ass house-slash-compound about fifty miles outside of Cairo. Dude is a real bastard."

Wyatt leaned back in his chair, rubbing his hand across his face. "Normally, we'd go the usual kidnap and rescue—K and R—route, see if Sayed made ransom demands, and work from there. But Andre is the son of a US ambassador. Went into the country despite being told not to. Relations between the US and Egypt are tenuous at best. We are being brought in to see if this can be handled off the record."

"Are you sure the kid and his cousin are still alive?"

Wyatt nodded. "My best sources say yes. But a snatch and grab isn't an option. Sayed's huge property is walled, well-guarded, and fortified. Basically impossible to get into without help from the inside or a full military assault. So we need you."

This was good. Maybe it would take his mind off the fact that yesterday, Wildfire—a.k.a. *Girl Riley* to the people of Oak Creek, *love of his life* to him—had canceled their scheduled video chat for tomorrow.

Long distance had been part of their relationship from the beginning—his profession required a lot of travel. But they'd both been committed to making it work, and it had worked very successfully for three years. Audio calls, video calls, text, chats, letters, visits—whatever either of them needed, they did it.

But for the past couple of weeks, Wildfire had been... distant. Their chats had been sporadic, her text responses shorter and shorter. And tomorrow, the first day he was going to be in a location with strong enough Wi-Fi for a video chat, she'd canceled, saying she had to *work*.

Yeah.

He wasn't calling her a liar, but he wasn't calling her a truther either.

So whatever crazy stunt Wyatt and Gavin needed him for to help Andre and Josh—Riley still wasn't sure what sandboarding had to do with it—he was in. At the very least it would take his mind off what was happening, or *not* happening, seven thousand miles away.

"Okay, how can I help?"

"Kendrick worked his computer voodoo in Oak Creek and was able to hack some of Sayed's files." Wyatt typed something into the tablet again. "Nothing exceptionally useful, but when we saw that he was into some adventure sports, we immediately thought of you."

"Let me guess, sandboarding?"

Gavin nodded. "Yes. But mostly FMX is his thing. He has his own FMX course inside his compound."

Freestyle motocross. It wasn't Riley's specialty, but he could hold his own. He didn't compete, but he'd done some stunts on his bike over the years. They were some of his most popular online videos.

"We're hoping you could put the word out on social media that you're making a last-minute trip into Cairo and hoping to do some sandboarding," Wyatt said. "That usually draws your fanboys, and according to his internet search history, Sayed is one."

"Even if he comes out to join me, he's not going to bring his prisoners."

Wyatt shrugged. "Your presence in Cairo will be a big deal to him. We think if you make it known you'd like to do some FMX while you're in town, Sayed will issue an invitation. We'll tag along as part of your crew and bust Andre and Josh out while you're wowing Sayed with your FMX sills."

"Doesn't sound too difficult."

Gavin glanced at Wyatt, then leaned onto the table with his forearms. "Phoenix, listen. We're not kidding about the government wanting to keep this quiet. We're here without backup. If we get caught, things will get ugly pretty damn quick. Sayed is known for being old-school brutal on his enemies."

Wyatt nodded. "As in, *ancient Egyptian* old-school brutal. The locals are terrified of him."

"So you're asking me to get invited into a known psychopath's house and distract him with my wit and good looks while you break out two kids who should've never been in the country to begin with, knowing we have no backup and are going to die horribly if we're caught."

Wyatt and Gavin glanced at each other, then both nodded. "Pretty much," Wyatt said.

"This is the worst plan ever." Riley leaned back in his chair and stretched his tattoo-covered arms up over his head. "When's our flight?"

Chapter 2

Riley and his team had traveled to Egypt several times over the past eight years. He and Damon had gone hang gliding over the pyramids of Giza and scuba diving in the Red Sea. Damon had even attempted a crazy Jet Ski stunt in the Nile River—which had ended with him crashing into the riverbed and breaking his collarbone.

Denied by De Nile. They'd teased him about it for weeks.

Damon and Michelle hadn't come to Egypt this time. They'd have a couple days off, then Riley would meet them in Sri Lanka.

Hopefully.

The sandboarding plan was both working and not working. Working, because his social media call had been answered in droves. Dozens of sandboarders, mostly teenage boys, and probably a hundred spectators had joined Riley at the posted time and location. Sayed's name had already been mentioned more than once. It was only a matter of time until he showed up.

Where the plan wasn't working was in how it was supposed to stop him from thinking about Girl Riley. He was supposed to be video chatting with her right about now, rather than getting desert sand in places he'd rather not think about. A couple of weeks ago she'd been messaging him about what color she was about to dye her hair this time—blue currently leading the race—and then something had changed.

Everything had changed.

And hell if Riley knew what or why.

He swerved to the left and pulled up into an unintentional half-cab 180-degree spin as some teenage kid cut into his path.

Riley wasn't sure if the cutoff had been an accident or on purpose. Both happened, sometimes because someone didn't know what they were doing, or sometimes because someone wanted to show off in front of the big dogs. Riley tried to take it all in stride.

The natives out here with him weren't so kind, yelling at the kid in Arabic, obviously upset with what he'd done. That was what usually happened if Riley just let it go. The sports world, even the extreme sports world, policed itself.

Riley added a mule kick near the bottom of the dune, a more basic stunt derived from skateboarding, then slid to a stop near a group waiting to catch a dune buggy back up the sand dune. Someone handed him a water bottle, which he opened and gulped.

"You going to yell at me too?"

Riley glanced to the side to find the boy who'd cut him off. Probably fifteen or sixteen years old. At least he was speaking in English so Riley could understand him.

"No. You either did it by accident or you did it on purpose."

The kid side-eyed him. "Which do you think it was?"

Kid had a high-end board, but it was well used. His moves had been pretty decent for the three hours they'd been at it. He knew what he was doing. "I'd say on purpose. You're both skilled enough and smart enough to have spun out of my way if you'd wanted to."

The kid nodded but didn't say anything.

"What's your name?" Riley finished the water bottle.

"Omar."

"You've definitely got some skills, Omar."

The kid loosened up a little bit. "We practice a lot."

Maybe this kid knew how they could get in touch with Sayed. "How about FMX? Any of that around here?"

Omar's eyes lit up. Perfect. This is when Riley's reputation would come in handy. "Yes. I'm better at FMX than sandboarding. You want to ride?"

Riley shrugged. He had to play this cool. "I'm always up for a great course, but sometimes it doesn't work out for me to do public courses. Somebody cuts me off with a sandboard and I can recover pretty quickly. Somebody cuts me off on a motocross bike…"

Omar grimaced and shook his head. "Sorry I cut you off. That was stupid. But I know the perfect FMX course. It's a private course owned by Mr. El Kadi. He's also a great rider."

Bingo.

Riley glanced over at Wyatt and Gavin, who were chatting with some of the locals while also keeping an eye on what was going on with Riley. He gave them a slight nod.

"Why don't you see if your friend Mr. El Kadi would be open for me and my team to come over? No filming. We'll keep it casual."

The kid had a smart phone in his hands ten seconds later, talking excitedly, this time in Arabic to whoever was on the other line. Riley hoped it was Sayed.

He wandered over to Gavin and Wyatt. "My friend

Omar over there knows somebody who has a private FMX course. Thought we might check it out."

Immediately the locals Gavin and Wyatt had been talking to started gushing about Sayed and his course.

It was setting up to be the perfect cover.

"Sounds like a great location to me," Wyatt said.

Omar came running up. "Mr. El Kadi says he would be honored to have you at his home to ride his course. He looks forward to personally challenging you."

Riley slapped the kid on the back. "That can definitely be arranged."

The crowd dispersed, and they all started packing up as the sun began to set behind the dunes. Riley kept up an easy banter with Omar and the other riders coming with them to Sayed's house. Wyatt and Gavin kept their heads down and helped pack things up like they were part of the crew.

Riley got into the small van with Wyatt and Gavin. They followed the other vehicles, forming a caravan heading to Sayed's estate.

The guys got Kendrick on the line once they had privacy.

"Update us, Blaze. We're heading into Sayed's compound." Gavin put his phone on speaker and set it next to him as Wyatt drove.

"Satellite footage shows two infrared signatures in the cellar near the barn. My spidey senses are telling me that's our boys."

"Security cameras?" Wyatt asked.

"Tons, but all pointing toward the outside. Once you're inside their walls, security cameras aren't really a problem. Roving armed guards on the other hand…" Kendrick sighed from his end of the phone. "I sometimes feel like a broken record saying this to you Linear guys, but you're going in there outgunned and outmanned. If things go to shit, you're going to be in trouble."

"Then we won't let them go to shit," Wyatt said.

Kendrick sighed again. "If the guards follow the pattern of the past few days, they're only checking on the prisoners once a day. So they shouldn't even notice they're gone until tomorrow—plenty of time for you to make it to Cairo and out of the country."

"Sayed might suspect you had something to do with it," Gavin said to Riley.

Riley shrugged. "I'm going to be with the guy the entire time, riding bikes. Based on his invitation, not my request. So he'll hardly be able to accuse me of anything when I'm kicking his ass at motocross."

"Just keep him riding until as close to ten p.m. as possible." Wyatt caught Riley's eye in the rearview mirror. "Like you're having the time of your life and want to stay until the last possible minute. So that when we do finally go, we have an excuse to drive like a bat out of hell toward the airport."

Riley nodded. "You guys just be sure to have them in the van by then."

"Charter jet is ready, along with private security screening," Kendrick said. "As long as you guys make it out of the compound and to the airport, you'll be fine."

They disconnected the call as the caravan pulled up to the gate.

The guard recognized Riley and was a fan, so Riley chatted with him for a few minutes—which was what he would do in a normal situation, and because it didn't hurt to build up some goodwill—before they made their way inside.

"Good luck, you guys," he murmured as they parked next to the huge house and he opened the door. "Keep safe."

"You too, brother," Wyatt said.

Omar rushed over to Riley, alternating between gushing

and playing it cool as only a teenager could. They all walked around the house toward the bike course.

It was already dark outside, but the industrial, stadium-strength lights provided more than enough illumination. Riley let out a whistle now that he could see the course clearly. Impressive.

"See?" Omar was grinning, obviously delighted that Riley was impressed. "I told you. I told you Mr. El Kadi has the best course, maybe in the entire country."

"Omar." A voice rang out behind them. "Our American friend has eyes. Let him judge for himself."

Riley turned and found a dark-skinned man, definitely of Egyptian descent, in his late forties, and already dressed in motorbike-riding garb. "Mr. Harrison, I am Sayed El Kadi. *Salām 'alaykum*. Welcome to my home."

"Hell of a course you've got here." Riley shook the man's hand.

He smiled. "That's because I'm a hell of a rider."

Riley grinned. He was never going to be friends with a kidnapper tied to terrorists, but he could respect someone who knew his own strengths. Although the man looked more like a businessman than a motocross rider. "What a coincidence, so am I."

"Then shall we have a little go at my course? You can change clothes in here." He pointed to a small building.

Riley was changed and on the bike they'd rented in Cairo in no time. Sayed hadn't been lying about his FMX abilities. He was good. And in riding the course purely for speed, especially with home-field advantage, he was even better than Riley.

But when it came to stunts and showing off, Riley had him beat hands down.

Riley knew how to work the crowd, knew how to perform stunts. After all, they'd gotten him millions of views on YouTube. Riley knew what flips looked harder than they actually were, and that a fall every now and again made everything seem much more dangerous and immediate.

For three hours, Riley made sure the attention was on him while doing his best not to irritate his host too much. Sayed didn't like to be beat and was used to being the best rider on the course.

Riley didn't have to downplay his own skills nearly as much as he would've thought. Sayed was that good.

Meanwhile, Riley trusted Gavin and Wyatt to get the job done. Because there was nothing he could do to help them besides play ringmaster at the circus.

He kept track of every minute, but as it neared ten p.m., he acted like he was caught by surprise. "Holy shit, Sayed, I've got to go. I'm barely going to make it back to Cairo for my flight, and I've got to be in Sri Lanka tomorrow."

Sayed took a sip of his water, as did Riley. Both of them had their hair matted to their heads from the sweat under the helmets.

"No, stay. Eat with us. I insist. Then we'll have another few goes at the track and see if you can finally beat me in a speed test. I'll personally escort you and your friends to the airport tomorrow and you can take my private jet to your next location."

Riley smiled tightly. This was an unexpected offer. If Riley hadn't known Sayed was a terrorist asshole, he might have taken the older man up on his offer. "I can't."

"Come on, Phoenix. Since when have you ever turned down a challenge in order to make a flight?" This came from one of the other guys who'd been hanging out and riding with them all day. Someone who thought he knew Riley because he'd watched all the Phoenix videos over and over.

He didn't know Riley.

But, then again, in this case, the guy wasn't incorrect.

Riley would never back down from a challenge like this just to make a flight. Of course, Sayed didn't need to know that.

Riley shot the guy an easy smile before turning to Sayed. "I hate to sound like anybody's mother, but my team and I have responsibilities in Sri Lanka."

Sayed gave Riley a smile of his own. "How about we race for it? If you beat me in a speed test on the course, you go tonight on your flight. If I win, you stay until tomorrow."

Turning this down would draw much more attention than they could afford. Riley took another sip of his water and winked at Sayed. "You got yourself a deal."

Cheers lit up all around them. Riley still didn't see Gavin or Wyatt. He sure as hell hoped they had Andre and cousin Josh already in the van.

Riley hadn't been able to beat Sayed in a speed test on the course. If he didn't do it now, they were going to have to think way outside the box on how to get out of here.

"I'm not going to take it easy on you just because you've been a great host." Riley kept an easy smile plastered on his face as they walked over to their bikes.

"You wouldn't be in the record books for so many different sports if you did." Sayed grabbed the helmet off the handlebars. "I know why you're here, Phoenix."

Oh shit. "Is that so?"

"I've known from the moment you first drove in here."

For the first time Riley glanced over to where Gavin and Wyatt would be, trying to figure out a way to signal them if necessary.

"Oh yeah? What's that, Sayed?"

"To win. You always chase the win—I've seen it in your videos. Too many people here are too afraid of me to truly give me a challenge."

Riley relaxed.

That's because you're a tyrant, asshole. "Trust me, I'm not afraid of you."

They got their bikes to the top of the hill and situated themselves. Riley took a deep breath, pushing all thoughts of Wyatt and Gavin and the mission from his mind.

When the large red light turned green, Riley didn't hold back.

Sayed was right. Riley was here to win. Phoenix never started a race he didn't plan to win.

Sayed knew the course better, but that wasn't as much of an advantage anymore after the past couple of hours, during which Riley had become familiar with it too.

And Riley was much more familiar with the art of riding itself. And it was an art.

True to his word, Riley didn't take it easy at all; he raced like his life depended on it—which it might. In Sayed's defense, there were a couple of times the man could've cheated, an ugly cutoff he could've made a la Omar, but he didn't. He stuck to the race rules. Clean.

Amazing how a criminal with blood on his hands could be so scrupulous in other areas.

In the end, Riley crossed the finish line a wheel's length in front of Sayed. It was close, but it was enough.

He was a little afraid he was going to have a fight on his hands, but when Sayed took off his helmet, he was smiling. "You gave me a fair fight. That's all I can ask for. Although, if you had seen my luxury jet, you might not have pushed so hard to win."

Riley shook Sayed's outstretched hand. "I always push hard. Like you said, chasing the win."

Fifteen minutes later, ten minutes past when they were supposed to have left, Riley was back at the van. Wyatt and Gavin gave him a silent nod as they helped him load his bike into the vehicle. That meant Andre and Josh were secure and hidden in the two large storage boxes near the front.

They drove out of the gate, Riley once again talking to the guard and distracting him from searching anything too thoroughly. As they left, he gave a little salute to the group waving them off near the gate, including Sayed.

Nobody said much, none of them daring to breathe until they finally reached the airport. They got Andre and Josh out of their hiding spot and cleared the private security area. Within minutes, they were all on board the plane and speeding down the runway.

As they took off and the lights of Cairo became smaller and smaller, Riley looked over his shoulder at Wyatt and Gavin. They were smiling. So was he.

Another win, chased and captured.

Chapter 3

"Riley, girl, I hope to hell we don't need all this stuff."

Riley Wilde studied the boxes of medical supplies stacked up in the RV camper. This would be her home for the next week.

It was, in fact, a shit ton of stuff.

"We've got fifty people racing over a hundred miles through some of the toughest Wyoming wilderness, hurling themselves through obstacle courses, rappelling down cliffs, kayaking through white water, and doing whatever else your fiancé has cooked up for them. All while trying to beat each other to the finish line." Riley looked over at her friend Anne Griffin, one of Oak Creek's best emergency physicians. "We probably don't have enough supplies."

The Wild Wyoming Adventure Race, or WAR, was starting tomorrow. What had started out as a multiday training exercise for the Linear Tactical guys five years ago had turned into a popular multistage race among endurance and adventure athletes—people looking for something challenging.

After all, who knew how to push athletes better than a bunch of former Special Forces soldiers?

"I'm just glad Zac is in charge of it this year instead of racing," Anne said about her fiancé. "Nearly gave me a heart attack last year, watching him. This entire thing is insanity."

Riley chuckled. "All the Linear guys are half insane. Why do you think Boy Riley gets along so well—"

She stopped talking, throat closing up in pain. She couldn't keep talking about Riley as if the two of them were still together.

What she could do was ignore the fact that her heart was in a million pieces on the ground, her life was falling apart, and her future was uncertain at best.

She could concentrate on medical supplies and a race that would, fortunately, require all her attention.

"You're allowed to talk about him, you know. I may not agree with what you're doing, but you can always talk to me about any of it. You need to talk to someone, Riley."

She shrugged off Anne's gentle hand at her back and moved to organize the boxes, even though they were fine the way they were. "What's there to talk about? I have multiple sclerosis, I'm eventually going to end up in a wheelchair, and that doesn't really jive with the lifestyle of the world's premier adventure sport YouTube star."

Not just YouTube. The Adventure Channel had contacted Riley about hosting his own weekly show, *Phoenix Rises*. He'd be traveling to even more remote and exotic locations than he already did. More excitement. More adventure. More of everything that Riley, *Phoenix*, was good at. He loved it, and people loved him for it.

Including her.

There was no fucking way she was tying him to her and this fucking condition.

She was already not adventurous enough for someone

like him. Throw in a deteriorating central nervous system in a body that was attacking itself…

The best thing she could do for Riley was to get out of his life.

Anne let out a sigh. "We've been over this. Every case of MS is different. You may not need a wheelchair until you're seventy, if you even need one at all. All the indications—"

"I know what the research says, Anne, but you and I both know there are no guarantees either way. Breaking up with Riley was the right thing to do."

She'd done it three days ago, when the confirmed MS diagnosis had come through. For weeks she'd been hoping otherwise, but deep inside she'd known. She'd been a nurse for too long not to figure it out.

The involuntary muscle spasms, dizziness, loss of balance, fatigue… Her body was turning on itself. The MRI had confirmed it.

She and Riley had been supposed to video chat the next day, but she'd canceled, telling him she had to work.

Her entire life had just been turned upside down. She couldn't face him—even from thousands of miles away, he would've known something was terribly wrong. Would've gotten the truth out of her.

So she'd called him the next day—he'd just been getting back from some unscheduled stop in Egypt—and told him their relationship was over. Some bullshit about distance and changing and growing apart. She had hung up before he could ask too many questions. She had been curt with, or ignored, his many texts since.

She hadn't quite been able to breathe since then. Or sleep. Or eat.

She couldn't go on this way. So she was glad to have WAR to focus on. Riley was in Sri Lanka, then heading to some other parts of Southeast Asia—a problem for another day.

"I just want to concentrate on the race and getting everyone through this safely."

"Okay."

She turned to face her friend. "Okay? That's it?"

Anni-e gave her the quiet smile she was near famous for. "Like I said, I may not agree with you not telling Boy Riley, but you're my friend, and I'll support you in whatever way I can. If that means avoiding the issue for a little while and watching grown-ass adults do ridiculously dangerous and stupid things for fun...I'm in."

Riley would be with the racers all week as medical support. Anne would be here off and on to provide backup as needed.

Anne went back to her list, and Riley turned back to the supplies, grabbing a box of gauze to move to the other side of the table. But she twisted the wrong way and knocked over a stack of ibuprofen.

"You okay over there?" Anne asked.

"It's not the damn MS, okay?" Riley snapped. "I'm just clumsy."

A pause. "Clumsy is allowed too," Anne said softly.

Riley scrubbed a hand down her face. She was being a bitch. Anne hadn't said anything about MS. Riley didn't even know if that was what the woman had been thinking.

But pretty soon it would be. Soon it would be all anyone thought when they thought of Riley. Her MS.

She refused to let it be all Boy Riley associated with her too.

Anne came over and silently helped her restack the fallen boxes.

"I'm sorry." Riley reached over and squeezed her hand. "I'm a bitch."

Anne shook her head. "No need to apologize. You're coming to terms with something life changing. Nobody would blame you for needing a minute to adjust."

How did one adjust to this? How did one adjust to the knowledge that one's entire life could change with one sentence from a doctor's mouth?

She was a nurse, for God's sake. She knew how much worse it could be. There were some people who'd just been given a diagnosis of cancer or a tumor or some other terminal illness who would give *anything* if their diagnosis were only MS.

Only MS.

Yet it was causing Riley's world to crash in pieces around her.

Enough already. "I think I've used up today's quota of self-pity and bitchiness. Are you ready to head to the starting line? We can help get the athletes checked in."

"Listen. I know you're throwing yourself into this race so you don't have to think about the diagnosis or the breakup"—Riley shot Anne a narrowed-eyed look and her friend held a hand out in a gesture of surrender—"and that's fine. Avoiding short-term is fine. It gives your subconscious a chance to adjust. But long-term, you're going to have to really deal with this. You need to talk to your friends about what's going on with you. Wavy or Peyton."

"You're my friend. I've talked to you about it."

Anne shook her head. "You've talked to me, *very briefly*, about medical specifics only. Concerns about your job, not about how you're feeling or processing everything happening to you. I'm more than happy to talk to you about that too, but you've always been close with Wavy and Peyton. They both would want to help."

She scrubbed a hand across her face. Peyton had just reconnected with the love her of life and Wavy had problems of her own. "I know. I will. I just…can't. Not yet. Not any of it."

Anne let out a soft sigh. "And Boy Riley…The MS diagnosis and all that comes with it is hard enough without losing the man you love in the middle of it."

She knew. Oh God, she knew. Felt the five-hundred-pound weight of it all on her chest every second. "I think getting all the hard over with at one time might be easier in the long run."

"You can't hide it from him forever, Ry. I know he wasn't raised in Oak Creek like so many of us, but he considers this home now. He's going to find out."

"I know." Riley looked down at her hand on the boxes. It was shaking. But once again it had nothing to do with MS. "But I'm not going to trap him with me—guilt him into staying."

"You guys have been together for three years. There's no guilt. He loves you. Honestly, we all thought you would get married."

"No. He knows how I feel about marriage. We've never even talked about it."

Except for once. But then the universe had sent a sign that it wasn't meant to be. And now it had sent another one. A big-ass one.

Anne bumped Riley's hip with her own. "I know your parents' marriage was bad. I didn't have the greatest example of marriage growing up either. But it wouldn't be that way between the two of you."

"It doesn't matter. Marriage isn't in the cards for us."

Anne let out a sigh. "Fine. But you've got to think about your support system. Alienating yourself from the people who love you is not the way to handle MS."

"I know. And I will come up with a plan that doesn't involve me living like a hermit with two dozen cats and screaming at kids to get off my lawn. But right now, I don't want to think about MS. I don't want to think about Riley. I just want to turn my brain off."

"Fair enough. As long as you know you're going to have to think about it, and him, sometime."

"Phoenix is in Sri Lanka. He's not scheduled to come back for another couple of weeks."

Actually, why would he come back at all? He might not. He'd texted her repeatedly on the day she'd broken up with him, but by yesterday, it had dwindled down to only a couple of messages.

Seemed like he was already moving on.

"I'm just going to worry about all that later. This week, I'm just focusing on the race and keeping everyone alive."

Seemed like a much better plan than focusing on the dumpster fire her life had become.

THERE WERE a lot of multistage races in the world, races where athletes ran twenty to thirty miles a day over multiple days, carrying their own supplies and equipment. These runs tested the physical endurance and mental toughness of those crazy enough to participate. They were available all over the world. Some took athletes through the hell-like heat of deserts, some took them over miles of unforgiving volcanic lava rock, and some tested athletes' sanity by pitting them against the vast nothing of the Antarctic.

Then there were the shorter one-day events that tested athletes' other skills: agility, marksmanship, situational awareness, orienteering, strength, and outdoor skills.

The Wild Wyoming Adventure Race was one of the few that combined the best—or worst, depending on how you wanted to look at it—of both types of events.

It was a grueling, multiday endurance race that required the athletes to not just run and carry their supplies ten to twenty miles each day, but also complete daily challenges in the middle of their miles.

WAR was considered one of the hardest all-around events outside of military-grade training.

And no real surprise there, considering it had been developed by the Linear Tactical guys because they'd wanted to see which one of them was the best. Word had gotten out about that quickly, and now WAR had a waiting list each year.

Anne had gone on to help Zac with registration, and Riley was getting a look at the monstrous obstacle course that would be part of the day-one event.

She shook her head, staring at the wooden walls, towers, and tunnels around her. "This thing looks brutal."

"Do you like my fiendish invention?" Gabriel Collingwood grinned from ear to ear. It made the hugely muscled man seem charming and almost boyish.

"Looks like you're going to be sending a lot of business my way. Just when I thought I was going to have a week off to enjoy myself."

Gabe rubbed his hands together, and Riley thought he might start jumping up and down any second. "This course has some of the most savage elements of my BUD/S training. I can't wait until they come at this thing all gung ho."

Unlike most of the Linear Tactical guys, Gabe had been a Navy SEAL. Their training was legendary.

And the WAR athletes would be hitting this obstacle course after a five-mile running loop and half-mile swim in water that would make polar bears think twice.

Yeah, Riley would definitely be getting some extra patients due to Gabe's fiendish obstacle course. "Do you wish you were competing?"

"I won't lie: a little. But when Zac asked me to design this obstacle course, I had to choose between that or participating. I decided I'd rather spend the week with my gorgeous fiancée."

"Wise choice. Jordan is definitely more beautiful than any obstacle course."

"More beautiful than anything," he murmured as he turned to tighten a rope.

Riley hid her smile. Gabe would just be embarrassed if she teased him, and besides, after what Jordan had been through, Riley was glad the other woman had her own personal guardian angel now.

"Maybe next year." She nudged him with her elbow.

"Oh hell yes. It's about damn time these army guys stop getting all the badassery credit."

"Well, I'm sure the racers will be cursing your name tomorrow when they get to some of these obstacles."

Gabe waggled his eyebrows. "If they don't, I haven't done my job right. We have a good group this year. Zac was saying the contenders to win are best-in-the-world elite athletes. Do you think Boy Riley will take the title again?"

She forced herself to ignore the fissure in her heart at the sound of his name. There was no Boy Riley and Girl Riley anymore, or soon there wouldn't be, once word got out about the breakup. There would just be Riley Wilde and Riley Harrison.

And soon America's adventure sport hero and the nurse with MS.

She studied the particularly wicked-looking rope climb. She could just picture Boy Riley scrambling up it at full speed to ring the bell at the top.

You couldn't pay her enough to try something like that— even if she had the upper-body strength to make it—but

Phoenix loved this sort of stuff. The bigger the challenge, the better.

No wonder he'd been at this race three years ago. That's where she'd met him.

He'd won it. And won her heart at the same time.

"I'm 100 percent sure Phoenix won't win this year."

Gabe chuckled. "Damn, Wilde. Betting against your man? If you don't think he's going to win, who do you have your money on? A couple of weeks ago, the guys were saying Bo Gonzales was the one to beat. Evidently he's having a good year at everything."

She knew Bo. Even at his absolute best, he'd never beat Riley. "It's not that I think Phoenix couldn't win, it's just that he's in Sri Lanka, so that would make it a little too difficult, even for him."

Gabe's dark brows pulled together. "That's not what—"

"Nope, Wildfire." Riley froze at the sound of the familiar voice behind her. "Sri Lanka had to wait. I decided I needed to make a detour."

Chapter 4

She'd gone with red for her hair, an almost purple color. It suited her.

He wondered what had made her change her mind about the blue.

Not nearly as much as he wondered why she'd ended their relationship with no real explanation, but he still wondered. Because today, like every single day since the day he'd met her, he wanted to know everything there was to know about Riley Wilde.

She stiffened at the sound of his voice and spun around.

"Uh, I'll leave you two to say hello," Gabe said slowly.

Riley glanced over at Gabe for just a second. "Good to see you, man. Looks like you built a beast for us."

"Sure as hell have. I'll catch you later."

Riley nodded as Gabe walked away, his gaze falling back on Wildfire.

Her beautiful hazel eyes were trained on him. Not narrowed, but carefully neutral. It was her poker face. It didn't give anything away. His girl was tough, and she didn't wear her heart on her sleeve, so he was used to seeing that guarded look on her face.

He just wasn't used to it being directed at him.

"You shouldn't be here," she said.

Something in his gut clenched. She really didn't want him here.

He'd been traveling nonstop for more than twenty-two hours to get back to Oak Creek, convincing himself the entire way that the breakup hadn't really meant that she'd wanted their relationship to end. That it was some kind of message on her part.

Maybe she'd been trying to tell him that she needed more from him—more face time, more calls, more *something* —but didn't want to come across as clingy or needy. That would definitely be something Wildfire would do.

They'd always agreed to tell each other if the distance was becoming too much, that they would figure out a new plan if needed, where his schedule wouldn't be such a weight. They'd been committed to each other from the beginning, to making it work no matter what.

He'd flown her out to places to stay with him when she could. They'd met for romantic weekends all over the world when her own nursing career had made an extended stay too difficult. He showed up in Oak Creek every chance he got. They had video chatting and sexting down to a science— every single day, without fail, for three years they'd talked to each other in some way.

He refused to accept that what they'd built together could just fall apart without any warning at all.

He'd hoped beyond all hope that when he arrived here she would be happy to see him.

She wasn't.

"I'm racing. That's why I'm here." That hadn't been the plan, but it could become the plan now.

"You shouldn't be here," she said again. "You're not on the registration list. The race filled up three months ago, and I know you haven't registered."

He let his backpack drop from his hand to the ground and narrowed his eyes. Now he was starting to get a little irritated.

"I don't have to be on any list. It's one of the perks of being a past winner. You can show up for the race any year and you're guaranteed entry."

Now her eyes narrowed. No doubt she'd be checking to see if that rule was actually true.

Let her check; it was.

"What about Sri Lanka? I thought you weren't coming back for another few weeks or…at all."

"Like I said, I made a detour."

People were starting to come out to get a look at Gabe's devious obstacle course. The Linear Tactical office was handling athlete check-in, so it made sense for them to see it before heading off to where they'd camp tonight.

But he didn't pay attention to them at all. His eyes stayed pinned to Riley's.

All he wanted to do was cross over to her and yank her to him. Shake her. Kiss her. Both.

Get her to tell him what the hell was going on and demand she explain how she could cut him out of her life with such surgical precision.

She crossed her arms over her chest. "You shouldn't have come here, Riley."

Goddammit. He was getting fucking sick of her saying that. "I don't need your permission to do anything anymore, now do I, *Riley*?" He spat out her name the way she had his.

More and more people were starting to mill around the roped-off obstacle course. Some of them were competitors, but some of them were their friends from Linear Tactical.

The fact that the two of them were having a standoff was going to be pretty obvious to everyone.

She stepped closer. He knew it was for privacy rather than a desire to be close to him, but his body didn't care. His body responded to hers the way it had from the very beginning: with complete awareness.

"I want you to leave," she hissed out.

"Too fucking bad, Wildfire. I'm not going anywhere. Now do you want to finish this conversation out here in public, or do you want to find somewhere private where we can talk? Because we are going to talk."

Her teeth gritted, but she knew him well enough to know he wasn't bluffing. If she wanted to fight out here, he would do it.

But he was going to get some answers.

She jerked her thumb toward the huge warehouse to her right. "Linear training facility. I'll give you ten minutes. And then you've got to go."

She looked almost scared.

Screw the Linear training building. Screw all the people around. He needed to know what was going on. *Now*.

He took a step toward her, but she sidestepped him before he could touch her.

"Hey, Phoenix," Bo Gonzales called out from a few yards over. "Didn't think you were going to make it this year."

He glanced over at the other man. "Never a hardship to show up and beat you, Bo."

Bo's lips pressed together as the other people around chuckled.

"Inside," Wildfire whispered as she slid past him. His body tightened in a primal way at her very scent. It took everything he had not to grab her and pull her to him.

He let her go.

But he wouldn't for long.

RILEY RUSHED AWAY without looking back at him, heart pounding in her chest. What the hell was he doing here?

Her hands shook and her legs felt weak, but it had nothing to do with MS.

And everything to do with how Boy Riley had always affected her.

She'd had to physically stop herself from touching him when he'd come close. God, all she'd wanted to do was reach out and touch the back of his head, run her thumb across his temple. That was how they'd greeted each other for years now, since sometimes more overt public displays of affection weren't appropriate.

The "hey, you," they called it.

She looked down at the fingers that had so wanted to touch him. The same fingers that had first given her the indication that she had some sort of problem a few months ago. The tingling and numbness were early signs of MS. She'd ignored them for as long as she could, her brain refusing to accept what could be happening, until other symptoms had also appeared.

She beelined it to the training warehouse. Nothing had changed in the situation with Riley. She had to convince him to leave, and she didn't want to do that in front of an audience, especially since she was afraid she might have a complete breakdown while doing it.

She walked inside the huge, empty building. Nobody would be using it today as everyone prepared for the race. The Linear guys used this space for all sorts of training, and Riley had been in here numerous times, so she knew where the lighting switches were. She flipped on the bare minimum, keeping the warehouse dim.

She and Riley wouldn't be in here long enough to need more than that.

She needed to be calm, but firm. Just convince him to go, not stick around for the race. He didn't really want to be a part of Wild Wyoming—hadn't ever talked about racing it again.

He was here because of her.

She breathed in through her nose and out through her mouth, trying to calm herself as much as possible. She just needed to convince him it was in both of their best interests to move along.

"Is there somebody else? Is that what this is all about?"

Her calming breath flew back out of her lips as she spun to face him. He came inside and closed the door behind him.

"I think I have a right to know," he continued. "If you've found someone else, you should've told me right away."

The emergency lights cast an orange haze more than they actually lit the space. She couldn't really make out his features. "There's nobody else."

As soon as the words were out of her mouth, she realized she'd made a strategic error. She should've lied. She should've told him she'd met someone else—it would've been the easiest way to make sure he didn't keep searching for the truth.

His backpack hit the ground with a thump as he left it by the door and crossed to her. "Then what, Wildfire? I've been over this from every possible angle in my head. A month and a half ago when we met in Paris, we were fine. Three weeks ago when we talked on the phone for five hours while you were repainting your kitchen, we were fine."

She nodded. Oh God. How was she going to get out of this?

He took another step closer. "And then something changed. I don't know what. I don't know why. You started ghosting me. Barely a word, barely a text. Just enough to keep me from panicking."

She grimaced and took a step back from him. He was too close. And he was too right. That was exactly what she'd done: talked to him just enough to make sure he didn't send everybody he knew in Oak Creek to check on her.

She shook her head. "I know it may be difficult to believe this, but sometimes people just change. Grow apart. Maybe a relationship with the great Phoenix just wasn't what I wanted anymore. That's allowed, you know."

He was on her with the speed of the world-class athlete he was. Not in anger. She never had to worry about anything like that from him. His eyes searched her expression. He wanted to see her face clearly in the dim light.

Ascertain if she was telling the truth.

Damn it.

"Are you allowed to get tired of me? Yes." His pulse pounded in his jaw. "Are you allowed to get frustrated and resentful of this life I lead? Yes. Are you allowed to decide you're too good for me and you want something better? Hell yes."

He stepped forward and she stepped back, realizing she'd made another strategic error when her back hit the wall. Riley's hands moved to either side of her head, caging her in.

All she could smell was him. All she could feel was the heat radiating from his body. She clenched her hands into fists at her sides to stop herself from touching him.

It was a physical pain. It seemed like everything in her genetic makeup screamed it was wrong to hold herself back from him.

She turned her head to the side, unable to look at him without touching him. Without breaking down and telling him everything.

"Do you just not love me anymore, Wildfire? Is that what this is?"

She barely bit back her whimper as he leaned forward and trailed his nose across her jaw, breathing in her scent.

She couldn't stop the shudder as one of his hands dropped from the wall by her head and trailed down the side of her throat. He knew her too well.

"I should go." The words were hoarse and tight coming out of her mouth. One last, desperate attempt at sanity.

His lips found her throat. "Should you? Should you go?"

He wasn't holding her there in any way. The only place his body was touching hers was his lips on her neck. All she had to do was put any effort *whatsoever* into moving away and he would let her go.

Move, Riley. Just move.

She didn't.

It was like she was rooted in place by a force beyond her control.

His lips made their way back and forth across her throat. "Of course, I *definitely* think you should stay."

His lips worked their way up to hers, stealing any words she might've said. The kiss sent electricity coursing through every part of her.

It had always been like this, always a ridiculous level of heat between them. From the moment they'd met, they'd never been successful at keeping their hands off each other if they were anywhere close.

Not that they'd ever tried.

His body moved up against hers as he deepened the kiss, pushing her back against the wall.

He rocked against her, his hand moving up to cup her breast, thumb and finger pinching the already tightened peak.

He knew exactly how to touch her to make her come apart. Quickly, slowly, whichever way he wanted.

It wasn't fair.

And it was exactly what she wanted.

She helped as he slid the thin jacket she'd worn over her scrubs off her shoulders, and it pooled on the floor at their feet.

His lips moved back to her neck, nipping this time, and her head fell back against the wall. When his fingers slid inside the elastic waist of her scrubs—damn them for being such easy access—and pressed inside her, she groaned. He bit at that place where her neck met her shoulder and she couldn't control her squirming, pressing up against him. Needing.

"Doesn't seem like all of you wants to leave me behind."

His deep voice only turned her on more. She grabbed him by the hair and pulled his lips from her neck up to hers. "Shut up, Phoenix."

She'd always loved his confidence. He could be so damn cocky, but she loved that too.

She couldn't wait any longer. She reached down for the buckle of his pants, feeling better when he let out a groan of his own as she wrapped her fingers around him. It had always gone both ways, this need they had for each other.

She tucked her face into his neck as his fingers worked her higher.

"Fuck, Wildfire. I want to be inside you. Are you still on the pill?"

"Yes," she said immediately.

Yes to it *all*. She slid his jeans down, freeing him as he yanked one of the legs of her scrubs down over her shoes, then slid them and her underwear until they were hanging off one leg.

It was unlikely anyone would come in here, especially

where they were, in the back of the facility. But taking off all their clothes wasn't an option. Not that either of them needed it. They might not even care if someone walked in on them.

His hand moved back to her breast, pinching her nipple just to the point of pain. She gasped, twisting closer to him, returning the favor by yanking his lips back to hers and giving the bottom one a stinging bite before soothing the slight hurt with her tongue. Now it was his turn to squirm as the breath shuddered out of him.

His fingers slid back to her core, curving in that way only he knew how, leaving her gasping for air and thrusting up against his hand. When he moved his fingers away, she couldn't stop the whimper that fell from her lips.

But it was only so he could reach around the back of her thigh and hike her leg up higher, positioning her where he wanted her against the wall. She hooked her legs around his hips, almost desperate to have him inside her.

He didn't make her wait. They both groaned as he slid inside her, filling her. Everything about it was so right. Had always been so right.

She slid her arms around his shoulders and held on as he drove them both higher. Her nails clawed into his back through his shirt as she gave herself over to him, over to the primal rhythm of their lovemaking.

It wasn't long before orgasm crashed over her, drowning her in sensation. A few seconds later he followed, calling out her name in a moan before thrusting one last time and slumping against her.

For a few moments, her brain was free of everything. All she could feel was the two of them breathing in unison, everything at peace, her body at rest in the knowledge that she was in Riley's arms, where she belonged.

After weeks apart, the first times were always like this,

almost manic in their desperation to be near each other. But now would come the slow and long and easy—

Like a rubber band snapping against her skin, reality came crashing back.

There would be no slow and long and easy this time.

There shouldn't have been anything at all.

She slapped at his shoulder. "Let me down."

"Wildfire." He didn't move.

"I mean it, Riley. Let me down."

She could feel the panic bubbling up inside of her. She needed to get away. He was going to want to talk now, and nothing had changed.

The only thing that had changed was he'd proved she still wanted him.

He backed away just enough for her to disengage their bodies and scoot over to the side to pull her underwear and pants back on.

"Wildfire, we need to talk."

She looked up to find him buttoning his jeans. "We really don't. This doesn't change anything."

She grabbed her jacket from the floor and kept herself pressed up against the wall.

She had to get out of here. If he touched her now, pressed her for the truth, she was going to crumble. She couldn't do that. Not to him. Not to herself.

A sob was choking up from deep inside of her. A scream. It had been there since she'd gotten her diagnosis, but she'd kept it buried inside.

She couldn't let it out now.

"Wildfire, talk to me. Whatever it is, we'll work it out together."

She pulled her jacket up to her chest and held it in front of her like a shield. "Not this time," she whispered. "Not all bad guys can be fought."

"What does that mean?"

What the heck was she doing? Being cryptic was just going to make him more concerned and curious, not less. She needed to make this cut as clean as possible.

She straightened, cleared her throat, and dropped the jacket to her side. "You shouldn't have come here, Riley. Yeah, the breakup sex was great, but that's over now. You need to leave. You know you have no interest in doing this race again. You're here because of us."

She pushed away from the wall. She had to show strength now. Any sign of fragility was going to have him trying to play protector. She slipped her arms into the sleeves of her jacket. "We're done, Riley. It's that simple."

"And if I don't accept that?"

"Sorry to tell you, you don't get a choice. You shouldn't be here. There's nothing left for you to win. So just go. Make it easier on both of us."

Without giving him a chance to respond, she turned and walked out the door.

Chapter 5

Her contagious laughter rang out through the entire camp. An animated, rowdy guffaw that ended with an adorable little snort.

Phoenix knew where the laugh was coming from without even having to look. But he looked anyway.

He wanted to look.

The young nurse with his same name. Although somehow Riley *sounded infinitely more sexy attached to her than it did to him*

He'd seen her every day in the four days since the race started, but they'd only been able to talk to each other in passing. She'd been busy assisting the older doctor in treating any injuries the Wild Wyoming Adventure Race participants had received.

Phoenix had never been so disappointed to not be injured in his life.

The cut he'd gotten on his arm today pulling a kayak out of the river definitely wasn't something he'd normally bother a medical professional about—barely more than a scratch.

But since the sexy nurse with the striking pink hair and I-love-life *laugh wasn't currently examining someone else, he thought now would be a good time to show her his mortal wound.*

As Phoenix, he'd parachuted out of airplanes, SCUBA dived with sharks circling around him, and snowboarded in the pristine snow of the Alps in areas only reachable by helicopter. None of those things stole his breath like the sight of the impish grin on this woman's face as she glanced up at him from her perch on the picnic table as he approached.

"Hi, I'm—"

"Phoenix," she completed for him. "I think everyone here knows who you are."

It was one of the few times he wished his recent YouTube escapades hadn't made him somewhat of a celebrity. But then again, without those he wouldn't be in this race.

Wouldn't be here with her.

"Phoenix is just a nickname. I'm Riley Harrison."

She held out her hand. "Riley Wilde."

He took her hand in his but didn't shake it. Just held it, eternally grateful when she didn't pull away and stare at him like he was some sort of creep.

Just let her hand rest in his.

"Everybody's already calling us Boy Riley and Girl Riley," he said, thumb stroking over the back of her hand.

"I guess that's better than other possibilities. Short Riley and Tall Riley. Crazy Riley and Nurse Riley."

"Beautiful Riley and the Riley Who Won't Leave Her Alone."

Her smile got even bigger. "This is the first time we've even really talked."

"I didn't want to bother you. You're working, treating the injured racers. I know that's important." He stroked her soft skin again, then let go of her hand. "Actually, that's why I came over. I almost mortally wounded myself today with a kayak."

Her hazel eyes grew serious, and she sat up straighter. "Why didn't you tell me you were hurt? Want me to grab Dr. Lewis? I'm just here shadowing him so I can take over medical supervision of the race next year."

"Actually, do you mind looking at my injury? I trust your medical opinion. But I'm afraid I might need an amputation."

He slid up his sleeve and held out his forearm to show her the tiny scratch.

She laughed softly—a sound he was becoming addicted to pretty damn quickly. "Wow. It's amazing you made it back to camp of your own volition with a wound this serious."

Her fingers slid over the scratch and their eyes met. "I'm very brave," he said, somehow able to keep a straight face.

Her smile.

God. Her smile.

"You are very brave, Phoenix." She stroked his arm again. It was the most decidedly sexual, non-sexual thing he'd ever experienced, and he wished there weren't dozens of people walking around them everywhere.

"I need a nickname for you. I can't call you Girl Riley." She let go of his arm, but only to reach down into the medical kit next to her and pull out a small adhesive bandage and begin taking it from its wrapper. "Do you have a middle name?"

"Nope. My mom and dad couldn't agree on one—one of the ten thousand things they couldn't agree on before they finally divorced—so I'm just Riley Wilde." She put the bandage over his tiny scrape.

He caught her hand again. She didn't pull away again. "Alright, Wilde, I'm going to call you Wildfire. Seems perfect for you."

She smiled, shaking her head. "You don't even know me."

"I know enough. I know I want to know more."

She actually blushed a little at that, rubbing her cheek against her shoulder, while still peering up at him. "Don't you have a race to concentrate on, Phoenix? I hear you're doing really well. Everyone is surprised a non-Special Forces guy is at the front of the pack. It's always been someone from Linear Tactical who has won."

"Not this year. I'm going to win."

Her smile grew. "Is that so?"

"If I win, will you go out with me, Wildfire?"

Dr. Lewis stuck his head out from the medical RV and called her name. Riley dropped her hand and she stood.

"Yes, I'll go out with you if you win, Phoenix."

He winked at her. "Good. Because I'm going to."

She grabbed the medical kit and turned towards the RV. "But I've got a secret."

"What's that?"

She glanced at him over shoulder, pink hair hiding part of her face, but not her smile. "I'll go out with you either way."

RILEY FLEW six feet before hitting the ground with a thud— dirt ground covered in about three inches of water. Just enough to cover half his body with mud, something he'd be wearing the rest of the fucking day now.

His shoulder took the brunt of the fall—certainly not anywhere close to the worst injury he'd ever had. But one that could've been completely avoided.

"Watch it there, Phoenix." Bo Gonzales snickered but didn't look down at Riley from his perch on the two-inch-wide balance beam over the pit of mud Riley had just fallen into. "I'd hate to see you break an arm on the first day and be out of the race. How embarrassing."

Riley swallowed his curse and ignored the man as Bo continued forward on the beam. Riley tracked back through the mud so he could make his way out of the pit and start the balancing element again.

He and Bo had been friendly, and occasionally not-so-friendly, rivals for years. Generally speaking, Bo was always a step, or second, or meter behind Riley in everything.

But not today.

Riley was completely unfocused, and Bo was right. If he didn't get his head in the game, he was going to end up with a broken bone and out of the race.

And how pathetic was it that the first thought that came

to mind was that if he broke a bone, he'd get to talk to Girl Riley again?

He had no idea what had happened yesterday.

The sex had been amazing. Of course, the sex always was. For three years, he'd been waiting for their lovemaking to become routine or ordinary, but it never had.

Yesterday in the Linear training facility, after enough blood had returned to his brain for him to form a coherent thought, he'd hoped that the amazing sex they'd just shared meant they could work out whatever was going on.

He took Riley's concerns seriously. She wasn't flighty or petty. She didn't make up drama in order to manipulate people around her. His girl was strong and independent and decisive.

She'd ended their relationship for a reason. He wanted to know what that reason was.

He'd thought he had a chance. In that moment after sex, when all they could feel was each other, he'd thought they could talk it out. Work it out. He loved feeling her so soft and content in his arms. Wanted to keep her that way forever.

He'd wanted to hear whatever she had to say. Maybe they were starting a new path together.

He knew he'd been wrong the moment she stiffened. The reconciliation he'd been hoping for was gone. She'd been back to angry and hard and distant.

There was something—something *important*—he didn't understand.

She'd told him to leave, but Riley had never been great at following directions. Especially not when it came to leaving behind the woman loved.

So as soon as she'd left—all but running out of the training building—he'd done the exact opposite of what she'd demanded and registered himself for the race.

If Wildfire was going to be on the WAR course, that's

damn well where he was going to be too. He still needed answers.

He'd spent the rest of the day running around Oak Creek prepping. WAR wasn't something you just showed up for unprepared.

Athletes were only allowed to use and eat what they carried with them in a backpack. Part of the challenge of the race was deciding how little you could survive on and still maintain optimal levels of performance. The race provided water and shelter. Everything else you packed and carried yourself.

The lightest sleeping bag and smallest amount of food—usually in the form of nutrition bars or MREs, Meals Ready to Eat—could make the difference between who won or lost the race overall. Running twenty miles a day, plus the daily adventure events of the race, required a lot of calories, but everyone also wanted their packs as light as possible.

Riley wasn't necessarily trying to win, but that didn't mean his competitive nature was going to just let him coast. He'd begged, borrowed, and bought what he'd needed to get him to the starting line with all his provisions this morning.

Now if he could just focus on what he was doing, he might survive the next five days.

He pulled himself out of the pit.

"You doing okay there, Phoenix?" Baby Bollinger gave Riley a little salute as he came up to the balance beam next to Riley. Baby was the younger brother of Finn, one of the founding members of Linear Tactical. "Saw you take a tumble. Looked pretty hard."

Riley took a confident step onto the beam. Lack of confidence when you had thirty feet to walk across was going to end with you down in the pit.

Of course, not concentrating the way you should would end with you down there too.

Riley nodded. "Momentary loss of focus."

Baby gave a good-natured chuckle as he moved slowly across the beam. "My brother and his buddies have made it so a *momentary lack of focus* in this race might get you killed."

They both moved across their beams, arms out for balance. "That's the damn truth." And it really was. Figuring out what to do about Wildfire was going to have to wait or there might not be anything left of him to worry about anyways.

She'd be here each day as race support. Until he figured out a plan, that was enough.

He finally made it across the damned balance beam with no more falls. He and Baby stayed together as they ran the quarter mile to the next element, a fifty-foot rope climb with two ropes. Every ten feet, there was a barrier requiring the competitors to swing from one rope to the other. Nets were set up to keep people from dying if they fell, but it was going to take a shit ton of time to get out of them and back down if they fell and had to start over.

"Shit," Baby muttered. "Gabe Collingwood is a sick son of a bitch."

They both shook their heads as they spotted a giant yellow sign with a huge smiley face on it. Under were the words *Remember, you paid to do this*.

They both flipped off the sign and ran over to two of the empty sets of rope.

Riley immediately used both his arms and his legs to shimmy up the rope. Times like this, he was glad he did functional strength training as much as possible rather than just hitting the gym. A gym could provide the strength element but didn't include other factors that came into play with a challenge like this: grip, agility, balance, and burst strength.

A lot of times, there were no gyms around when he was

filming stunts in the middle of the jungle, wilderness, or mountains. So functional training had been the only option. Hell, one time in Nepal, he'd spent his mornings pulling a cart of yak dung five miles.

At least the smell had encouraged speed.

Riley pulled far ahead of Baby as he reached the top, rang the bell, and climbed back down. But considering Baby wasn't a professional athlete, he wasn't doing too badly. Being a mechanic was its own sort of functional training.

Riley took off for the quarter-mile run to the next obstacle, smiling as he caught sight of the front-runners just a little farther head. He was making up time. He grinned even harder when he saw what was slowing them down.

A team element, a fifteen-foot vertical wall that no one was going to be able to get over by themselves. Riley could understand why an obstacle like this would be included in Navy SEAL training, where team building was of critical importance. But in a competition where there was only one winner, requiring athletes to work together was just cruel.

"Sadistic bastard," Riley said with a chuckle.

He added extra speed into his gait so he could catch up with the three men ahead of him. When he made it to the wall a few minutes later, the athletes were still arguing over the best way to handle this.

"How's it hanging, fellas?"

Damon had decided to bypass Sri Lanka and join Riley in the race. He stepped to the side now and pointed over his shoulder, revealing Amber Lowe.

Shit. Everyone knew Amber. Or had known her brother, Felix Lowe. Riley hadn't realized she'd be racing here.

"Sorry, Amber. I didn't realize you were racing. Good to see you."

She nodded and gave him a small smile. "They let me take Felix's spot, since it was already paid for."

Felix definitely wouldn't be racing it.

Riley patted the woman on the shoulder, wishing he wasn't so awkward. "That's what he would've wanted."

Everyone around them murmured their assent. Felix had run in the same adventure and extreme sport circles as all of them until a skiing accident last winter. Riley and Damon had been there. Had seen Felix lose control and go over the side of a small cliff.

The fall had left Felix paralyzed. Then, unable to handle it, he'd committed suicide a few months later.

Riley had wondered every damn day since that accident if there was something he could've done to have changed the outcome of what had happened.

"I'm not trying to be an asshole, but are we just going to wait for everybody else to catch up with us or are we going to do this?"

Good old Bo. Always ready with his unfiltered comments.

"You're an asshole, Bo," Gunnar Jefferson muttered.

Riley didn't know much about Gunnar except that everyone called him Iceland since that's where he was from. He was known more for endurance races than the stunt stuff Riley and Damon did. The man generally kept to himself. But if he was up here at the front of the pack, then he was definitely a contender to win WAR.

"What, Iceland?" Bo shrugged. "I'm just saying what everyone else is thinking."

Riley doubted anybody else had been thinking that.

"Bo is right," Amber said. "Look, somebody else is on their way. Let's get moving."

"You need to send me up first," Bo said. "I'm tallest and the only one who's going to be able to reach that top. I've got the upper body strength to pull over everyone else. I'll do my part."

"What's to stop you from jumping down the other side if we lift you over first?" Damon asked. It was a valid question.

Bo rolled his eyes. "I've already told you I'll do my part. Now let's quit bickering like old women and get past this thing so we can get on with the race."

Everybody looked over at Riley to see if he would voice an objection. Since he didn't have anything better planned, they might as well get going with this one.

"Hoist him up."

Riley and Iceland got into position at the bottom of the wall with their hands cupped. Damon and Amber stood to the side, ready to provide support if needed. Bo jogged a few meters back and turned to face them. He counted it down and ran toward them at a full sprint. Riley and Iceland both grunted as they caught his weight—bastard was fucking solid —and pushed him toward the top of the wall.

Bo grabbed it and pulled himself up the rest of the way. They were all a little bit surprised when he swung one leg over for balance but remained up there.

"I thought he was going to bolt," Damon murmured.

They all grunted in agreement.

"Send up the chick," Bo called out.

"Chick's name is Amber, asshole." Amber sounded so much like her brother Riley had to smile.

Bo rolled his eyes. "Whatever, sweetheart. We're wasting time. Let's go."

"You want a hoist?" Damon asked her.

She nodded, then stepped back and turned to sprint at the wall. She stepped into Damon's waiting hands, and he was able to propel her much higher than they'd gotten Bo. Bo grabbed her hand and pulled her the rest of the way, and soon she was sitting opposite him over the wall.

The two of them would be able to help get everyone else over.

But then Bo gave them a little salute. "Okay, I think we can agree I've done my part." Without another word he slipped his leg over the other side of the wall and slid down out of sight.

Iceland shook his head as they watched Bo sprint out from behind the other side of the wall and leave them behind. "That guy really is an asshole."

"All right, people, it's not like we weren't expecting something like this." Riley looked up at Amber. "Can you pull someone up by yourself?"

"Yeah. Send Damon. He's lightest."

They set back up to send Damon up to the top. True to her word, as soon as Riley and Iceland hoisted him, Amber grabbed his hand and pulled him the rest of the way.

Her brother would've been damn proud.

Iceland went next and by that time Baby had caught up to them.

"Got room for one more to your little party?"

Riley nodded. If they didn't help Baby now, he'd have to wait until the next three or four people made it. Actually, Baby would be pretty damn useful.

"I can hoist you up, the guys will catch you, but then you've got to hang and let me crawl over you. Then they'll pull you up."

"Wow, just the sort of fun I was hoping for when I signed up for this crazy race."

Amber got down off the back of the wall as Iceland took her place. Double-checking that Damon and Iceland were both ready, he and Baby jogged back to position. "I'm three seconds behind you so that the guys don't have to bear that weight too long."

Baby nodded. "Roger that." A couple seconds later, Baby burst toward the wall. Riley caught his foot and gave the man as much of a boost as he could.

Iceland and Damon caught Baby, both of them grunting as they lowered him back down.

Riley backed up, then flew at the wall. Parkour had never been his area of expertise, but he kept his footing as light as possible as he grabbed Baby's shoulders and basically climbed up his back. He pushed off Baby, leaping for the top of the wall, grabbing the edge, and pulling his weight up so that the other guys didn't have to hold both him and Baby any longer.

All said and done, it took less than eight seconds, but they were all breathing heavily by the time they were up and over the wall.

But they had done it.

They leapt down to the other side.

"Now let's go finish this hellish course and catch that cheating bastard."

Chapter 6

Boy Riley didn't leave.

But then again, she hadn't really expected him to. After all, why would he when she'd basically torn her own clothes off to have sex with him the first time they were alone?

That didn't exactly suggest she was serious about the breakup.

So, when he'd shown up this morning at the starting line in race gear and with a race backpack rather than his regular one, she'd known he planned to stay.

Never mind that he hadn't specifically trained for WAR like so many of the athletes had. Never mind that he probably hadn't had most of the needed supplies. He'd shown up, determination in his eyes.

Whether it was to get answers from her or win the race— or *both*—she wasn't sure.

She'd stayed away from him as he'd listened to Zac's briefing and chatted with the other athletes. He hadn't come near her. Hadn't tried to talk. Thank goodness.

Damn heat between them. She had to make sure they

weren't alone for the rest of this race. She couldn't let that happen again. Her heart couldn't take it.

So she would just ignore him. Or treat him like every other athlete: with detached respect. If he needed medical assistance, she'd help, of course. And she would clear him to race each day like she had to do for everyone.

But that was it. Besides that, she would pretend she didn't even know him.

Which worked perfectly as she pretended she didn't even notice him taking off at the start line for the eight-mile loop that led the athletes to the obstacle course.

Then she had pretended not to watch him on the obstacles themselves.

It definitely hadn't been his best day. She'd winced with every fall, felt every bruise as if it was her own.

But even unfocused and at a disadvantage, he'd still been beautiful to watch.

He was always beautiful to watch. There was a grace to him, the way his body moved. It was something only the most elite athletes possessed.

She'd always been sort of awed by his physical prowess. Whenever they'd done anything together, she'd always felt clunky and slow and cowardly.

Watching him just reminded her why they had to remain broken up. The physical differences between them from the beginning had been bad enough. The MS would just make it all unbearable.

At that point, she'd turned away from the obstacle course to drive back to the camp where everyone would be sleeping for the next three nights. She needed distance.

"Nobody has died yet, have they?" Zac smiled as he walked over from the supply truck to where she was standing outside the medical RV a few hours later. "I only expect that face if someone needs to be taken to the hospital."

Zac didn't know about her diagnosis. Anne would never tell him even if it wasn't for all the privacy laws. Riley had gone to Reddington City for all her tests to make sure no one in Oak Creek found out.

She found a smile for Zac. "I'm just preparing myself for all the whining about to commence. You know how endurance athletes are. Big babies when it comes down to it. Second only to Special Forces soldiers when it comes to whine." She elbowed Zac's rock-hard abs. He, like most of the other guys who made up Linear Tactical, had served in the Army Special Forces.

And they were definitely not whiny.

"If you think they're going to be boo-hooing today, you should see what we have in store for them tomorrow."

"Tomorrow's the kayaking, right?" The specifics of the race were a closely guarded secret until the night before, when Zac, as race director, would hold a briefing about what the athletes could expect the next day. Riley had been sworn to secrecy, and even she didn't know all the details.

"Yup. Rapids navigation and kayaking skills. Everyone will have two choices: the long and safe route, or the shorter and much more likely to get you killed route."

She rolled her eyes. "I don't even have to guess which route most of them are going to take."

"Well, the river will filter out those who can't handle it. They'll never be able to make the turn to get to the harder rapids. But I'll have most of the Linear team out ready for emergency water rescue tomorrow in case they're needed. How's Phoenix on the kayak?"

She tried to hide her flinch. "He wins. Like he does everything."

Zac ran a hand up over his hair. "Damn, I'm sorry. I heard you guys broke up. I'm just so used to you being—"

She touched his arm. "Don't worry about it. Everyone is

used to the two of us a unit. It'll take a while for us all to adjust."

It should only take her thirty or forty more years. "And Phoenix is better on a kayak than a lot of people might think," she continued, forcing a smile. "It's less his paddling skills and more his situational awareness, I think. He sees stuff sooner than most people do."

"That's why he's a world-champion athlete."

She nodded. It was exactly why he was a world champion in so many sports.

"He would've made a damn fine soldier also." Zac poured water into a large pot and set it over the portable stovetop to heat. The athletes would start coming into camp not long from now. They'd need hot water for their MREs or freeze-dried meals. "You know Phoenix has helped Linear out more than once in some kidnapping situations. Gotten our men into places they wouldn't have been able to access otherwise."

"I know. He loves making a difference." How many hours had they spent talking about the missions he'd helped with?

God, she couldn't keep thinking about this if she didn't want to end up crying like some whiny Special Forces soldier.

"Okay, so tomorrow." She changed the subject. "It's not the kayaking itself that's going to give me the most business, but getting up and down to and from the river. Gashes, sprains, that sort of thing?"

He nodded. "Hopefully, everyone will take it slow and easy and no one will take the riverbank too fast and end up with a concussion."

They looked at each other and both rolled their eyes. The chances of the participants, particularly the elite athletes, taking it slow up or down the path into the river were slim to none.

Riley laughed. "I'll be ready."

This camp would be home base for the first three nights. The tents were already set up for the participants, although they had to clear out the tent each morning and take everything with them in their backpack. Self-sufficiency was part of the challenge of this race, requiring the athletes to figure out what was necessary for optimum output.

They looked at each other as both their walkie-talkies went off. It was the volunteer stationed about a mile out from camp. "We've got our first athlete coming in."

Riley waggled her eyebrows at Zac. "Let the whining begin."

They walked together toward the camp's entry point. "You got your bets on anyone?" she asked Zac.

He shrugged. "I would've said your... I would've said Boy Riley on principle, but..."

"Yeah, he was looking a little rough out there on the obstacle course this morning. Unfocused. I think it's probably jet lag, or honestly, lack of training for this specific race."

"Phoenix can handle anything thrown his way. And his training at any given point is better and tougher than most of these athletes' hardest week."

She shook her head. "Yeah, but did you see him today? He was making some pretty basic mistakes."

Zac raised an eyebrow at her. "I saw him. I'm not saying he wasn't struggling. I'm saying it wasn't a physical problem. He had...other things on his mind."

Her. She was the other things.

She pretended to rub off a speck of dirt on her pants. "He's going to have to get focused. No matter what he's got on his mind."

So was she.

It wasn't Riley who made it into the camp as the first-day winner. It was Bo.

She swallowed her disappointment. There was absolutely no reason to be disappointed. First, because this was day one. There were still five more days to go, and it was the combined finishing times that mattered.

Second, she did not care how Riley Harrison did in this race. She. Did. Not. Care.

She glanced over to find Zac watching her.

"Yeah, honestly, I also thought even after his rough start it would be Riley coming in first."

She gave him a one-shouldered shrug. "I don't have an opinion. I'm just here to make sure everybody is fit to continue the race."

Zac nodded, but she caught his smile as he turned away.

Damn it.

She was going to have to find a better poker face when it came to what she was feeling. Or better yet, figure out how to turn these feelings off altogether.

The race volunteers—it took about two dozen to successfully put on a race this size—cheered for Bo as he made it across the camp finish line. He stopped to talk to a few of them as he walked to the tent area. The athletes got to choose which tent they stayed in—some were in better locations than others, closer to the bathrooms or the water. It was one of the perks of being one of the early finishers.

"I'm going back to the RV to get ready. They'll be arriving regularly now."

"I'll send Bo over to you after I talk to him."

Her fingers were starting to get a little tingly. And she was tired.

Those had been some of her first warning signs that anything was wrong, back six months ago. She'd ignored them, blaming the odd feelings on a dozen different other things.

It was only after Anne had finally talked her into seeing a

neurologist in Reddington City that Riley had finally gotten her answers.

Although, she definitely hadn't gotten the ones she wanted.

She walked inside and sat down at the small desk that held everyone's files. Sitting felt good.

She reminded herself that being a little tired and having tingly fingers didn't necessarily mean anything. Sitting had always felt good. She was on her feet all the damn time as a nurse.

But discouragement weighed on her. The hardest thing for her right now was figuring out what was MS and what was just everyday life. MS affected every person differently. She was constantly waiting for the other shoe to drop to see how it affected her.

There was a knock on the door a couple of seconds before it opened. Riley turned around to face Bo.

He grinned at her. "I'll bet you didn't expect to see me in here first."

She gestured for him to sit in the patient chair near the back of the RV. She washed her hands, then walked over to him.

"I'm neutral." But her smile was tight. "My only concern is making sure everybody makes it through this race with the fewest injuries possible."

"Come on, surely you wish it were your boyfriend in here first."

Bo and Boy Riley had been in a lot of competitions against each other, so she'd gotten to know the man in the past couple years. She didn't dislike him but didn't plan on becoming chummy with him either.

"Honestly, neutral. And Riley and I are no longer together, so *doubly* neutral."

Damn it, why couldn't Boy Riley have just stayed away?

She rubbed her fingers as they began tingling again. Dealing with the MS was enough without a constant reminder of him too.

"I'd heard something of the sort, but I wasn't sure if it was true. I'm sorry." Bo nodded at her.

"Thanks. So, first day is over. How are you feeling? Any injuries?"

"Nope. The only thing I'm feeling is that this is going to be my year."

She had no idea what to say about that. If Riley continued the way he had today, this very well could be Bo's year.

She marked down the abrasions and cuts in Bo's file, then sent him on his way. Iceland was the next to show up, also with no injuries to talk about but an interesting story about Bo leaving them during the team event.

Riley wasn't surprised. These guys could be cutthroat in their competitiveness. But technically Bo hadn't been cheating, so it was something the others had to deal with.

All was fair in love and WAR.

Her stream of patients was pretty solid for the next few hours. Everyone had to be signed off each day by her, or Anne when she was here, as okay to continue. Most of the time, that just meant a few seconds of conversation, especially today, since there'd been nothing too tough. It would get progressively more difficult on the athletes going forward: blisters, sprains, cuts, and bruises. Hopefully nothing much more serious than that.

During a lull, she walked back outside, continuing to talk to racers. It was midafternoon and nearly everyone had made it in for the day. There had been no major injuries, and no one had decided to quit after just one day. That had happened in the past.

Everyone seemed in relatively good spirits as they ate and

rested, talking about the obstacle course and its brutality. She wandered around, listening and smiling. There were a few more people she wanted to examine more thoroughly, mostly those who'd listed the Wild Wyoming as their first foray into adventure racing. For anyone else left, she'd just do a cursory check and observation.

Including Boy Riley. She'd heard the announcement when he'd arrived in fourth place, just after Iceland and Damon, but she'd refused to come out immediately and check on him.

Of course, her intentions didn't matter. Her eyes found him now, automatically sizing him up to see how he was doing.

He seemed fine as he talked to the two middle-aged women who were the last to come in for the day. No stiffness that would suggest injury or undue pain.

He looked up and caught her studying him, and she let out a curse before looking away. They were just too damn aware of each other.

She wandered more, talking to different participants, looking for anyone who might be struggling. So far, everyone seemed ready to tackle day two.

She was on the opposite side of the camp when the first spasm in her leg hit.

"Fuck." She sucked in a breath and let it out slowly, willing herself to relax. Sometimes the spasm lasted just for a moment.

Her leg jerked again.

Damn it, there was no way she was going to make it back to the RV without someone noticing something was wrong. But she wasn't going to stand here and just flop around for everyone to see.

She turned away from the camp and began walking toward the lake just a hundred feet away. The spasms probably wouldn't last long. She'd just sit by the lake in the cover of the trees. Once she had control of her muscles again, she'd go back to camp.

Generally speaking, relaxing tended to be the best thing she could do for any minor MS flare-ups right now. Relaxing would be much easier if she didn't have to worry about fifty people watching her.

She walked steadily toward the lake, feeling better and better as her muscles loosened as she moved. She was already relaxing. Maybe she'd overreacted. Maybe the spasm back at camp had just been a one-time thing. That happened too.

She made it to the large rock by the lake and just stood, feeling herself become more and more calm as she stared at the water. False alarm. Crisis averted. Everything was going to be—

A surprise gasp fell from her lips as the muscles in her legs and lower back seized up once again. There was nothing she could do but curse herself for getting so close to the water as she flopped in face-first.

Chapter 7

"Glad you finally decided to join us, Harrison. Thought maybe you'd already thrown in the towel."

Riley had arrived at camp in fourth place. He'd said earlier that he wasn't trying to win WAR, but he was used to watching everyone else come in behind him, not having the earlier finishers wave to him with a smug smile.

Yeah. Fourth place didn't sit well with him.

"Some of us don't cheat, Bo, so it takes a little longer."

Bo chewed the bite of food in his mouth and grinned at Riley. "Spare me the lecture. You're just pissed because you weren't in first place the whole day. If it hadn't been for that team obstacle, I would've left you all in the dust a lot earlier."

Riley gritted his teeth. He couldn't deny the truth in the other man's words. He had been off today. He knew why, but that didn't change it. The fact that he didn't know how to fix it made it even worse. "It was still a bitch move, Gonzales."

"Whatever. I'm not here to make friends; I'm here to win." Bo got up and threw his empty meal package into the trash bag. "And I'll tell you what I'd tell anyone who looked like you did out there today."

"Yeah? What's that?"

"If you can't give the race the concentration and respect it deserves, you have no business being out on the course. You'll get yourself killed. One wrong move on a course like this can result in a broken bone or much worse."

Damn it, Bo *still* wasn't wrong. "I'll take that under advisement."

Bo gave him a cocky little grin. "Maybe you need to face that your time as the best is over. You've risen for the last time, *Phoenix*. If you can't hack it anymore, you should just sit this one out. I'd hate to see you get hurt. Especially since I hear you don't have a nurse girlfriend to coax you back to health anymore."

"He's egging you on," Damon whispered as he and Iceland walked up behind Riley. "He didn't technically break any rules by leaving us behind, but if you start a fight, you will be. That'll be a time penalty against you."

"Ignore him," Iceland said.

Riley nodded. There was nothing he'd like more than to get into it with Bo, but his energy was better used elsewhere.

WAR was a long race, and this was just day one. It was the overall combined time that counted at the end, not who made it to camp first today.

Bo didn't know it, but he'd just made a legitimate competitor out of Riley. Now the race wasn't going to be just about Wildfire.

He was going to win this thing.

Damon slapped him on his back. "Let's make dinner and get off our feet. It's going to be a long-ass day tomorrow."

He nodded and unzipped the door to a large eight-man tent. He changed out of his running clothes and into his camp clothes, which were basically the same thing, just a little warmer. In order to keep the packs as small and light as possible, all the athletes traveled with just two sets of clothes.

Basically, the sweaty set and the non-sweaty set—one to wear during the day and one at night.

Neither set would smell very good by the time the week was over.

He walked down to the lake to rinse out his muddy clothes, not needing a reminder that he hadn't even been able to make it over a balance beam without falling, then took them back to hang out to dry near the tent. Hopefully they'd be fully dry by tomorrow—putting on damp clothes in the chilly dawn air completely sucked.

He grabbed one of his meal pouches and headed out to get the hot water to make it edible. Nothing about these MREs was very appetizing, but they were calorie and nutrient dense, so all the athletes forced them down. Between the events each day and multiple miles carrying a fifteen- to twenty-pound backpack, they were burning a shit ton of calories.

He wanted to talk to Wildfire but knew that interrupting her now when she was in the middle of talking to racers about potential injuries was a bad idea.

But he kept an eye on her—always aware of where she was and what she was doing. Of course, that had always been true.

He could almost feel her eyes a moment later looking up and down his body, which he might've taken as a sexual invite if he didn't know the truth. She was looking for injuries, looking to see if he was hiding any pain or stiffness in his movements. He'd seen her do it dozens of times over the years as he'd finished a stunt or a trip.

When she realized he was watching her in return, she immediately looked away, then turned to talk to some other people.

He filled his MRE pouch with water and zipped it shut so it could take the ten minutes to rehydrate. He stopped to talk to various people—careful to stay out of Wildfire's way —and applauded with the others as the last of the racers came in for the day—two middle-aged women smiling and covered in mud. The race attracted all types, from serious contenders to people who only planned to ever try this sort of thing once in their lifetime.

When he saw Amber sitting by herself, he walked over. "Mind if I join you?"

She shrugged, barely looking up from her food. "Sure."

"Are you doing okay?"

She took another bite of her food. "That's a tricky question to answer."

He waited, but she didn't say anything else. Her brother had died only seven months ago, four months after his skiing accident. The fact that she was here at all was amazing in and of itself.

"I just want to say that I think Felix would have been really proud of you today. The way you powered through and got Damon up that wall? It was impressive."

"I hope so."

"It's obvious that you're athletic too. Must run in your family."

"Maybe. He and I were both really active in sports, growing up. I feel like I…" she shrugged, trailing off.

"Feel like what?"

"Like since Felix's death, I haven't done enough. I feel like I've been in a holding pattern but now it's time for me to move forward. To put the past to rights."

"I really hope this race can do that for you." Maybe competing in her brother's place would give her a sense of closure.

She stood up, giving him a little nod. "It will. It has to."

She gave him another nod and walked off to throw her

meal package away. Damon smiled at her as they crossed paths, but she didn't really look at him.

"She's a tough nut to crack." Damon made a sour face and slid down beside him.

"Please do not tell me you are going to try to put the moves on Felix's sister. That's just wrong."

Damon put a hand over his heart as if he were mortally offended. "Of course not. At least, not while we're on the race."

Riley shook his head, stirring the food pouch that was almost ready to eat. "I don't remember Felix very well. But he had no business being on that slope that day. I should've tried to talk him out of it."

"Hey, Felix was an adult. Everybody has to know their own boundaries. You can't walk around with a checklist. Plus, like you said, we didn't really know the guy."

"The man broke his back, then committed suicide. We should've tried harder." He ran a hand through his hair, then rubbed the back of his neck. "Done something. If not then, then afterward. Maybe we could've made a difference."

Just because he hadn't known Felix well didn't mean Riley couldn't have stopped by the hospital or his house a few times to chat. Maybe it wouldn't have changed anything, but maybe it would've. Now Amber and her family were paying the price.

"Leave Amber alone," Riley said to Damon. "She needs friends, not…whatever you are to women."

Damon began to wax poetic about how he could be both the best friend a woman ever have and the best lover, but Riley was only half listening.

Something had just happened with Wildfire across the camp. She'd stiffened and a look of panic had fallen over her features.

No one was around her, so he had no idea what was

making her look so grim. She glanced over at the RV across the camp, then slowly stepped back into the trees behind her.

What the hell?

He waited to see if she would come back into camp, but she didn't.

Leave her alone.

Just like he'd just told Damon about Amber, Riley needed to leave Wildfire alone. Chasing her wasn't the way to handle this. He knew it, but that didn't stop him from setting down his barely touched meal pouch and telling Damon he'd catch him later.

Then Riley faded back into the tree line himself.

What the hell was she doing? What the hell was *he* doing?

Maybe Wildfire just wanted some time for herself.

Jesus, maybe she was meeting someone out here for some sort of rendezvous.

Maybe he was just losing his damn mind.

It didn't take long for him to make it around to where he'd last seen her and pick up her trail from there. She was going to the lake. That was the only thing in this direction and Riley had always loved water. He spotted her as she stopped at a rock at the water's edge.

He was an idiot. She just wanted a minute alone and he was following her like some pervert.

This was not the way to win her back.

He was just turning and walking back to camp when Riley's body did some sort of weird flailing thing, propelling her into the water.

"Riley!"

Chapter 8

He bolted for the water's edge. It was way too cold for her to have jumped willingly. Had she tripped and fallen? Passed out?

By the time he reached the water, she'd turned and clasped the rock.

He was just happy she was conscious.

"What are you doing?" she yelled, teeth already chattering from her submersion.

"What am *I* doing? What the hell are *you* doing?"

He didn't wait, just reached down and grabbed her under the armpits, yanking her out of the water. Even literally soaking wet, she didn't weigh much.

"I tripped. I fell."

"It didn't look like you fell. It looked like you were doing some sort of goddamned chicken dance and flopped into the water." He kept his hands on her shoulders.

"I—I..."

"Let's get you back to camp so you can dry off and get warm."

She looked a little panicked. What the hell? Was she in shock?

"Okay look, let's get you out of your wet clothes. At least your top half. You can have my jacket."

He thought she was going to argue, but she just nodded. He let go of her shoulders and reached down and pulled her jacket and sweater over her head. It was a very mild November day, but being soaking wet could get miserable quickly.

His mouth watered a little at the sight of her standing there in her bra, because hell, he was never *not* going to appreciate her breasts, but he didn't waste any time. As soon as her clothes were off, he stripped off his own lightweight jacket and pulled it around her.

A look of bliss crossed her face as she slipped her arms in and he zipped it up. "Thank you."

He locked his arms around her and pulled her up against his chest, relaxing a little when she didn't pull away. "I'm glad you're okay. It's a little chilly for swimming without a wetsuit. What the heck were you doing?"

"I, uh, thought I saw a spider, and I guess I overreacted."

"I thought you said you tripped."

She was silent for a moment. "Yeah, I meant I tripped because I saw a spider."

He wanted to pull her away and look her in the eyes. Tripped because she saw a spider? Her story wasn't really making sense.

But the need to hold her close won out. She could keep her reasons for her icy jump to herself if she wanted.

Before long, she pulled away. "I need to get back so I can change. And so you can get your jacket back."

He'd stand out here stark naked for hours if it meant he could be holding her. But instead, he dropped his arms.

Damn it. He hated that he wasn't sure exactly what to

do. He'd never had any sort of indecisiveness when it came to Wildfire. From the very beginning, there had been a solidness between them—unshakeable and steady. He'd always wanted her close. Had always been able to pull her close. But now that was missing.

"Okay." He took a step back, feeling the cold more from the distance between them than from the actual temperature. "Let's get you back to camp."

She took a few ginger steps, and he held a hand out at her back in case he needed to assist. Was she dizzy? Was something wrong?

He was about to ask when she seemed to find her center and begin walking normally back toward camp. Maybe he'd just imagined it.

They were almost back to camp when she turned to him. "I'm going to go around the back way so no one can see me." She gestured to his jacket. "I'll get this back to you in a few minutes. Thanks."

She didn't quite meet his eyes before turning and walking away.

Shaking his head, he watched Riley sneak around the outside of the camp circle so no one would see her.

Was she embarrassed that she'd fallen in the water? Is that why she didn't want to walk into camp?

He rubbed the back of his neck. The Wildfire he knew would've marched into the camp, trumpeting what had happened and providing descriptive details about the spider, the water, and her own hysteria. She would have made it into a huge, funny story about her own clumsiness. Would've used it to make the first-time racers feel more at ease.

That was one of the things he'd always loved about her —her ability to find joy and humor in everything, even her own mistakes. She'd never been self-conscious or embarrassed about them. Never one to sneak around camp to hide them.

Yet here she was sneaking around the back of camp to her RV so no one would see her.

He watched her go. When had she become that person who felt like she had to be embarrassed by her mistakes? Had he just been oblivious to changes happening in the woman he loved?

He scrubbed a hand over his face as he walked back into camp. He needed to cut her some slack. She was here in a professional capacity. If she didn't want to announce that she'd fallen in the water because she was afraid it might hurt her effectiveness as a medical professional, that was certainly her prerogative.

Or maybe she wasn't embarrassed by the fall into the lake at all. Maybe she just hadn't wanted to walk back into camp with *him*.

Shit. This just kept getting worse.

Baby, sitting down on a giant fallen log to eat, lifted an arm to wave at him. He grabbed the now half-cold MRE he'd left and sat down next to his friend.

The only thing that tasted worse than rehydrated beef and rice was half-cold rehydrated beef and rice.

"Did I just catch a glimpse of you walking with Girl Riley? I heard you guys broke up. Sorry, man."

"Yeah. It only happened four days ago. How does everybody know what happened?"

"That's small-town life for you. Everything moves slowly except the gossip."

Riley wasn't from Oak Creek but had been hanging around long enough to know that was the gospel truth. "I was pretty much blindsided. Everything seemed fine, and then I got a call saying our relationship wasn't what she wanted anymore." He forced himself to chew a bite of his barely lukewarm meal. "I thought maybe there was another guy involved, but she said there wasn't. Riley isn't a liar or a cheater."

Baby took a bite of his own food. "If it helps, I haven't seen her around with anyone. Although…"

"What?" Riley prompted when Baby trailed off. "Anything is better than knowing nothing."

"I've been pretty busy with Cade and Peyton. It's not every day your best friend finds out he's a father, so my intel may not be great because I've been dealing with that. But it seems like Girl Riley has been pretty distant over the past couple weeks."

That wasn't good. "Any particulars?"

Baby shrugged. "You know Riley, she's pretty independent, doesn't wear her heart on her sleeve. Last time I saw her was about three weeks ago for a girls' night out when they all showed up at The Eagle's Nest. Riley seemed fine except…almost too fine, you know? Like she was determined to be happy or die trying."

Three weeks ago. That was just about the time the weird behavior had started.

Baby shrugged. "Sorry I'm not more help. And I'm really sorry you guys broke up. Everybody always thought it was pretty amazing how you two made it work even with all the distance and the fame and everything. Plus having the same name. Seemed like it was predestined or something." Baby shifted to grab his water bottle and groaned in pain. "When Finn told me to do this race because it would be a life-changing experience, I didn't know he meant it would be because I would want to kill myself."

Riley chuckled. "I would tell you it gets easier as the days go on, but we both know I'd be lying."

Baby groaned again. "That's what I'm afraid of. Siblings, man. They're trouble. Got any brothers or sisters?"

Riley nodded. "Older sister. Well, half-sister."

"She do crazy stuff like this? Extreme sport stuff?"

"Oh hell no. Quinn is a college English professor. I'm pretty sure she disapproves of anything even remotely as immature as extreme sports."

Baby's fork stopped midway to his mouth. "Does she teach at Wyoming Community College?"

Riley let out a bark of laughter. "A community college? Dearest half-sister would never set foot in such a place. She teaches at Harvard."

This whole conversation reminded him that he needed to call Quinn. They'd never been particularly close. An eight-year age gap meant she'd been out of the house before he'd gotten old enough to really know her.

He'd only seen her one time in the past couple of years —his schedule was always crazy. They talked on the phone every once in a while, but not often enough.

Yet another person he was letting down. A lot of that going around.

"Yeah, community college. That's for people who can't hack it in real college, right?"

"Don't ask me, man. I've been putting off college for years, much to Quinn's dismay. There'll be time enough for that once this part of my life is over. Where did you go to college?"

Baby laughed, but something about it was forced, not the natural chuckle everyone was so used to, the one that put everyone at ease. "Me? I didn't even make it all the way through high school. Your Harvard sister would probably think I'm the biggest moron on the planet."

"Naw. Quinn isn't that way. She's never mean, just too smart for her own good." At least, book smart. Quinn tended to close herself off in her academic tower. The two of them couldn't be more different.

"Book smart. Yeah, that's definitely not me," Baby muttered. "I'll just stick with my cars."

"Nothing wrong with that. I mean, unless you want to go to college."

Baby just shrugged. "Some things aren't meant to be."

Riley finished his last bite and stood and stretched. He was also feeling pretty sore for it only being the first day. Bo was right. Riley was going to have to get his head out of his ass and into the game if he had any hopes of avoiding injury, and forget winning.

Wildfire opened the door to the RV, clothes now changed and looking dry and warm. "Baby, you're up for your medical check. Get in here."

"Coming, Mom!"

With a salute to Riley, Baby stood and jogged off, tossing the food packet into the trash as he went.

Riley watched as Baby said something to make Wildfire laugh, then swat at his shoulder as he entered the RV. Riley wasn't worried about it; Baby wasn't going to make a move on her.

But if Riley couldn't figure out how to fix whatever was wrong between them, he would have no say over who Wildfire dated. A knife twisted in his gut.

"Briefing in ten minutes," Zac called out to everyone. "We'll be going over tomorrow's course and what evil events we have in store for you."

Baby exited the RV just a couple minutes after he'd entered, obviously no serious wounds. But the knife was still twisting in Riley's gut when Wildfire walked out just before the briefing started.

She looked warmer and drier but still had that pinched look in her eyes.

He pulled her over to edge of the group gathering to

hear what Zac had to say. "Enough of this nonsense. I want you to tell me what's going on."

"There's nothing going on. Thank you for your jacket. I have it hanging over the heater in the RV. It should be dry by morning." She turned away, but he shifted so he was in front of her and she couldn't escape. "Move, Phoenix."

"Aren't you going to give me the required medical check?"

She glanced over him for a brief second. "You look fine."

He raised an eyebrow. "You're seriously not even going to check me out? Now my feelings are hurt."

"I won't be seeing everyone every single day. If you have medical concerns, you can let me know, and I'll be sure to keep an eye on it. Otherwise, I'll walk through camp for checks on some of the athletes. There's no need for you to come to the RV."

"Is this because I've seen you half naked twice in the past two days? Afraid you won't be able to resist me again?"

It was a dick thing to say, but it got her attention riveted back to him.

Everybody was quieting down as Zac stood up in front of them to give the briefing. Riley dropped his voice to a whisper. "You check out everybody else except me. That's because you know what happens when we're alone together."

"Or," she shot back in the same low voice, "it's because I've been watching you do stupid shit so long, I know when you're hurt or in pain and when you're not. So don't flatter yourself."

"Are you ready to tell me what's really going on?"

"Fuck off, Phoenix."

She said it just above a whisper, but it happened to be right as everyone got quiet so Zac could start the brief.

Everybody heard.

After a startled moment, everyone chuckled.

Everyone except Wildfire.

She shot Riley a look that had him checking to make sure he wasn't on fire.

Zac cleared his throat. "You might not want to make an enemy of our medical staff there, Phoenix. After I explain what we have in store for you over the next couple of days, having someone qualified to save your life might come in handy."

If so, by the looks of it, Riley was in trouble.

Chapter 9

Riley woke up before the dawn on the third day of the race. She'd always been an early riser, no matter what sort of shifts she worked at the hospital. Watching the sunrise had always been a favorite part of her day.

Even when she was pretty successfully screwing up her life.

Fuck off, Phoenix.

It had been the running joke around camp all day yesterday since everyone had heard her say it to him during the briefing the night before that.

Boy Riley had taken it all with his good-natured smile. Which just made her feel like an even bigger bitch. None of this was his fault. She knew he was trying to process the situation without having all the info.

And she was feeling more and more like she was drowning under all the weight of the info. About to crack.

She walked out of the RV into the fading darkness. The sun would be coming up soon. She gave a small wave to the volunteer who was setting up the hot water for the race participants. But right now, all the athletes were sleeping, their bodies needing as much rest as possible after the first two grueling days of the race.

She sat down at the edge of the bench and just looked out at the purple sky. She'd always found such centering and peace during the sunrise moments. But lately those moments had been missing. Was she ever going to be able to find any sort of emotional peace ever again?

Was this one more thing MS would steal from her?

Because right now, it felt like that damn condition was stealing everything important to her.

She wanted to scream up at the dawn. Just bellow with rage and pain and despair. But what good would that do except confirm to everyone around her that she was bat-shit crazy? She was on the constant verge of a panic attack. Her mental state had gotten so bad yesterday that Zac had pulled her aside to ask her, as gently as possible, if he needed to replace her.

Shit.

She'd been mortified. Wanted to go crawl under a rock somewhere.

Not once in her medical career had she been reprimanded for not doing her job thoroughly. To be reprimanded when it wasn't even MS at fault, but her own basket-case mental state, had been a cold, hard slap in the face.

The talk had at least gotten her back on track. And just in time too. Like Zac had predicted, the physical demands of day two were rough on the athletes' bodies, particularly getting up and down the hill to the river.

She'd been needed to treat multiple cuts and bruises. One person had needed stitches, one was out of the race completely with a broken wrist, and another she'd observed closely all evening due to a possible concussion. He'd have to be checked out this morning before she cleared him to continue the race. If she cleared him.

So yeah, her focus was needed here. These racers needed her to concentrate on them.

Being busy had also given her an excuse to ignore Boy Riley. Thankfully, he hadn't pushed. After he'd seen her fall into the lake, and then her none-too-gentle outburst everyone had heard at the briefing, distance had been necessary. It was all she could do yesterday to hold it together. Arguing more with him—or sidestepping more of his questions—would've just put her completely over the edge.

She hated feeling so weak. She closed her eyes and rubbed her cheeks with her hands.

So weak.

She felt the warmth of steam against the back of her hand and looked up.

For a second all she could see was a coffee mug in front of her face—the collapsible kind the racers carried.

"I don't want to fight." Riley's voice was soft as he sat down beside her. "I just want to have a cup of coffee and enjoy the sunrise with you."

Like they had so many times in so many places. He didn't say it, but she knew he was thinking it. They had experienced sunrises together all over the world, had sat in comfortable silence with each other as a new day had formed.

She didn't have the strength to fight him. Didn't want to fight him. Just wanted to watch the sunrise with him.

She took the cup and brought it to her lips, sighing at the dark, earthy taste. This was coffee from his personal stash.

"I shouldn't drink this. I know you're limited."

"I brought a little for you, don't worry."

She nodded and took another sip. She recognized it for the gift it was. Riley loved his coffee. In a race where the participants spent hours getting their backpack weight down as low as possible, he had deemed coffee necessary enough for his survival to be carrying it with him.

To offer her some now meant a great deal more than it would under normal circumstances. Participants were only allowed to consume what they carried themselves. Boy Riley wouldn't be allowed to drink any coffee she offered him, and to offer her some of his was a peace offering she couldn't turn down.

Not that *he* was the one who needed to be making the peace offering…

"Thank you. I'm sorry about everyth—"

He shook his head, his little smile just visible in the early light. "No sorry. Just sunrise."

She passed the cup back to him so he could take a sip. She sat next to him, sharing the coffee, watching the sunrise.

The weakness pooling inside her seemed to fade away with the darkness as dawn rose around them. Having him next to her, not demanding anything, not expecting anything…strengthened her.

Maybe her energy was feeding off his strength. God knew he had enough of it.

And how she missed him.

Lord, how she missed him being hers.

He handed her the cup once more, not saying a word as promised. He just sat with her to enjoy the sunrise. She'd thought falling in the lake and losing control of her body had been the most stressful part of the MS diagnosis.

She'd been wrong.

This was the most stressful part of her MS so far: not having her best friend to talk through it with.

"Thank you for the coffee," she whispered.

"Thank you for sharing the sunrise with me."

Only a couple of other racers were starting to peek their

way out of their tents. The start wouldn't be for another couple of hours. Everyone wanted to stay in their warm sleeping bags as long as possible—but they had to get up sometime.

"Was the river what you'd expected yesterday?"

Inviting conversation with him probably wasn't the best of plans, but she couldn't help herself. She missed just talking to him. She just needed a little more time with him.

"Yes." He tilted back the mug to get the last sip of coffee. "Remember the Youghiogheny River? When we decided to explore that offshoot and almost got ourselves killed?"

She couldn't help but laugh. God yes, how she remembered. Boy Riley had world-class athletic abilities; almost everything came easy to him. But water activities—kayaking, canoeing, white-water rafting, even snorkeling and scuba diving—had always been where she was most evenly matched with him. "And in that storm in Bali when we were out in that canoe? We almost died that time also."

He slid up the jacket she'd returned to him yesterday to expose his forearm. A stunning tattoo depicting a beach with the sun trying to peek out from behind angry clouds. "How could I forget?"

She touched the tattoo, one of dozens that covered his body. How could either of them forget? They'd found shelter inside a cave and spent hours making love waiting for the storm to pass.

She swallowed. "That was quite a storm."

"We've ridden out a lot of storms together."

"And experienced a lot of sunrises."

What was she saying? What was she doing? He was going to push now, want to know why she'd broken up with him.

But instead, he just looked back at the sun, which was now over the horizon. "Yes, we have." He didn't say anything else, just folded the collapsible coffee cup back down into its smallest form.

"You're not going to push?" *Fuck.* Did she want him to push? *Shut up, Riley.*

"Nope. I promised this morning was just for coffee and sunrise."

She relaxed. She couldn't help it. This. This closeness. They'd had lots of exciting moments over the course of their relationship, but it was these moments where Riley was just *Riley*, not Phoenix the international superstar, that had made her fall in love with him. "You worried about the navigating today? I hear the puzzles are a bitch this year."

He looked over at her and grinned. And her heart flip-flopped.

That grin. That cocky grin. She couldn't deny she'd fallen in love with that too.

How was she supposed to fall out of love with him at all?

"Today's where I'll stop screwing around. It's time to win."

She wasn't surprised to hear those words come out of his mouth. One, Riley didn't know any other way than to win, to be the best. Plus, she'd seen his face during last night's briefing, when Zac had been talking about what the athletes would face today. Some of the course's most challenging running, then navigation and puzzles.

It was the sort of stuff Phoenix loved to do.

"Bo is gunning for you. You better watch your back. He thinks it's his year to win."

"Let him think that. It's not going to happen." He stood up. "Thanks for sharing the sunrise with me, Wildfire."

She stood also. "Thanks for sharing your coffee. And for teaching me how to drink it black over the years so I can enjoy it anywhere."

He smiled and looked like he was going to say something but stopped himself.

"What?" she asked.

"Nothing. Sunrise—a new day. I'll see you later today after the navigation. Be on the lookout... I'll be coming in first."

Chapter 10

"You're grinning like a pretty big idiot for someone who is barely in the top five on day three of a six-day race. There's no way you're going to win, Phoenix."

Riley just grinned bigger. Bo was right; Riley had been smiling all day despite his standing in the race, which had neither gone up nor down in this morning's running segment.

The running had been brutal. A lot of hills, which required the athletes to either slow down or burn through calories they didn't have with their limited food supplies. Rough terrain that made the backpacks more cumbersome and everything just more difficult.

And Riley wasn't a runner. Not like Iceland was. The slender, quiet man had been gaining ground all morning. The best Riley could do was just hold his own and not *lose* any ground. He was still in fourth place.

Fourth place didn't sit well with him.

But Bo was right; Riley was smiling. He'd basically been smiling since this morning, when Wildfire had touched the tattoo on his arm with such a wistful look on her face.

She. Still. Loved. Him.

He didn't know what was going on, and he wasn't sure exactly how to fix it, but she still loved him. That was the best possible starting-off point he could hope for.

"Don't you worry, BoGo,"—Bo hated that nickname —"you'll still be crying at the end of the race when I beat you once again."

"Whatever, asshole. Just remember I'm a full lap ahead of you." Bo filled his water bottle from the tank the race provided.

Riley's smile didn't slip. They were in the middle of running four three-mile loops that brought them back around to camp each time. Each loop took them out into a different direction, with different terrain, each progressively more difficult to navigate with their packs.

And like Bo said, he was in fact a full lap ahead of Riley. Bo thought it was because he was so much faster, but it was really because of Riley's physical ailments.

So many physical ailments that had required he stop and be checked out by the race medical staff—Wildfire—every time he came back through camp.

Riley would gladly move into last place if it meant he got to talk to her every time he came through.

"I'm sure I'll catch you during the navigation section." He winked at Bo. "I'm not worried about it for a second."

Bo muttered something under his breath and took off from the camp down the new trail. Riley couldn't help but chuckle. Bo was young, almost ten years younger than him. He still hadn't quite developed his game face or a genuine respect for the experience of racing.

All Bo could see right now was the destination. The journey was lost on him.

Riley had been that way for a long time also. It had only been in the past few years, mostly since he'd met Wildfire, that he'd started to appreciate the race, the journey, the sunrise…not just the winning.

Of course, he still liked the winning. And planned to win this race.

Planned to win all the way around.

He slipped the backpack off and watched Wildfire rush over to him from the RV, worry clear on her face. Let Bo get ahead. Riley had more important things to do at this moment.

"You're stopping again?"

He almost felt bad that he was putting that look of concern in her eye, although he could admit he was happy to see it there. She was right to be a little concerned. Under normal situations, he would've been near death before stopping for medical attention three times in a row.

She put her hands on the rotator cuff of his shoulder, pressing to check for inflammation or soreness, since this was the "injury" he'd had last time he'd come through camp about forty minutes ago. "Does this hurt?"

Hurt? Hell no. He had to hold back his groan at how good her hands felt on him. He shook his head. "No, it's feeling better."

She narrowed those hazel eyes at him. "Let me get this straight. Your knee was hurting when you came in here the first time. That was feeling better when you came back around the second time, but your shoulder was hurting. Now you're telling me your shoulder is not hurting, yet you're stopping again?"

He could barely keep from smiling. He'd known Wildfire was too smart to fool for long. He was surprised he'd even made it to the second round.

He slid both his sleeves up, then held up his elbow and pointed to it. "I was injured going through the woods and got scratched. Zac has us on the most menacing trails out there."

Her eyebrow was raised so high she looked like an emoji.

"What?" he asked, all innocence. "I think I might need stitches."

She finally looked down at his elbow. When he heard her little chuckle, he thought his heart might actually burst out of his chest.

That's what was wrong.

It came to him so suddenly it almost floored him.

Wildfire hadn't been laughing. At all. Not with him, not with anyone else. She was so lively and full of life that the absence of her laughter was completely foreign and unnatural. Her laughter had been the first thing he'd ever noticed about her.

He'd been going about this all the wrong way, thinking about their breakup from a purely selfish standpoint—why had she broken up with him? That wasn't the question he needed to be asking at all.

What had caused her to stop laughing?

And even more importantly, how could he bring the laughter back?

He definitely couldn't bring it up directly. He knew her well enough to know that. Whatever was going on, he couldn't force the details out of her. He was going to have to *gentle* the details out of her.

Court her. Woo her. Make her understand there was nothing in this world she couldn't trust him with.

She shook her head, looking down at his arm. "I can tell it really hurts by the way you're holding up the *wrong elbow*, Harrison."

Shit. Ha ha. He quickly brought up the other elbow, which did, in fact, have a tiny scratch on it. "Yeah, this one. I have elbow dyslexia."

She touched his arm, then looked up at him, fighting off a smile, and shook her head. "Stay right here while I go get my amputation kit. There's no saving a limb with a wound this terrible. Almost like the first time."

She remembered the first race. Their first time talking. Good. He wanted her to remember.

He nodded solemnly. "That's what I was afraid of."

"What are you doing, Ry?" she whispered.

"Just spending a little time with my favorite nurse, getting myself checked out."

She rolled her eyes. "I think you need to get your head checked out."

"We've both always known that."

She opened the first aid kit in her hand and pulled out a bandage. He gave her his best scared face.

"Is it going to hurt as you cut my arm off?"

She chuckled again as she opened the bandage. "Only if I accidentally slip and chop off your head instead."

She placed the bandage over the tiny scratch. "There. Now get out of here with all your boo-boos."

He winked at her. *Someday soon you'll be kissing my boo-boos and making them better again.*

He was wise enough not to say it out loud, but there was no doubt in his mind that it was true.

"If you'll come watch me rappel tomorrow, I won't stop next time unless I'm actually injured."

She shook her head. "You're incorrigible. But yes, if I can."

He slipped his pack back on and took off at a sprint. He had a race to win.

Chapter 11

The next time around, as promised, Riley didn't stop to have any of his wounds tended. He gave Girl Riley a little salute as he ran past, grinning as he heard her call out, "What? No amputations this time?"

God, how he loved that woman.

It was time to move on to one of his favorite portions of the race: navigation and puzzles.

So much of what Phoenix did on a regular basis was physical in nature—after all, physical danger made for exciting viewing. But that didn't mean he didn't like mental challenges also.

The navigation portion of the race wasn't *physically* difficult, but if a participant wasn't careful, these puzzles could add a lot of minutes to their overall race time. The race had been won or lost here before.

Every competitor's route was different in this segment. They each had a particular color that corresponded with their puzzles and were given only a compass and a rudimentary map. They had to complete each puzzle to gain the flag and move on to the next segment, puzzle, and flag.

It required patience and mental acuity, both of which weren't always easy to find when your brain and body were exhausted from two and a half days of brutal racing already.

Riley pulled his focus inward, blocking out everything else: his exhaustion, discomfort, real and pretend booboos, and even what was going on with Wildfire. He'd need all his focus and concentration to make it through this segment as quickly as possible.

This was where being a world-class athlete came in handy: he knew how to focus his mind.

It was time to make up for lost ground.

He moved competently for the first two hours through the easier clues and puzzles, running into various other athletes on their quests. Since everyone was looking for different colored flags, it didn't matter that they were all roaming the same woods, and it certainly wouldn't help a competitor to follow someone else.

He studied his map and the natural markers it provided —rivers, boulder, ledges—then used his compass and found where the next puzzle should be—near a tree where a small creek turned south.

But it wasn't there.

Riley looked all around in case it had fallen but didn't see it anywhere.

Finally, with a curse, he backtracked to where he'd found the last puzzle box, completed it, and gotten the flag. He must've made some sort of error in his navigation.

He recalculated everything, forcing himself to slow down and follow the map more closely in case he'd made a mistake. Even the smallest of errors could have pointed him in the wrong direction.

But even that slow, he ended up at the same place. Still no puzzle. Without the puzzle, he couldn't get the flag. *Shit*. He could continue, but he'd be penalized.

Out of the corner of his eye Riley caught sight of someone. He turned to ask the person if they had seen the puzzle box or were having difficulties.

But no one was there.

Okay, so now this was getting a little weird. He'd been talking to various people all afternoon. All of the competitors were crossing paths during this event. Talking to each other and egging each other on had been part of the of navigation camaraderie.

It was pretty damned suspicious that someone would take to hiding at the same time and near the same location where Riley's puzzle box was missing.

Riley wanted to know who it was.

He walked casually in the opposite direction until he reached a large fallen tree, then ducked behind it and doubled back to where he'd first seen the unknown person near some low shrubs.

There was no one there.

Goddammit. Riley looked around, crouching down to the ground. Someone had been here. He'd spent enough time with the Linear Tactical guys, Dorian —*Ghost*—in particular, to have picked up some tracking tips.

He could see where someone's knee had made an indentation in the muddy dirt closest to the bushes. A little bit further over, some branches were bent and broken, most likely from the person trying to move in a hurry once Riley headed that way.

But regardless, it didn't matter. Whoever had been here was gone. If they'd had something to do with why he couldn't find his fourth navigation puzzle box, he wasn't going to be able to prove it anyway.

With a curse Riley headed back one last time to where he'd finished the previous puzzle. He worked his route out again, hoping this time it would be different, but it wasn't, of course.

Damn it, he was going to have to take the penalty. An event that should have been helping him catch up in the race was now going to put him further behind.

He went back to where he knew the puzzle should be and began the last segment from there. He wouldn't get the points from his missing flag at stage four, but he could still get the flag for stage five.

He used his map and compass to figure out the location of the fifth puzzle. That basically proved that he'd been in the correct location for the fourth stage. There was no way he could've gotten to the fifth stage correctly if he'd been wrong for the fourth stage.

This wooden puzzle box was the most difficult, but Riley forced himself to say calm and focused, ignoring the frustration eating at him over the missing flag.

The puzzles used the same part of his brain that designed and organized his stunts. He took his safety seriously. Before he ever jumped off a cliff or tried a new motorcycle flip or launched a skydive trick, he made sure the science worked. That same thorough thinking and logical approach worked in his favor now. It wasn't long before he had the puzzle box open and was accessing the flag inside. From there he sprinted back to camp.

He was in second place coming in for the day, behind only Amber. Good for her. Riley didn't have any recollection of Felix being particularly good at navigation or puzzles, but that didn't mean his sister wasn't a whiz.

And Amber should at least be safe from Damon's advances for a few hours. He would take a huge hit in time today—probably knocking him out of the top five. Mental challenges weren't his strong suit. He was much better at the physical ones.

Iceland, Baby, Bo... Riley wasn't sure how they would do.

Especially Bo.

Riley walked over to the check-in table where Zac was sitting.

Zac grinned up at him. "Phoenix, now this sort of result I was expecting out of you. I'm not surprised you're coming in second."

Riley slapped the four flags down on the table.

"Four?" Zach's brow furrowed. "You couldn't figure out number five?"

Riley flipped them over so Zac could see the numbers on the back of each flag. "Nope, the puzzle for four wasn't where it was supposed to be."

"You sure you weren't just in the wrong spot?"

"If I navigated to the wrong spot for puzzle four, then I would've been off for puzzle five also. I was at the right place. The puzzle wasn't there."

Zac's eyes narrowed. "What exactly are you trying to say?"

"Somebody moved it."

Zac signaled for one of the volunteers to come over, one of the teenage kids that lived in town. "Adam, can you check in everyone as they get here? Mark their time on the paper."

The kid nodded.

"Everything okay? We need some sort of amputation?"

Just the sweet sound of Wildfire's voice was enough to calm some of the angst inside him.

"Can you help Adam man the table if he needs it?" Zac asked. "Phoenix and I need to go check something out in the woods."

"Everything okay?" she asked.

Riley nodded. "Zac and I just need to double-check a couple things."

She smiled. "No problem. We'll hold down the fort."

"Stay off your ankle as much as possible." Zac grabbed a folding chair and set it up for Wildfire behind the table. "Have runners come to you."

Riley turned to ask her what had happened but was taken aback when he saw the look in Wildfire's eye.

Fear.

Fear directed at *him*.

What the hell?

He'd dragged her all over the world, taken her rock climbing, scuba diving, hang gliding, all sorts of scary things.

And she might've been nervous about some of them, but he'd never seen that look of unadulterated fear in her eyes.

He wasn't even sure how to process it.

"What? What happened?" He dropped down next to her, eyes searching over the rest of her body, the same way hers had searched him so many times, trying to ascertain if there was some bigger injury he couldn't see.

"I'm okay," she said, reaching out to him. "I just tripped. Barely twisted my ankle. Zac shouldn't have made a big deal out of it. I'm okay."

He studied her again, scrutinizing her for signs of pain but found none. She really did look fine. "Really?"

She looked away for a second, but when she turned back to him her eyes were bright. The fear was gone. "Just got clumsy and tripped. It won't even hurt in a couple hours."

He still had the overwhelming urge to pull her into his arms and just hold her. To shelter her from some foe he couldn't see and that probably didn't even exist.

He'd never been overprotective of Riley. There was not one thing about her that gave off a damsel-in-distress vibe. She could take care of herself—it was one of the things he most loved about her. So this urge to grab her now and fight her demons was a little unsettling, especially given the fact that she'd wanted more distance between them, not less.

He held a hand out toward her. He wasn't even sure what he was reaching for, what he was trying to do. "I don't understand what's happening."

His heart broke a little as she took a step back and sat in the chair Zac had set up for her. "I know."

What did that mean? He wanted to push, but this wasn't the time.

She turned to Zac. "I'm fine. We've got everything under control here. You guys go on."

Whatever emotional vulnerability he'd sensed was gone. His Wildfire, independent and capable, was 100 percent back.

Zac turned to him. "Ready?"

He nodded. Girl Riley was already talking with Adam and they were setting up a system to check the athletes in.

He and Zac began walking back the same route Riley had used coming in to camp.

They weren't very deep back into the woods before he had to ask. "When did Riley hurt her ankle? I ran through camp multiple times this morning, and she seemed fine."

Zac had never been overly chatty, but he was quiet for so long Riley didn't know if he was going to answer. But that just meant Zac had something further to say about Girl Riley's hurt ankle. He would've already answered if had just been some random fall like she'd said.

"Did you do something stupid?" Zac finally asked.

Riley let out a short bark of laughter. That wasn't what he'd been expecting the other man to say. "I'm afraid you're going to have to be a little more specific. Or at least give me a timeframe if you want me to start listing all of my stupid."

Zac chuckled as he made his way through the woods. It

was good to hear the sound. Before his fiancée Anne came along, Zac hadn't laughed much. Losing a wife and toddler son did that to a man.

"Fair enough. Specifically, I'm asking if you did something stupid like cheat on Girl Riley to make her break up with you."

"Wow, Cyclone, didn't realize you had taken over the position of Oak Creek's lead gossip."

Zac flipped him off without even looking at him but chuckled again. "I'm a man of many skills. Look, I don't need details. I was just wondering if you'd been a complete dumbass and that was what had put the look I've been seeing on Girl Riley's face the past few days."

Riley stopped. "You need to tell me exactly what you're talking about. No, I did not cheat on Riley. I would never cheat on Riley. I can't even imagine anyone else in the world capturing my attention the way she does. I would never hurt her that way."

Zac nodded and started walking again. Riley had to walk or get left behind, so he started walking.

"So you guys broke up because it just wasn't working for you anymore? A mutual decision?"

He'd worked with Zac multiple times, here in Wyoming and when he'd helped Linear with some missions overseas. So he and Zac had spent their fair share of hours conversing. But this was by far the weirdest, most personal conversation he'd ever had with the man. "If you must know, she broke up with me, and I have no idea why."

Now it was Zac who stopped and turned to look at Riley. He nodded, no surprise anywhere on his dark features.

"What exactly are you asking, Zac?"

"Why are you here, Phoenix?" the man shot back.

Riley started walking again, this time leaving Zac to

follow or not follow. "I'm here to win this race again. To become the first two-time champion."

"Is that it?"

"Is that not enough?"

"I don't know, is it?"

Riley let out a sigh. "Zac. Whatever it is you have to say, just spit it out."

"I've known Riley for a long time. For most of her life. She's an amazing woman. Smart. Independent."

"You're not telling me anything I don't already know and wholeheartedly agree with."

Zac shook his head. "She's fearless. Maybe not in the way you are with the stunts, but in life. If I had to pick a single word to describe Girl Riley, it would be *fearless*. That's why I always thought you two were a good fit. She would never be scared by your antics."

Riley raised an eyebrow. "I'm still sitting here parked at the corner of Already-Know-That and No-Duh. What's your point?"

Zac crossed his arms over his chest. "Last few days, something with Girl Riley has changed."

"The fearlessness is gone." The words were out of Riley's mouth before he was conscious of thinking them. *Wildfire's fearlessness was gone.*

Zac nodded. "Thus, my original question about whether you'd done something stupid. I know you being here has affected her, but I wasn't sure you were the root cause of whatever it is that is weighing on her."

Riley thought about the look on her face a few minutes ago. "You brought up her ankle in front of me on purpose."

Zac gave him a one-shouldered shrug. "Yes. I wanted to see how you both would react."

She'd been scared. Why? That was the question he needed to figure out. They started walking again.

"Most people wouldn't have caught that I'd done that on purpose." Zac glanced over at him. "You would've made a good Special Forces soldier. You've got the physical and intellectual drive it would take."

"I've never been great at following orders. And somehow, I don't think the army would approve of some of my antics." Riley ran a hand through his hair as they continued.

Zac chuckled. "Probably not."

"I'm here to win her back." He stepped around a fallen log. "Or at the very least find out why she broke up with me to begin with."

Zac stepped over the log. "Something is hurting her. It might be you. And if that's the case, you're going to have to decide whether your answers are worth the pain you're causing her."

That was something Riley hadn't considered. The last thing he wanted to do was cause Riley pain.

But, Jesus, he wanted answers so bad he could taste it.

They continued on in silence.

"Okay, show me where you feel like the puzzle box should've been."

Riley got his map out to make sure he was going to the exact same place. He led Zac back to the tree he'd been at three times already today.

"This is it. Every calculation I did led me right to this point."

"I'm sure it did." Zac pointed down to a rock resting against the tree. Sure enough, there was a box, about half the size of a shoebox, in Riley's color.

He grabbed and opened it, finding the puzzle inside.

"Motherfucker." Riley looked over at Zac. "I'm telling you, that wasn't here. I scoured everything in a ten-foot radius of this tree. That box was not here."

Zac nodded, then looked down at his watch. "If you want to do the puzzle right now, I'll clock your official time in from the moment you're done. It's less of a penalty than not having the flag."

Riley took out the papers and immediately began working on the puzzle. It was number and logic based this time. When he finally figured out the answer, he used the digits to open the combination lock inside the box and pulled out the flag.

Zac nodded. "Okay. I'll record this as your official time."

Riley got up, handing the flag and box to Zac. "I'll take it. But I'm telling you, that box was not here when I was looking for it.

Zac nodded. "On one hand, I believe you. I really do. You'd have to be damn near blind not to see this thing. Plus, you made it to the fifth puzzle's location. You never would've been able to do that if you weren't at this spot to navigate from."

"Thanks."

"But on the other hand, your brain is not fully in this race, Riley. I've seen people make mistakes more stupid than this, and that was just after the *normal* mental wear and tear of this race. With what's happening with Girl Riley, you're going through a lot more."

"Shit." Zac was right.

Was it possible that he'd just totally missed the box? Had he been so caught up with some stupid premonition that someone was hiding in the woods that he'd missed what was right in front of his eyes?

Had Girl Riley been trying to tell him something for months and he'd missed that too?

"I want to say it's impossible that I didn't see the box, but I can't with 100 percent surety." For someone who'd made a career out of situational awareness, this was a tough thing to admit.

Zac shrugged. "Ultimately, it doesn't matter. You take the time hit, but it's not unrecoverable."

"Yeah. Thanks for even giving me that much."

Zac slapped him on the shoulder. "Let's get back to camp. A few hours rest will probably do you wonders. Tomorrow is rapelling, another of your strong suits. You'll be able to make up even more time."

If Riley could keep from sabotaging himself, which might be what had happened today.

Jesus, was that also true about Wildfire? Had he been sabotaging their relationship and been oblivious to it?

He needed a few minutes alone to get his head clear.

He nodded at Zac. "You go on ahead. I'm right behind you."

Zac nodded and took off. Riley stood for a while looking at where the box had been.

No. There was no way he'd missed that.

He turned and made his way over to the place where he'd been sure someone had been hiding and watching.

He blinked, muttering a curse under his breath. The broken branches that had convinced him someone was there were now gone.

"Fuck."

First the box, now this.

He didn't know what to do if he couldn't trust his own mind.

As he began to back away, he looked down at the ground. Damn it, even the place where he'd seen an indentation from a knee was gone.

But wait. He leaned down closer. There was no indentation, but the dirt there was a little too perfect. Had the person come back and covered their tracks?

Or was he just taking a bad scenario and making it even worse, justifying his own neuroses?

For the first time in his life, not only was Riley unsure what his next steps should be, he didn't know which of his past steps were true either.

Chapter 12

Riley knew there was a problem as soon as she saw Zac returned to camp without Boy Riley. She stood up from behind the table. Her ankle really wasn't a big deal. She wished he hadn't said anything in front of Riley at all.

She'd been terrified Riley was going to ask for details, and that she was going to have to figure out a way to explain away the random spasm that had caused her to trip as she was coming down the RV steps.

MS strikes again. She'd just been glad only Zac had seen the misstep. But then he'd tattled on her, damn it.

She left Adam at the table and walked over to Zac. Most of the elite athletes had already checked in for their official times. The ones coming in now were those in the middle of the pack, not the ones so worried about time.

"Did you kill Boy Riley and need me to help you hide the body?"

Zac smiled. "No. He should be back in just a few minutes."

"Had the box been destroyed by an animal or something?"

Rumors about the missing box were already floating around camp. She and Adam had spent some of their time discussing what might have happened to it. They were in the middle of the Wyoming wilderness, after all, so there were lots of options for demise.

"No. It was right there, exactly where it was supposed to be."

The camp around them got unnaturally silent—a telltale sign that the competitors had been listening in on the conversation. Zac didn't look concerned.

But Riley couldn't believe what he was saying. "Are you sure? He wouldn't have just skipped it. He loves puzzles and navigation. Not to mention he's way too stubborn to have given up and just come to camp early. He'd still be out there now trying to figure the puzzle out if he hadn't been able to do it." She had not one doubt about that.

"Probably. Riley's timing in the navigation segment the year he won WAR was unparalleled. Faster than anyone had ever done it by far."

"You can't really believe he would go from that to not being able to finish. Riley is too good for that."

Everyone was still listening. She didn't really want to have this conversation in front of everyone, but Zac was leading them farther into the camp rather than toward the cabin he'd been using as an office.

He was making sure everyone could hear.

"I found the puzzle right where it should have been."

She shook her head. "He really just missed it?"

"No. He never would've been able to make it to the fifth box and flag if he hadn't made it to the fourth. Riley feels certain the box was not there earlier this afternoon. Yet, there it was."

"I can't believe it. Riley doesn't make mistakes like that."

"I agree."

Someone made a smirking noise behind them, although no one said anything outright.

Riley could understand their frustration. The rules and penalties for this part of the race were clear. Riley had come in without one of the flags. Zac couldn't just ignore that.

But if he penalized Phoenix, it would effectively eliminate any hope Riley had for winning the race.

"Riley led me directly to where the box should've been without any difficulty. And honestly, he would've had to be damn near blind to have missed it. I allowed Riley to complete the puzzle in front of me and recorded his time as the point at which he finished it."

"Okay." She didn't like it, but it was better than the multi-hour penalty he would have taken for coming in without the flag.

"I'll have to look at everyone else's scores to know where that puts him overall."

There was silence for another moment before everyone resumed their normal conversations. Evidently, everyone thought Zac's ruling was fair.

The person this would most negatively affect was Riley. This should have been his event to catch up on.

"I couldn't give him any unfair advantages," Zac said in a voice that didn't carry to anyone else. "Not that he wanted me to."

"Yeah, I know." She wasn't surprised. That wasn't how Riley would want to win.

"He's struggling, you know."

Because of her. Zac didn't say it, but it was still true. She just nodded, unable to say anything. Zac squeezed her shoulder and turned to the check-in table. She walked over to the latest racers to arrive to see if they had any medical concerns. Even though today wasn't nearly as risky as yesterday, everyone still had to be cleared.

She almost wished for yesterday's more serious physical ailments. Those had at least kept her attention riveted to what was happening.

She couldn't stand the thought that Riley was hurting. But of course he was. How could he not be? She'd broken up with him out of the blue, then had been ping-ponging back and forth ever since.

This race was designed to push athletes to their limits physically and mentally. Riley definitely had an added handicap by having to deal with their emotional fallout also.

It would've been so much easier for both of them if he'd left like she'd told him to.

She just needed this race to be over so that she could get away from him and try to keep the MS from him. That was so hard when all she wanted to do was lean into his strength.

"What's that sigh all about?"

She turned to find Bo standing behind her. "Just trying to keep all you crazy racers in one piece."

"I'm sorry about the shit today with Phoenix. Truly. This race is hard enough without having a breakdown during one of your best events. I'm sure he's frustrated. Anybody would be."

"I'm concerned about him, just like I'm concerned about you all."

"Okay. Right." Bo looked sympathetic, though incredulous too.

"How about you? How's the body holding up?"

"Some cuts and scrapes like everyone, but I'm feeling great overall." She looked him over. He had a couple of cuts on his palms as well as some scrapes and bruises from getting up and down to the kayak yesterday. He had stiffness in his shoulder from the obstacle course that might give him some discomfort over the next couple of days, but she was sure he would ignore that.

These athletes would ignore almost everything until the race was over. Her job was to make sure there was nothing wrong with them that couldn't afford to be ignored. Bo didn't seem to have any of those worries.

She slapped him on the back. "Looks like you're in pretty good shape, just where you want to be halfway through this race. How are you feeling mentally?"

Unless someone showed obvious signs of mental deterioration, she wouldn't really be judging anyone's emotional stability, but it never hurt to give somebody a chance to express themselves.

Bo shot her a beaming smile. "I feel great. This is really my year. I'm going to win." He grimaced. "I guess I shouldn't say that to you."

He was so enthusiastic about winning it was hard not to be caught up in it. "No, it's fine. Really. For more reasons than one."

"I'm sorry about you and Phoenix." Bo shrugged. "I'm not good at interpersonal communication stuff. But, you know, I'm sorry."

Coming from the big guy, it was a sweet gesture. "Thank you."

"If you want to talk about it or anything…" He shrugged awkwardly. "Now, or even after the race sometime."

He touched her on the arm. It was all she could do not to flinch and jerk away. Nothing about the touch was inappropriate, but she still didn't want it.

She was never going to date Bo. She didn't want to date anybody in the adventure sport world if it wasn't Riley. She didn't want to date *anybody at all* if it wasn't Riley. She wasn't sure that would ever change.

"Can I see you in the medical RV for a couple minutes?"

She jerked at the sound of Boy Riley's voice behind her. As she turned, she caught sight of Bo's sly little grin.

Fucker. He'd been using her to poke at Riley. These guys would do anything to win.

"You really are bad at this interpersonal shit," she murmured.

Bo ignored her, his attention now on Riley. "Glad you finally made it in, Phoenix. Sorry to hear about your missing box trouble. I was offering Girl Riley here a shoulder, or more, if she was ready to level up in her love game."

Oh, this guy was about to need a lot more medical attention than she'd be able to give him. "Watch it, Gonzales," she murmured.

"It's okay," Bo said, actually stepping closer to her as if both she and Boy Riley weren't about to kill him. "You guys are broken up. You're free to do what you want. If you want a better man—*a winner*—nobody would blame you. Looks like Phoenix is going to lose the girl and the race all in one year."

Boy Riley's eyes narrowed and he took a step closer.

Shit. Bo was pushing all Riley's buttons on purpose, trying to start a fight. Once Riley lost his temper, there would be no stopping his fists.

That would be another penalty at best, complete disqualification at worst.

"Riley—" she started.

He took a step closer, his eyes on Bo. She held an arm out toward him and he glanced at her. The tiny smile he gave her—the one they used to communicate with each other that everything was okay—warmed her heart in a way she didn't want to think about.

It also meant he wasn't going to let Bo goad him into anything. Phoenix was in complete control of himself.

When Boy Riley's gaze fell back to Bo, all traces of warmth disappeared. He continued walking forward until he was right up in Bo's face.

"One," Riley poked him in the chest, "Girl Riley is way too good for me, which makes her ten times too good for you. So you can touch her all you want. She's perfectly capable of breaking your fingers herself."

Had her heart been warmed by his smile? That was nothing compared to how his words made her feel now.

Because she damn well *was* capable of breaking the fingers of any man who touched her without her permission.

"Two," Riley lowered his voice so nobody but the three of them could hear, "that's a nice dirt stain on your knee, BoGo. Funny how your knee got muddy in today's events. Only one knee got dirty."

She had no idea what Riley was talking about.

But evidently Bo did.

"You can't prove anything."

"Can't prove what?" she asked.

Neither man answered her, attention caught on each other.

"Plus, we're in a race that has us all filthy," Bo continued. "How the hell am I supposed to know how my knee got dirty?"

Boy Riley reached up and brushed an imaginary piece of lint off Bo's shoulder. He leaned in closer. "You should've opened with that argument, Gonzales."

Bo grimaced.

"What is going on?" she demanded. Whatever was happening between these two guys, she didn't understand it.

"Nothing. Bo was just leaving, weren't you, buddy?" Riley turned to her. "And I need you to look at my hands."

Bo stomped off without another word. She turned her glare on Riley. "What just happened?"

"Gonzales decided to up the game. I was just letting him know I'm up for the challenge."

She narrowed her eyes. She still didn't understand what was going on.

Before she could even ask him what was wrong with his hands, he was moving toward the RV. She had to hurry to catch up with him.

"Hey, are you okay?" she asked as he reached the steps leading up to the RV door. "Zac said the box was there. I don't understand that. And your hands are hurt? What's going on?"

She looked down at his hand. The knuckles were bloody.

"Inside." He reached for the door, leaving her to follow behind.

Alarmed by his tone and everything that had just happened with Bo, she immediately followed. The door closed behind her.

"Riley." She slapped him on the back. "What the fuck is going on—"

The breath left her body in a huff as she found herself slammed up against the door, her body trapped by his, his lips pressed hard against hers.

"Tell me to stop," he said against her lips. "Tell me I'm hurting you physically or emotionally, and I swear I'll back away. But God, Wildfire, I can't stand to see another man touching you. Not Bo, not anyone."

She should stop this. She knew she should stop this, but everything about it felt so good. Everything about his body fit so perfectly against hers. Everything he was doing was what she needed.

"No, don't stop. It doesn't change anything about our situation, but don't stop."

He was dragging her jacket off before she even finished her sentence. She did the same to his, trying to take care of his fingers, but he wouldn't let her.

"What happened to your fingers?"

"Lost a fight with a tree."

The race was really wearing on him. "Riley." She pushed him back until he was against the bench seat and lowered himself to sit.

She climbed onto him, straddling his hips. He hooked a hand around the back of her neck to bring her in for another hard kiss, but she resisted, threading her fingers into his hair behind his ears and rubbing her thumbs down his temple so she could look into those brown eyes. "Riley."

She could almost feel the adrenaline buzzing through him. He pulled away and nipped down her jaw. She didn't mind being his outlet, she'd been his outlet for this on more than one occasion, but she wanted to make sure he was all right. "Phoenix. Hey."

She closed her hands around his cheeks, holding him still. He closed his eyes, then leaned his forehead against hers. "I'm sorry. What am I doing? This isn't fair to you."

"I'm okay. It's you I'm worried about."

"Shit. Zac was right."

His face was so agonized. She ran her thumbs over his wrinkled forehead. "Right about what?"

"I'm hurting you."

She ground her hips down against his. "Trust me. Nothing about this hurts." He shook his head but didn't turn away when she brought her lips in to kiss him. "It's okay, Phoenix. I want you."

She wanted him now more than ever. She'd regret it, but she wanted him.

He wanted her too. The evidence was rocking up against her, driving her crazy. "Kiss me, Phoenix. Make me burn."

He let out a strangled groan, and she knew she'd won.

His lips fell on hers with a ferocity that left her gasping. His hands locked around her shoulders and pulled her tighter against him. When his lips fell to her neck, she let out a sigh. Whatever price she ended up paying for this would be worth it. But at the small sound, he stopped. His hands fell away from her hips and his lips moved from her throat.

"What's wrong?"

"I know that sound."

"What sound?"

"Resignation."

She cupped his cheeks. "Riley, I want you. You are not coercing me in any way."

"But you also know you're going to be paying a price for it later."

She sat, staring at him. He knew her too well.

"I don't know what's going on with you, Wildfire. I don't know what it is you won't share with me. But I'll be damned if I'm going to add to whatever weight it is you're carrying. I love you too much for that."

He took her weight at the hips and gently moved her until she was sitting next to him on the bench, then stood up.

"What about you? Are you okay?"

He stopped but he didn't turn around. "Honestly, no. I haven't been okay since you called a week ago and ended my world as I know it."

Without another word he walked out the door.

Chapter 13

Day four of the race involved no backpacks.

The packs were all getting lighter each day as the athletes ate more and more of their food, but today the packs were left in the camp since the fifteen-mile course would end with rappelling and climbing.

Fifteen miles was still a long way to go, the terrain as rough as yesterday, their bodies more worn down.

But Riley was focused. There would be no more stopping and flirting with Wildfire. Last night's kiss had singed him, but Zac's words were a constant echo in his head.

Something was hurting her. Something was making her afraid.

And somehow, it was tied to him.

He didn't love her any less, but he needed to regroup and decide the best way to approach this whole situation with her. The direct approach wasn't always the most effective. Spending time with a bunch of former Special Forces soldiers had taught him that. It was true in war.

It was true in love also.

In this case, those things were the same.

He'd had coffee with her again at dawn this morning, again not saying anything, just needing to be close. He'd asked her if she would come watch him during the rappelling today. She'd said she would try.

He was going to shove the entire situation out of his head today as he pushed his body hard. Winning with Wildfire might have to wait. But he was damned well determined to win this race. Whoever had messed with his puzzle box yesterday had just cemented it.

It was time to stop screwing around. Phoenix was about to rise.

Running without the backpack felt so much easier. Riley pushed, the miles melting away as he focused on nothing more than the next step in front of him. By midafternoon, he'd made it to the cliffside where the rappelling would take place, the route having looped them back around so they were about a mile and a half from camp.

The climbing and rapelling were set up in multiple stations. Just like with the kayaking, there were safer routes that weren't as technically difficult but were longer. The less experienced athletes would go with those.

Riley didn't even slow down as he passed them on his way up to the more dangerous rappelling stations. Most of the elite athletes would do the same.

There were three separate rappelling stations set up at the top of the cliff. Only one person could be on one rappelling line at a time, so if all three were taken when you arrived, you just had to wait.

Everyone had to rappel down the cliff, move over to the sides, and climb back up again in an area more suitable for climbing, then rappel back down before running back to camp.

There were two people already in the process of climbing back up. The one near the top was definitely Bo.

The other near the bottom was slower, maybe Baby. Somebody else was on one of the easier rappelling lines, moving pretty slowly. Looked like Iceland.

Riley didn't waste any more time. He got into the rappelling harness and strapped himself in. Less than five minutes after he'd arrived at the edge of the cliff, he was making his way down.

Riley didn't play it safe, but Zac had chosen a location that didn't make the rappelling easy. Some of it required horizontal jumps, and the trickiest parts required participants to move both down and to the side at the same time.

None of it fazed Riley. He was laughing out loud and had passed Iceland by the time he reached the canyon floor.

Iceland wasn't mad, just waved him on. It was going to take the other man a while.

Riley unhooked himself from the rappelling line at the bottom and ran over to the climbing area. Bo was already near the top. Catching him would be hard, probably impossible. Baby was halfway up. Riley might very well catch him if not in the climb, then back on the second rappel. There was no way Baby was as fast as him on that.

The climbing was treacherous and free solo for the first fifteen feet to a ledge, meaning the athletes had no safety ropes to catch them if they fell. That was one of the challenges of the harder section. A fall from fifteen feet wasn't going to kill you, but it might knock you out of the race for good. In the easier section there would be no free solo climbing at all.

As he ran over, a flash from the top of the cliff wall caught his eye. Based on the location, it looked like Wildfire had kept her word to come watch him.

That just made him move faster and with more purpose.

He'd never needed to impress her with athletic feats before, but damned if he didn't want to today.

He studied the cliff wall for a couple moments, determining the best route. Once he had a clear path in his mind, he didn't hesitate.

All thoughts of everything, even Wildfire, disappeared from his mind as he focused on the climb. If he'd thought the rappelling route was treacherous, this climbing route put it to shame.

Keeping the path he'd established clear in his mind, he began to move. His muscles, which had already been used to run more than thirty miles in the past three days, including the equivalent of a half marathon today, made their abuse known as he pushed himself to fly up the vertical wall.

This wasn't like the rock-climbing walls in gyms with nice little manmade hand- and footholds. This was a canyon wall carved out by Mother Nature, who damn well had not planned on having anyone climb it.

His legs were screaming by the time he reached the fifteen-foot marker and hooked his harness into the safety ropes. The safety restraints were a bare minimum. All they were going to do was stop someone from plummeting to their death. There was enough give in the rope to allow the climber to choose which route he or she wanted.

Which also meant there was enough slack to allow the climber to fall far enough to break an arm or leg before the rope caught.

Heights had never been a problem for Riley—he wouldn't have made it far in his career if they had been. Normally, he enjoyed climbing and made sure to take time to appreciate the view around him as he climbed.

Not today. Today he focused, pushing his body harder and harder.

He caught up with Baby just as he made it to the top.

"How's it going, Bollinger?" Riley smiled at his friend. "You're hanging pretty tough with the big boys today."

"Thanks, man. I'm a little slower than I want to be. Stomach upset issues. Four days of MREs aren't sitting well with my digestive system."

Riley chuckled. He understood that crazy. He'd spent many a race ducking behind bushes in ways nobody would ever want to know about. "That's never pretty."

"Believe me, I just want to make it up this cliffside without embarrassing myself."

"Suffice it to say, I'm glad I'm next to you rather than below you. But you're making good time, digestive issues considered."

Baby shot him one of his famous grins. "Having a brother like Finn and living in this area all my life means I've definitely done my share of rock climbing and rappelling. I may spend most of my time in the garage, but I love climbing. Picking out the angles to get me where I need to go the quickest? That's my kind of brain-work right there."

Riley stretched to reach the next handhold. "Are you sure you dropped out of high school? You're talking about some pretty advanced geometry."

Baby's smile became a little forced. "Yeah, believe me, I'm sure."

They made it to the top of the cliff. Both were breathing heavily as they pulled themselves over the top and unhooked themselves from the safety lines.

"I'll let you go on ahead." Baby gave him a little salute. "Nature calls, literally. I'm sure you'd pass me anyway."

Riley waggled an eyebrow. "I am the professional. See you at the bottom."

Baby waved and rushed toward the nearest set of large bushes in the opposite direction as Riley jogged back toward the top for the rappelling. He stopped when he rounded a boulder and found Amber walking back toward him, face crestfallen.

"Hey, you're going the wrong way."

Tears welled up in the woman's eyes. "I know."

He reached out toward her. "Whoa. Everything okay?"

"Yeah. I was up at the rappelling station for a while. I've been training to go down the harder rapelling line, but I sort of freaked out when I got there."

"It happens. Even to those of us who do stuff like this for a living. We all freeze up some time." And they weren't even carrying the emotional baggage of a brother who'd met tragedy going over the side of a ledge.

"Yeah, I guess so. Finally, Bo and Damon showed up for their second rappel, so I decided to leave. Standing there staring wasn't going to do me any good."

"Do you want to come back up here with me, and maybe I can talk you through it? I'm sure once you get over the edge you'll be fine. Hell, once you're over the edge, what choice do you have but to keep going anyway?"

She gave a little laugh, but at least the pinched look was fading from her face. "Damon was up there. He tried to help."

Riley rolled his eyes. "I'm surprised Damon didn't offer to carry you down in his big manly arms. Damon is a sucker for what he sees as a damsel in distress."

"Oh, he basically did. But that's not what I wanted. Plus, Bo was there, delightful as always. He was fighting with Damon over which rig he wanted to use."

Riley rolled his eyes again. "I think, if anything, we've all learned an important lesson in this race."

"To keep going, no matter what?"

"Well, no. Mostly that Bo is an asshole, and we should all ignore him." They both laughed. "But seriously, I'm more than willing to talk you through this if you want me to. I'm sure you can do it."

It was the least he could do. Hell, he should've been doing a lot more for the Lowe family since Felix's death.

She gave him sad smile. "Maybe. I've, ah, been seeing a therapist since Felix killed himself. I had a lot of anger."

"That's understandable."

"She wasn't sure I should do this race at all. Said it might be more damaging in the long run." Amber shrugged. "Maybe she's right. She also said forcing things could make the situation worse. I didn't listen to her about the race, obviously, but I think it's probably better to follow her advice and not force it with this. Go do the easier route."

Riley wasn't exactly sure how he should advise Amber. His normal inclination would be to tell her to face her fears and just go for it, but maybe if someone had told Felix not to take such a big risk on that ski hill, he'd still be alive today.

"You have to do what's best for you," he finally said.

"Yes. For the first time I feel like I'm doing that."

That settled it then. "Good." He smiled at her. "Follow your gut."

"Thanks. Now you get going. We can't let Bo win this thing."

"Oh hell no!" With a wave, both of them took off in their opposite directions.

"Bo swears the rig on the far left is the fastest one!" she called out as they ran.

"Thanks!"

Riley was glad Amber was working through this. Was glad she'd chosen to go the safer route. Recovery looked different for everyone, and he would hate for her to have a setback just to prove something that ultimately didn't matter.

When he got to the rappelling stations, Damon and Bo were long gone—already down on the ground. Baby was making his way down the cliffside. He'd chosen the left rig, the fastest one. Riley didn't waste time worrying about it. He hooked himself into the middle rig a few feet over from Baby's and got himself lined up correctly.

A few moments later, with a laughing yell, he launched himself over the side. That first drop was always a thrill he'd never get used to and would always love.

He took the cliffside even faster this time, his pace almost reckless. He wanted to catch up with Bo and Damon. He caught Baby about halfway down.

"I thought that was supposed to be the fast rig, Bollinger."

Baby laughed. "Fast one? Definitely isn't with me on it. I don't know why going up the cliff is so much easier for me than going down. Story of my life, I guess."

Riley chuckled. "Well, you're still in first place for the nonprofessional athletes. So you're doing pretty fucking good."

Riley swung himself over toward Baby to give him a high-five.

Which saved Baby's life as something happened to his rig much farther up, toward the top of the cliff. Baby began to tumble backward, falling with nothing to catch him but the bottom of the canyon still another seven or eight stories below them.

Riley grabbed for Baby with his free hand, years of honing his reflexes allowing him to catch his friend's wrist. He grunted at the weight.

The emergency rope had failed. The only thing keeping Baby from falling were their grips on each other's wrists.

"What the fuck?" Baby's eyes were huge as he reached up to grab Riley's wrist with his other hand.

"Shit." Riley gritted his teeth. Damn it, Baby was no lightweight. "I don't know. Something happened to your rig."

Riley had no idea what and there was definitely no time

to figure it out now.

Yells were coming from the bottom of the cliff wall, and at least one of the voices was Wildfire's. No doubt Zac and the others were doing everything they could.

But nothing could be done quickly enough to save Baby if he fell.

"We need to get you hooked to my rig." He bit out the words. "You're going to have to crawl up me."

Baby was already moving as Riley spoke, letting go of Riley's wrist with one hand to wrap his arm around Riley's waist.

Neither of them wanted to let go of each other's wrist so that Baby could make the transfer, but both of them knew it had to happen.

"Ready?" Every second they hesitated was more strain placed on their bodies. Exhaustion would become a factor quickly.

"Yup." Baby's voice was tight. Riley couldn't blame him.

"One. Two. Three."

With a groan, he swung his arm back. They both let go of each other's wrists and Baby's other arm wrapped around Riley's waist. Baby immediately reached up and grabbed Riley's harness. It was still a lot of pressure on Riley's body from the added weight, but at least it wasn't all on his arm now.

He could hear Baby's deep breaths behind him. They were in a less precarious situation than a moment before, but still dangerous.

"Man, I don't think I can hoist myself enough to clip onto your harness. I think we should just get down as fast as we can."

"How's your grip?" Even as Riley asked the questions, he began inching down the side of the cliff. A controlled, slow descent was harder on the muscles, especially with a two-hundred-pound tagalong, but actual rapelling with leaps and slides wasn't even an option with Baby's precarious grip.

"Not going to lie. I definitely wish I were holding a cold brew right now rather than staring straight at your ass."

"Hey, while you're down there…"

Baby chuckled. "No offense, but if I'm going to be this close to someone's ass, I prefer it to be the female variety, and not while I'm dangling off the side of a cliff."

"Dude, you better just hope I don't get any sort of stomach upset like you had a few minutes ago." Another few steps down. Slowly. Painfully.

"If you'd be so kind as to notify me ahead of time if that's going to happen, I'll just go ahead and let go and plummet to my death."

Riley continued to move as quickly and steadily as he could, ignoring the strain on his own muscles. "Yeah, can't blame you. Definitely the less agonizing of the two options."

He could hear the sounds of people below much clearer now—multiple voices in various stages of panic, yelling different things.

He ignored them all, except for one. "One step at a time. One step at a time. One step at a time."

Riley blocked out everything else except the sound of Wildfire's steady voice. She wasn't the loudest, definitely wasn't the most frantic.

But she knew exactly what he needed to hear.

Every step down the cliff wall was agonizing on his quads. The harness, not meant to support the weight of two fully grown men, was digging into his chest and shoulders to the point of drawing blood.

"Hang in there, Baby," he said through gritted teeth, ignoring the stinging sweat dripping into his eyes.

"Hey. Nobody puts Baby in a corner."

Riley would've chuckled if he'd had the extra energy.

Instead, he continued to move downward until finally they were close enough to the ground that the people there were able to grab Baby and help him off Riley's waist.

The relief of no longer holding Baby's weight was instantaneous. Riley lowered himself the rest of the way to the ground, leaning back against the cliff wall as someone reached over and unhooked him.

There was chaos all around as volunteers shot dozens of questions in their directions, checking the gear, and looking over him and Baby for injuries.

He found Wildfire. She looked up from examining Baby's hands to meet Riley's eyes.

He gave her a slight nod, communicating with her in the way they had for years, when it hadn't always been easy to talk outright with one another.

She needed to know he was okay.

He needed to give her that reassurance.

He wanted more. Wanted to pull her into his arms and just breathe in her scent.

This wasn't the first time he wasn't able to do that. They'd traveled to places all over the world where public displays of affection were completely unacceptable, if not illegal.

But always before, he'd known it was just a matter of time until he had her in his arms where he wanted her.

She looked away, and frustration pooled in his gut.

Damn it, there wasn't anything he could do about the situation with Wildfire right now. And for the first time, that was okay because there was plenty of other stuff to be furious about.

Like how one of his friends would've been dead right now if it hadn't been for a random, midair high five.

"Where the fuck is Bo?" Riley asked. "He's got some god damn explaining to do."

Chapter 14

"You're frustrated, Phoenix. It's been a hard few days for you. Your girl breaks up with you. You're not doing as great in the race as you would like…"

It was all Riley could do not to leap across the table and punch Bo in his smug face.

"Enough, Bo." Zac pointed at the other man from where he sat. "Or Wyatt and I are going to step out of the room and completely ignore what happens in here for the next thirty minutes."

Wyatt had arrived as race support with Anne, who'd been helping with medical. He'd gotten there just in time to see this afternoon's fiasco.

But neither Wyatt nor Zac would need to leave for thirty minutes. It wouldn't take that long for Riley to beat the shit out Bo.

Bo just shrugged. "What? Look, I'm sorry about what happened to Baby. And I'm really glad he wasn't hurt. But the fact is, I didn't have anything to do with that equipment malfunction. Phoenix over here just wants to blame someone for everything because he's not winning."

Riley's eyes narrowed and he slammed his fist on the table, ignoring the pain. "You went too far. Way too far. It's one thing to mess around with my navigation boxes. It's another thing entirely to do something where somebody could've gotten killed."

"Like I said, you're pissed. I get it. But don't go blaming me for every single problem that happens in this race." Bo leaned back in his chair, arms crossed over his chest.

They were in the cabin Zac had been using as an office since the race started. This conversation needed to take place in private. Baby wasn't here—he thought what almost everyone else was thinking: that the whole situation had been an unfortunate equipment malfunction.

Riley thought otherwise.

"I'm not accusing you of every single problem. Just the ones that keep happening when you're around. Interesting how that worked out. Damon already said he left before you did. Would've given you time to mess with the rig." He turned to Zac. "We could have been carrying Baby out in a body bag. This is bullshit."

Bo shook his head. "What, Phoenix? Trying to get Zac and Wyatt to cancel the race? Is that what you do when you're not in first place?" He shook his head, tsking. "Trying to get Zac to cancel the race so you don't lose?"

Riley gripped the arms of the chair to keep himself in it. "This is bullshit," he said again.

Bo stood up. "Can I go? I had nothing to do with what I'm being accused of and unless there's some sort of proof, I'm not going to sit here and argue with someone who is just upset that the race isn't going his way. And unless you really are going to cancel the race to placate Phoenix, my time is better spent preparing for what's ahead of me tomorrow, not whining about what happened today."

Riley stood too. This motherfucker was going down. But before he could move Wyatt's hand fell on his shoulder.

"Get out," Zac said to Bo, tilting his head toward the door. "But I advise you to stay well clear of Riley and the other competitors. And you better hope nothing else goes wrong right after you were the last person to be near it."

Bo's eyes narrowed, but he kept his cool. "Fact of the matter is, I don't have to cheat to win. And I think everybody in this room knows it."

Nobody said another word as Bo walked out.

"This is not about me wanting to win." Riley sat back down. "This is about Baby nearly dying today."

"Trust me, we'll be keeping a close eye on Bo to make sure he's not up to anything sketchy." Zac ran a hand over his face.

"We looked at the ropes and rigs ourselves." Wyatt came to sit down next to Zac. "There was no overt evidence of foul play. Just some fucking really bad luck—the anchor system bolt had loosened and the stopper knot at the end of Baby's rope had come untied. Both of them happening at one time was high unlikely but, unfortunately, not impossible."

Riley rubbed his eyes. Jesus, he was exhausted. "We all know that no overt evidence doesn't mean there was no tampering. Just because Bo didn't leave a handwritten note doesn't mean he didn't mess with it."

Zac leaned his elbows on the table. "Riley, think about what you're saying. You're saying Bo was willing to *kill* someone for this race. It doesn't make any sense. It especially doesn't make sense to take out Baby."

Bo hadn't been trying to take out Baby. He'd made it known that the left rig was the quickest. If Baby hadn't already been on it, that's the one Riley would've chosen. But he didn't have any proof of it.

Yet.

He wasn't going to say anything until he did.

"We'll keep an eye on him," Zac assured him once again. "And whether you like it or not, Bo's not wrong about the stress you're under."

"We robbed you of your downtime for the mission in Egypt, then you had the breakup with Riley, and then you went straight into this race." Wyatt shook his head. "Don't discount the stress all of that is putting on you."

"I guess I ought to hit the sack then." Riley stood up.

"Go see Riley or Anne," Zac said. "You've got to get cleared before you can start tomorrow."

He nodded. "Okay."

"Phoenix…"

Riley turned back to look at Zac.

"Get some rest. I know that's hard in a race like this. But it will make a big difference."

The guys didn't say anything else.

The hell of it was, they weren't wrong about anything they were saying. Bo wasn't wrong. Riley *was* stressed. He did need rest. WAR probably hadn't been a good idea with so little preparation time.

But he also knew in his gut that what had happened today hadn't been an accident.

He wouldn't be getting much rest anytime soon.

Chapter 15

It was a full four hours after watching Boy Riley's harrowing attempt to get Baby down the cliffside, and Riley still didn't feel as if she could manage a full breath.

Something had changed inside her, watching that. Baby might have been the one in the most immediate danger, but Riley hadn't been safe either. She knew enough about rappelling to know that a harness could only support so much. It wasn't meant to hold the weight of two. They both could've plummeted to the ground.

Not only that, she knew as a nurse there were a dozen other ways Riley's career could've been ended with an accident like this: injured back, neck, rotator cuffs... Any could've meant Phoenix would be out of the extreme sport world for a long time, if not for good.

Standing there, willing him to make it safely to the ground, had been all she could do.

"Are you okay, kiddo?" Anne asked. Riley forced herself to stop her pacing next to the picnic table and sit down next to Anne. All the competitors were in the main section of the camp. Riley was waiting for Boy Riley to get out of his meeting about what had happened today.

"I just need to check him out for myself, make sure he's okay. You know, professionally."

"And personally," Anne said. "I want you to say it. You need, personally, to know that Riley is all right."

"Okay, yes. Personally too."

She was too discombobulated to even pretend like she wasn't about to lose her mind over what had happened.

They'd already examined Baby. He was bruised, and his hands had taken some abuse even under his gloves, trying to hang on to Riley, but besides that, he was basically fine.

Shaken, and more reserved and pensive than Riley had ever seen her friend, but physically fine.

Riley's body had taken the brunt of the abuse.

"He's going to be okay." Anne rubbed Riley's back. "If there was anything serious, Zac would've sent him to see us rather than take him into a meeting."

Anne's words were true. Boy Riley wouldn't have been able to hide it if his shoulder were dislocated or something equally damaging. He probably had some bruises, abrasions.

She just needed to see him with her own eyes. Touch him.

"How could something like this happen?" She started her pacing again.

"Zac and Wyatt inspected the rigs themselves a couple hours ago. It looks like it was just a horrible accident."

Riley shook her head. She knew these things happened in a situation where the athletes wanted to use every time advantage they could get—safety concerns took a backseat to speed.

"The equipment was checked when it was put out yesterday, but something could've happened. Plus..." Anne faded out.

"Plus what? Just say it."

Anne lowered her voice a little further. "Riley is accusing Bo of cheating. Said that he moved Riley's puzzle box during the navigation portion yesterday and then did this today."

Riley rubbed her eyes with a weary hand. This explained the weirdness happening between the two men yesterday. "Honestly, someone moving the box would make more sense than Riley just not seeing it. And everybody knows how much Bo wants to win."

"Maybe. But it's a huge step to go from hiding a puzzle to sabotaging somebody's rappelling rig. Plus, it wasn't even Riley's, it was Baby's. Baby is barely in the top ten—it wouldn't make sense for Bo to go after him."

Anne was right. "Either way, it was scary as hell. I don't even know what I would do if something happened to Riley."

As soon as she said the words, she realized how ridiculous that sounded.

Thankfully, Anne didn't point out that she was a complete moron. "Why don't you go over to the RV and start refiling everyone's paperwork? We left it a mess. With that big storm coming in, our jobs are just going to get more hectic."

Anne was giving her busywork. Riley couldn't blame her. She was as big a mess as the paperwork in the RV. "Okay."

"Write in Johnson's sprain and the two stitches in Iceland's hand. Keep Boy Riley's file out. We'll need to add to it after I examine him."

Riley wanted to growl at the thought of anybody else examining him. But Anne was the doctor, a very well-respected trauma physician.

Not to mention a little more neutral when it came to Riley.

But still… growly.

When Riley looked over at the cabin door again rather than heading straight for the RV, Anne stood up and got right in front of Riley. "Remember that time you got me all fancied up in red cowboy boots and sent me out on my date even though I was scared to death?"

Riley dragged her eyes away from the cabin door. "Yes. You looked really hot, if I do say so myself."

Anne dropped her hands on Riley's shoulders. "You have always been a good friend to me, even though when I first moved back, I was a stuttering mess and just wanted to bury myself in my work. You encouraged me to take a chance on Zac, and now we're getting married in a couple of months. That might have never happened if it weren't for you."

Riley brought her friend in for a hug. "It would've happened. I saw the way Zac looked at you that very first moment in the hospital. He would have needed to hit his head a hell of a lot harder than that to not have wanted you."

Anne actually blushed. She might not be so socially awkward and suffer from so much anxiety anymore, but the doctor was always going to tip on the shy side. Riley had always felt protective of her, although she didn't need to anymore—Zac Mackay would stomp all over anyone who dared hurt his sweet fiancée.

"Anyway." Anne pulled back from the hug with a smile. "You were very kind to me when you didn't know me at all. I'll never forget that."

"It was nothing—"

"And my point is now it's *my* turn to help you a little bit. You head back to the RV and get your mind off Boy Riley. I promise I will grab you if there is anything you need to know about his condition. Anything."

Riley grimaced. "I know I'm acting like an idiot."

"You're not acting like an idiot. You are acting like *some-*

thing, but I'll leave you to figure that out on your own. Right now, go do the filing."

Riley almost pressed Anne on what she meant but was afraid she already knew. Riley was acting like a woman who was worried about the man she loved.

Yeah, better to leave that alone.

She walked to the RV and opened the door, startled at the silhouette of someone sitting at the back table, studying the medical files.

What the hell? Those files contained confidential medical information. No one should be accessing them except for her, Anne, or someone officially tied to the race.

"Excuse me, you shouldn't be in here without permission."

As she stepped closer, the long blond hair of the woman at the table came into view.

"Amber?" Regardless, she still shouldn't be going through the files.

Amber didn't turn around or move from the table.

"Really, you're not allowed to be reading those. You shouldn't be in here at all."

She crossed back to grab the files and realized the other woman wasn't looking at the files at all; she was just hunched over them, crying.

Shit. "Amber, oh my gosh, are you okay?" Riley knelt down next to her and put her arm around the other woman's shoulders.

"I'm sorry," Amber finally got out. "I know I'm not supposed to be in here, I just needed somewhere where no one else was around."

"I understand. This race is really stressful. It can get the best of everyone."

Amber began to cry even harder. "That should have

been me out there today. If I hadn't been such a coward, *I* might've been on the line Baby was on."

"What?"

Amber nodded. "I stood up at the top of that cliff wall, trying to get up enough nerve to use the hard rappelling stations rather than going back down to the easy ones. I looked over that edge and all I could think about was the pictures of my brother's mangled legs after his skiing accident. He lost control and went over a small cliff and broke his back."

Riley hadn't known Felix personally, not the way Boy Riley had, but she remembered hearing about the accident when it had happened last winter. Felix's paralysis had hit Boy Riley and his inner circle pretty hard.

"Amber." She grabbed a box of tissues and pushed them in her direction. "Anybody would understand you not rappelling down the hard section after what happened to Felix, and thank goodness you didn't. I'm sure your brother's fall and paralysis has been hard on you and him."

"Hard enough on him that he killed himself."

"Holy hell, Amber." Riley scrubbed a hand across her face. She wasn't a great counselor at the best of times. "No wonder you're upset. Hang on, let me go get Anne for you to talk to. She's much better with stuff like this than I am."

Amber grabbed her arm. "No. Please. I don't want anybody else to know I was in here having a breakdown. Everybody already worries about me because of what happened to Felix. They think I shouldn't be at the race at all."

"That's not true. What happened to Felix on the ski slopes was a tragedy and everybody hates that it happened. But nobody thinks you shouldn't be here. I'm sure they all respect what you're doing in his memory."

"I wish I didn't have to do it. I wish he were here doing it himself. He loved all of this stuff."

"I'm so sorry. It has to be so hard." She patted Amber's back. Jeez. Could she be any more woefully inadequate?

"I'm just so pissed off all the time. I'm so angry."

Riley nodded. "That's understandable."

"Felix never should've been out on that ski slope to begin with. I wish someone had just told him to go back to the chalet. To sit this one out."

"You know how these guys are." She imagined someone trying to tell Riley he couldn't do a stunt. He would never listen to them. "They are convinced of their own immortality. If your brother was anything like Riley and his crew, he wouldn't have listened even if they had begged him not to ski."

Tears welled up in Amber's eyes again. "I knew from the moment they told Felix he was paralyzed that it was just a matter of time before he took his own life. I tried to get through to him, but I was never anything more than his kid sister. He was never going to listen to me." The anger was back in her features.

"I don't blame you for being mad. It sucked for everybody, not just him. You have a right to be angry."

Amber's laugh was bitter. "I've been seeing a therapist, you know, to talk through my feelings. I'm not sure how helpful that really was. I decided I'd rather take action and do something than just sit around and talk about how losing Felix makes me feel. I want to do something about it."

"Like this race?"

"Yeah. Felix was still on the Wild Wyoming Adventure Race mailing list. When I got the notification about his race spot, I decided to take it, to do something about his death rather than just sit around talking about it."

Riley wasn't sure that competing in WAR had or would

actually help Amber process any of this tragedy any better, but who knew? "Doing is almost always better than sitting around, I think. But talking things through is good too."

Riley was probably the least qualified to give advice on how to work oneself through a trauma. Look at how she'd been handling her diagnosis.

"Yeah. My therapist was skeptical when I told her I was doing WAR. But I thought it might give me some perspective." Amber got up and began pacing, her movements jerky. "I'm here to put the past to rights."

At least she wasn't crying anymore. Riley wasn't great with crying.

But anger, she understood.

Riley looked at the files on the desk. The drops from Amber's tears could be seen on a few of them. And, of course, Riley's was open on the very top.

It was like she couldn't escape him. He was everywhere.

She closed his file. She was glad she'd caught Amber in here having her breakdown. Everything they'd talked about had made Riley realize something important.

She needed help. If she couldn't turn to Boy Riley, then at the very least she needed to talk to a professional. How many times had she suggested grief counseling for someone in the hospital? It wasn't just for when someone died. It was for all sorts of traumatic life changes.

Like a multiple sclerosis diagnosis.

"I'm such a coward," Amber whispered, jerking Riley out of her thoughts. "Maybe nothing would've happened if I had gone on that rappelling line. I may not be super experienced, but I'm a lot lighter than Baby. Maybe if I had just faced my fears and gone over that ledge, everybody would have been safe and okay."

Riley slapped the files down on the table. "No offense, but that's bullshit. First, let's remember that everybody *is* safe and okay. And you know what I think? I think you got to a point where you were over your head, but instead of powering through it like your brother"—or like Riley had been trying to do with her MS diagnosis—"you reevaluated and made a wise choice."

Amber stopped her pacing and stared at Riley, brows furrowed. "If Felix had done that, he would still be here."

"Exactly. So maybe it was his spirit or whatever telling you to turn around and stay away from those harder rappelling lines. Baby and Phoenix both ended up being fine."

At least she hoped so. She was still itching with the need to see him.

"Yeah." Amber nodded. "You're right. It worked out for the best. Of course, if Riley had been on that rig rather than Baby, it might've been different. Riley weighs more. Baby might not have been able to support him."

A shudder ran through Riley. So many things could've gone impossibly wrong. "Yeah."

"I guess none of us ever know what the future holds."

Chapter 16

The storm moved in overnight.

Wyoming storms weren't to be trifled with at the best of times. They definitely weren't to be messed with when you were out in the wilderness fifty miles away from the nearest substantial shelter.

Zac and Wyatt, in their uncanny Linear Tactical/former Special Forces voodoo way, had known the storm was coming long before the sky started pouring. They'd warned all the race volunteers and competitors.

But a change in weather didn't stop WAR. It just made the competition more miserable for the competitors.

Boy Riley was most miserable of them all. Everyone else had already left to start their racing for the day, but because of the time penalty from the navigation and puzzle segment two days before, Phoenix was starting an hour and a half after everyone else.

"It's like watching a kicked puppy, isn't it?" Anne shook her head as she joined Riley at the RV window to look out at him.

Riley sighed. "It really is the most heartbreaking thing I've ever seen."

Phoenix looked absolutely miserable. Since the camp location was moving today, all the tents had been taken down after the athletes had gone. Some of the athletes had waved to Riley as they'd left.

Bo, classy as ever, had flipped him off. Amber, the last one to leave, had yelled at Bo not to be an asshole, then given Phoenix the most awkwardly endearing hug, nearly falling into him.

It was almost sweet enough for Riley not to have her fingernails digging into her palms at the sight.

Once Amber left, Phoenix had then been left alone to sit under the tiny overhang of the lone cabin at the campground. It wasn't keeping him dry at all, and there was only so much a waterproof jacket could do.

Not only was it cold and rainy, his need to get moving was strumming through him. He'd looked down at his watch four times already in the past thirty seconds.

Girl Riley wanted to do something. She wished she could offer him a cup of coffee like he'd given her the past three mornings, or even shelter inside the RV. But she couldn't. Any of those things would be considered outside help and would just add more minutes to his time penalty. So all she could do was sit there and watch him be miserable.

"In case you're wondering, that's pretty much the same expression you've had on your face ever since the official MS diagnosis came through."

Fitting. "Probably because that's pretty much how I've felt since the diagnosis came through."

Anne shook her head. "You're being an idiot. You need to tell him. You know he's going to find out eventually."

Riley stared out at the man she loved. Yes, he looked miserable, but that didn't diminish his strength or virility.

Some people didn't take Riley seriously because he did crazy stunts on motorcycles and jumped out of airplanes. They wrote him off because he'd mastered the art of entertaining viewers on YouTube. They thought he didn't have much depth because he sought out thrills and danger.

But anybody who thought Riley Harrison was shallow or empty made that mistake at their own peril. There was so much more to him than his tattoos and reckless smile would lead people to believe.

"He would stay," Riley whispered so softly she wasn't even sure Anne could hear her. That didn't matter; she wasn't sure she was talking to Anne anyway. "If I walked out into that storm right now and told him about my MS and that I needed him, he would drop everything for me. He would stay here and take care of me. He would give up the life he has for me."

Her fingers came up to touch the glass of the window, as if she could reach through it and touch Riley himself. "Because that's the man he is. The man I fell in love with."

"Riley…"

She dropped her fingers, wiping the drops of condensation on her pants. "So, the answer is no. I won't let that happen. I'll work through this myself and figure out a plan. By the time he hears about it, there won't be any ties between us anymore. He loves me because I'm capable of handling things. I'm capable of handling this too."

But, oh God, she didn't feel like it sometimes. Hated that her own body was turning against her in a way she couldn't understand or fight.

"While I appreciate the tragic backstory and your willingness to fall on your sword so completely unnecessarily, I feel like you're being a little melodramatic here, bitch."

Riley spun around with wide eyes to stare at Anne. She'd never heard such language come out of her friend's mouth.

"Good," Anne was smiling. "See, I can use the bad words when they're called for."

Riley couldn't help but laugh. "You've got my attention. Say your piece, Anne."

"After what happened with the rappelling yesterday, I've been thinking. I know I said I would support you either way, but I'd be remiss if I don't kick you in the ass a little bit."

"You think I should tell him. You've never made that a secret."

"Well, first of all, you're making it sound like you're going to be in a wheelchair tomorrow morning. Hell, you may *never* be in a wheelchair. You may outlive us all. You may only have the most minor of MS symptoms. There's no reason to think that things are going to be the worst-possible scenario. Multiple sclerosis is a spectrum. We don't know yet where you're going to fall on it."

"I know, but—"

Anne held out a hand to stop her. "MS is also a timeline. We don't know how quickly or slowly you're going to move in your progression. But based on your initial tests, there is no reason to think it's going to be a rapid onset of symptoms. Hell, Riley, you could have good days ninety-five percent of the time for the next twenty years. That's more than the average non-MS person has."

Anne was right. "I know. But..."

It was the *but*. Because yes, everything Anne said was true, but not guaranteed. She might still be having mostly great days in twenty years.

But she might be in a wheelchair next year.

Adult diapers.

Unable to remember things.

"I can't take the risk." The words felt ripped from her throat. "Not with Riley's future."

There was a world of sympathy in Anne's eyes. "Here's

my ultimate question. What would you do if the roles were reversed? What if, like Felix Lowe, Riley went out tomorrow and broke his back in a stunt? Would that be it for you?"

Riley shook her head. "I know where you're going with this—"

"Just answer the question. If Riley were unable to do all his crazy stunts, if he were unable to even walk or pick you up in those strong arms, would that change who he is to you? Would that change how you feel about him? Would you stop loving him?"

Of course she wouldn't. It would be hard, it would be tragic, but Riley was much more than just what he could do physically.

Of course, Anne wasn't asking any of this because she needed real answers. She was making a point.

But it wasn't the same.

Boy Riley was so amazing, brought so much to the table.

The walkie-talkie went off, saving her from answering Anne's question.

It had already been a crazy morning—the worst possible day for the volunteers to have to move all the tents and the athletes to have to cross multiple rope bridges.

Then the storm had caused a landslide over a portion of the course the racers would need to run through. The entire support staff had left to help fix either the landslide problem or to set up the new camp.

After yesterday, Zac was taking safety beyond seriously. Wyatt was here to help. Aiden and Gavin had also come out from Oak Creek. There would be no more chances for sabotage, if that was what had really happened.

Every harness at every rope bridge had been checked and double-checked today. The Linear guys would be following the racers discreetly—meaning none of the athletes would ever know the men were around—to make sure nothing hinky was going on.

"Annie, we need you over at the western Flat Creek bridge." Zac's voice came through the walkie-talkie. "We've got a competitor who blew out his knee."

"Damn it," Anne muttered under her breath. She clicked on the walkie-talkie. "Roger that. Do you suspect more foul play?"

"No, just tripped over a root. This weather is hell out here."

"Okay. Stabilize it as best you can."

"Does Riley mind staying there and releasing Phoenix at the correct time? Honestly, I trust him on his own recognizance, but this will squash any doubts that might arise."

Riley nodded to Anne.

"No problem, she's got it," Anne told him.

Riley helped grab the medical supplies Anne would need to stabilize the patient until they could get him to the hospital.

"Don't think somebody's agony gets you off the hook," Anne said as Riley helped her into her rain jacket. She'd have to walk nearly an hour to get to the bridge. "It's just the two of you guys here. Now's the perfect time."

Riley rolled her eyes. "Lord, Anne, he's having a hard enough race as it is without me dumping that on him."

Anne looked like she was going to argue further, but Riley just raised an eyebrow and pointed at the door. This would have to wait.

Anne walked out into the rain. Riley watched from the window as she stopped for a second under the cabin's small overhang to talk to Boy Riley. She was obviously explaining the situation, since he glanced at the RV and then nodded.

Riley forced herself to look away from the window. She

returned to the filing she'd never gotten to yesterday because of Amber's breakdown. But it didn't take up nearly as much time as she would've liked.

Damn it. Riley still had twenty-four minutes before he could leave. She couldn't stand the thought of him out there all alone, so she got on her rain gear and walked out.

Boy Riley slid over to make room for her under the overhang. "I hear you're my babysitter."

She gave him a small smile. "Worst possible day for a torrential downpour. Most of the team is trying to get the new camp set up. There was some sort of mudslide that took out part of a path, and now someone has blown out his knee."

"I hate to hear that, but I'm a little glad I'm not the only person having a shit day."

"Yeah, Anne and I thought you might make a run for it a couple times."

"Believe me, I thought about it." That little half smile. God.

She looked down at her watch, ignoring the fact that it used to be his and he'd given it to her. "Nineteen minutes to go."

He leaned his head back against the wall behind, closing his eyes.

"You doing okay?"

He nodded and then shrugged. "I guess everything has really started to take its toll. Not to mention nobody got much sleep last night. When it's raining like this, tents leak no matter how good they are."

"Yeah, it was really hard being all safe and dry inside the RV."

He chuckled but didn't open his eyes. "Wench."

"As soon as you finally get your ass on the road, I'm driving the RV to campsite two. I'll still be nice and dry."

"Be careful."

She shook her head. "You're telling me to be careful? You're the one out in this ridiculous weather."

"Yeah." He opened one eye to look at her. "It starts at Brickman's Bridge."

They both knew it way too well. It was where he'd kissed her for the first time when they'd met on the race three years ago.

It was also where he'd told her he loved her for the first time a few months later.

And it very definitely wasn't a bridge. At best, it was three ropes across the ravine. You snapped yourself in with a harness and carabiner and then used the two ropes at waist height to keep your balance as you walked across on the third.

"That's going to be fun in this weather."

"Nothing to worry about. We've done that enough times, I could do it in my sleep."

He was probably right. He'd been so patient with her that first time she'd tried to cross it. She'd been terrified. He'd coaxed her across with kisses and the sweetest, kindest words.

He'd been the one to say *I love you* first, but her heart had belonged to him well before he'd said it.

They sat in silence until it was finally time for him to get ready to go.

"Will you come watch me, for old times' sake?"

"Yeah." She knew she shouldn't, but she told herself she would do it for anyone. Just to make sure they made it safely across and to the next checkpoint.

Yeah, right.

But it would be good. Full circle. She'd given him her heart there. That was where she would take it back.

She stood. "Okay, one minute."

She expected him to jump straight up, but he seemed to need the cabin wall for assistance.

"Whoa there, Phoenix, are you sure you're okay?"

He winked at her. "Just a little stiff. Not all of us had a nice, dry, warm RV to sleep in last night."

She nodded but was still worried. What else was she going to do? Unless she pulled rank and said he was medically unfit to race, he was leaving here in just over forty-five seconds. "Look, be careful out there. I know you want to make up time, but don't push too hard in these conditions."

She rolled her eyes at her own words. Telling Phoenix not to go at something full force was like telling the sun not to shine.

Full force was the only way he knew how to go. And she loved him for it.

"I'll be careful. And I'm sure once I get a few minutes under me, I'll be feeling fine. Just had too long to get stiff."

"Okay. Ten seconds."

He smiled at her. "I'll see you at Brickman's Bridge. I'll be the one zooming across it faster than anyone you've ever seen."

He winked at her, then turned and ran. She glanced at her watch. It had been exactly ten seconds. She had no idea how his brain kept track of things like that, but timing had always come intuitively to him.

She walked back to the RV and made the final preparations for the move to camp two. Riley had to run a couple of miles before getting to Brickman's Bridge. She could walk a much more direct path, but he'd be running much faster so she didn't wait too long.

Why had she agreed to do this? What part of her was so incapable of completely cutting him from her life?

All the parts.

She wouldn't go. That was a better plan. Forget the full-circle bullshit. She would get in the RV and drive to camp two and explain to him what had happened once he arrived there later.

Mind made up, she took off her jacket and put it in the passenger seat, then got behind the wheel.

She'd hadn't gone more than five feet before she stopped again with a curse. She put the RV back in park and thumped her head on the steering wheel.

Riley would stop and wait for her at the bridge. She didn't know how long he would wait before he figured out she wasn't coming, but she knew for a fact he would stop and wait.

Because she'd told him she'd be there.

"Goddammit, Riley. You're such a dumbass." She didn't know if she was talking to her or him or them both. The advantage of having the same name: more efficient cursing.

She got out and slammed the door behind her, cursing even more foully as she jogged around to get her jacket on the passenger side. She was wet by the time she put it on and fuming at herself as she marched off toward Brickman's Bridge.

She got there and found a little shelter in some small trees. Unfortunately, all she could do from there was look out across the rope bridge to the very spot where Riley had first told her he loved her.

She'd been so surprised. It'd been so crazy that someone as well known and vivacious as him would fall for her. They'd been dating for five months at that point. Five months of whirlwind weekend trips where he'd flown her out to wonderful places, and even a couple of surprise visits where she'd gotten off work and found him waiting in the parking lot.

They'd gone camping and ended up here. They'd made it across that rope bridge, and he'd been so proud of her for doing something she'd been so scared of that the *I love you* had just fallen from his lips.

She'd been shocked, joked that he could take them back.

He hadn't. He'd loved her, and he wasn't afraid to tell her.

They'd barely made it to a nearby emergency cabin before ripping each other's clothes off.

She rubbed her chest as she stood there staring off into the past.

God, she'd thought they would be together forever.

"Okay, I'm finally here."

She was startled back into the present by Riley's words and his laborious breathing.

"Jesus, are you okay?" His face was bright red like he'd been sprinting for the two miles. He should know better than to be trying to move at that speed so early in the day. There was way too much race left for him to be expending that sort of energy.

"Yeah, just haven't worked all my kinks out yet. I…" He trailed off.

She reached for him, but he turned away to look at the bridge, so she let her hand drop.

"I wanted to try to talk to you while we were here. I thought it might…" He shook his head and trailed off again, not looking back at her. "But I think I better just get across. I shouldn't stay here."

She had to swallow a sob. This was what she'd wanted, right? For him to move forward. For him to leave her behind.

But oh God, did it have to be right here where everything had first started for them? Maybe it did. Full circle.

"Yeah, you should go," she said.

Just be strong for a couple more minutes.

Do you love him enough to give him a clean break? A fresh start?

Her fingers itched to reach for him, her nails biting into

her palms inside her jacket pocket. "Just go, Phoenix. Just go."

Because if he didn't, she was about to break down and tell him everything.

He hesitated and her heart thumped in her chest. If he turned around now and told her he loved her, she'd break.

But he didn't. He grabbed the harness on the ground, slipping his backpack off and putting the harness on his body. Without a word he put the backpack back on and hooked himself into the line, double-checking the carabiner for safety.

Not once did he look at her. He didn't crack a joke. He didn't wink or tease her about the dry RV.

But when his hand grasped the stability rope, it was shaking.

He had to know. He had to know that this was the actual end for them.

He stopped. Seemed almost paralyzed.

"Just go, Phoenix. You'll be okay. You can do it."

She had to wrap her hand over her mouth to keep back her sob. He could do it. But could she?

Without a word he took the first step onto the narrow rope, balancing himself with the two higher ropes. If he fell, he wouldn't go far because of the safety harness.

But she knew Phoenix. He wasn't going to fall. And he wasn't going to look back.

Once he was a few feet out, she turned away. Why torture herself? Why watch him make it across to the new future and leave this gaping ravine between them?

She began to walk away, her heart shattering into more pieces with each step.

But call her a glutton for punishment, because as she got to the last spot where she could turn around and still see, she did so. She had to look at him just one more time.

Shock flew through her system at what she saw.

He was barely halfway across, stiff, when he should've already been almost to the other side by now.

And then his body began to shake, and he let go of the hand ropes, collapsing. It was only the connection to the safety harness that kept him from plummeting to his death.

"Riley!" she screamed, running back toward the bridge.

He didn't move.

Chapter 17

She ran back up to the rope bridge, still screaming his name. The way he'd fallen had pushed him about two-thirds of the way across the narrow ravine, hanging at an unnatural angle from his harness.

He was out cold.

Or worse.

She grabbed one of the harnesses and slipped it on herself, then clipped herself into the safety rope.

She didn't let herself even stop and think about what could happen, the things that could go wrong if her MS decided to make itself known right now.

Riley needed her.

Her heart was threatening to leap from her chest.

She cursed herself for not bringing her gloves. The rain wasn't unbearably cold, but the rope was stiff and rough on her palms, not meant to be handled by naked skin. She moved one step at a time, forcing herself to remain steady, looking in front of her rather than at the ten-story drop beneath her.

She'd been over this rope bridge before, she reminded

herself. Had traversed higher and wider ravines than this one. Riley had made sure of it. He had always found a way to bring out the most adventurous side in her—bring out the impossible in her.

He'd never goaded her or tried to talk her into things she wasn't ready for. He'd just helped her learn skill after skill until one day, she found she was ready and able to do the crazy things.

They'd rarely done normal date stuff, and now she was thankful for it.

Oh God. He was just dangling here.

"Talk to me, Phoenix," she yelled out over the sound of the rain. "Riley!"

All the things that could've happened to him—aneurysm, seizure, heart attack—ran through her mind. He wouldn't be the first athlete to die of natural causes while in the middle of an event like this.

It felt like eternity to get to him, although it was probably less than two minutes.

"Riley! Talk to me, baby."

Relief flooded her system when he groaned and moved slightly. She still couldn't see his face, but he obviously wasn't conscious. But he was alive. That was the most important thing.

She needed to get closer to him to evaluate his condition. That meant she was going to have to let go of the waist-height balance lines.

As soon as she did so, she was going to fall. Her safety rope would catch her.

But fuuuucck. Knowing one small rope and harness were all that kept her from certain death—especially after watching what had happened to Riley and Baby yesterday—did not give her the warm fuzzies.

But she didn't have time to feel uncomfortable. Not with Riley dangling unconscious.

Gritting her teeth, she crouched down on the walking rope and let go of the balance ropes. She gasped past the sickening lurch in her stomach as she fell the few feet before the safety rope pulled taut on her harness, stopping her fall.

She reached over and grabbed Riley. He was struggling to breathe. His face was swollen.

Anaphylaxis.

Her brain spun into overdrive. He could've been bitten or stung by any number of creatures, causing a reaction that was blocking his airway. She had to figure out a way to get him off this damn rope bridge. There was no way she was going to be able to hoist up his dead weight, and she wouldn't be able to balance him even if she could.

He didn't have that sort of time. He needed epinephrine right now.

The nearest EpiPen was back at the RV. It would be much quicker to just leave him here and bring her med kit back.

But God, just leaving him here, dangling off the bridge in this storm? There was lightning. He could be hit before she got back.

She felt almost paralyzed with indecision.

Think, Riley.

She had to leave him. It was dangerous, but attempting to get him off this rope bridge was going to take time she didn't have until she got the EpiPen.

Thunder boomed overhead, almost mocking her decision.

"Riley!"

She had no idea if he could hear her. "I'll be right back!"

Decision made, she didn't waste any more time. She hooked her leg back over the rope and pulled herself up.

God, that took a lot of energy. She needed to be careful not to fall; it would take too much time to get back up.

She fought her way through the rain and wind, moving as fast as she dared along the rope. The balancing rope continued to bite into her hands, but there was no way around that. If she loosened her grip, she was going to fall.

If she fell, it would waste minutes Riley didn't have.

Her breathing was already labored by the time she made it back to the ravine's edge. She unclipped her harness, mostly numb fingers wet with rain and blood from her palms, and ran for the RV.

She was soaked to the skin and breathing raggedly by the time she made it. She found her med bag exactly where she'd left it, already packed and ready for any emergencies. She threw the walkie-talkie inside, slipped it all on and ran back out into the cold.

Every step toward the rope bridge seemed more impossible, but she ignored the screaming of her lungs and muscles and pushed forward faster than she thought she was capable of.

Riley would do the same for her. She knew it without a shadow of a doubt.

By the time she made it back up to the bridge, the storm had decided to make things more interesting. Rapid bolts of lightning and cracking thunder echoed all around her.

Wyoming storms were notorious for a reason. Going out on that rope bridge might very well be suicide.

It didn't matter. She was not leaving him out there. Seeing him dangling so completely still had her heart lurching in her chest. Was she too late?

"No. No, no, no, no."

She strapped the safety line back onto the harness, cursing herself for not grabbing some gloves while she'd been at the RV, and went back out on the rope.

This time she ran.

She kept her balance longer than expected and was almost to Riley before she felt the sickening lurch of the fall again. But the safety rope held, and she used her momentum to swing closer to him, catching his dangling body with her legs.

Please let him be alive. Please let him be alive.

She didn't even wait to check his pulse, just drove the EpiPen into the muscle of his hard thigh.

It was only then that she allowed herself to take his pulse, nearly sobbing with relief when she found one.

He was still alive. That was the most important thing.

If there was one thing the Linear Tactical guys preached like a pastor in church, it was that survival was the most important thing. Everything else was secondary.

Of course, neither of them was going to survive if lightning struck the bridge. She was going to have to drag him. She wasn't sure she could do that. She'd used up the last of her reserves just getting to this point.

Dragging him back the way she'd come would be the best option. If he needed further medical attention, the RV was his best bet.

But getting him off this bridge was the most important thing. If she collapsed halfway, they both could die here.

She'd have to take him the shorter way. Even that was going to be hard enough.

"Talk to me, Riley. Open your eyes and talk to me!"

"Wildfire." The word was mumbled and barely discernible, but it was something.

"Ry, can you pull yourself up?"

He made a movement with his arm, trying to grab the rope, but then his hand fell back to his side. He was completely out of it.

"Okay. It's okay. I'm pulling you to the edge."

Silence.

"I'm going to hook one of my safety lines to you to pull you over." It was the only way she'd be able to move him.

She reached up and unclipped one of her safety ropes and clipped it into his. She crossed over him and began shimmying toward the ledge about ten feet away.

The second rope was taut enough to start pulling Riley's weight. Instantly, it took a huge effort from her exhausted body just to move a couple of inches.

She forced herself to keep pulling.

"Talk to me, Riley. Say something. Anything."

Another yank on the rope, another few inches moved.

No sound from Riley.

She could feel hysteria growing inside her.

"Come on, Phoenix. Open those eyes and talk to me."

The last word came out in a sob as she pulled again.

She felt some movement on the rope, and when she pulled again it was slightly easier. She looked back at him in a panic.

He had unhooked his backpack, allowing it to fall into the ravine. It didn't help much, but it meant less weight she was trying to move.

When he saw her looking, he held up a hand briefly. At least he was conscious. Breathing.

She renewed her efforts, ignoring the rope biting into her palms. Ignoring the screaming of every single muscle in her body.

She set her gaze on the end of the ravine and gritted her teeth. She was not stopping until she got there.

Riley had taught her that. He'd taught her the importance of focusing on the goal and moving toward it, even if it was only the slightest bit at a time.

She sobbed in relief when she finally reached the edge

and climbed up. She turned and pulled the rope until he was resting against the cliff.

It took every bit of her strength and a lot of help from gravity to pull on that rope until he was against the ledge. She finally shoved her hands under his armpits and then just threw her body weight all the way back, bringing him with her. And that only worked because somewhere along the way, he'd become coherent enough to use his legs to help.

As she lay on the grass with him at her side, her legs began spasming. She didn't know if it was MS or just what she'd been through in the past thirty minutes. Either way, it didn't matter. She'd gotten them off that bridge and Riley's breathing was already clearer. The EpiPen was working.

She needed to get them to shelter, but there was no way she was moving from this spot.

She'd done everything she could do. Her body was done.

She didn't even try to fight the blackness that overtook her in the middle of the storm.

Chapter 18

There had been quite a few times over the years when his life had flashed before his eyes, but none of them had been like he was stuck in some sort of molasses.

He'd been feeling weak by the time he left camp. He'd written it off as just being pissed at having to start so much later than everyone else. But by the time he'd gotten to the rope bridge, he'd known for sure something was wrong.

Riley took risks all the time, but well-calculated ones, ones where he was fully aware of the danger and had accounted for it. This had been totally different.

By the time he'd gotten to the rope bridge, he'd known he needed to stop. Get help. He couldn't breathe. Couldn't think.

But then Wildfire had been there. And she'd told him over and over to just go.

Her voice had been all he was able to process, and he trusted her above all others, so he'd gone.

Taking a step out onto that rope bridge, he'd *known* he was going to make it across because Wildfire had told him to go. He would do anything for her.

From there, it all became blurrier and blurrier. Literally.

Not even being able to see enough to take the next step.

Lying suspended in his harness, unable to muster the strength to get himself back up on the bridge. Trying just to fill his lungs with air.

Wildfire screaming his name.

He looked out at the rope bridge now. Had she come out to get him?

She'd been nearby, yelling his name. A sharp pain in his leg, then he'd finally been able to take a full breath a few seconds later.

He remembered unstrapping his backpack. Why had he done that?

And now the love of his life was lying next to him, unresponsive, unconscious.

"Wake up for me, Wildfire."

This storm was a bitch. He needed to get them to shelter. Make sure she was okay. Make sure *he* was okay. He had no idea how he'd gotten to this side of the ravine.

Everything was still so fucking fuzzy. The last time he'd felt this way was years ago when a doctor had given him penicillin without checking his medical chart to find out he was highly allergic.

Nobody was giving him penicillin out here, so he wasn't sure what had happened.

He reached an arm around Riley and moved her gently so she was lying beside him. She groaned the slightest bit, which was a good sign.

Then he caught sight of the blood on her jacket.

Shit. She was hurt. He forced himself to focus through the fuzziness that still wanted to wrap around his brain.

He unzipped her jacket, searching through the rain for any sign of wounds or any further blood but found nothing.

She groaned again and shifted, her hand falling open beside her.

Holy hell, that's where the blood had come from. He took a look at her other palm and sure enough it was just like the first.

Those were wounds from the rope bridge. He'd been in trouble, and she'd come to get him, tearing her hands up to do it. He still didn't understand all the whys of it.

But he did understand that they needed to get out of this storm right fucking now.

He sat up, breath hissing with the dizziness and stiffness. He squeezed Riley's shoulder. "Time to get up. We need to get out of this storm."

She didn't move.

He shook her harder. "On your feet, Wildfire. We've got to move."

She groaned and turned away from him, huddling into herself for warmth.

"Let's get somewhere dry where I can build a fire. Don't you want to get warm?"

He didn't have any feeling left in his extremities, and he had a good fifty pounds on her. A lot more muscle mass to keep him warm.

"Tired. Rest." Her words were whispered through wet lips that were turning blue.

If he was piecing the situation together correctly, she'd used all her energy getting him off that rope bridge. Now that her body was coming down from the adrenaline high, her blood sugar had bottomed out. There was nothing left in her tank.

"I know, sweetheart. I know you're tired. You've done so good. But this storm is getting worse. Let's get to some shelter."

He knew the exact one they could go to, had been to

before. Who said lightning never struck in the same place twice?

Thunder rattled overhead.

"I was just kidding," he murmured to Mother Nature.

Riley still wasn't moving. He didn't want to drag her, but he wasn't at all certain he'd be able to carry her without injuring them both.

She needed to walk a few hundred yards.

He pulled her up into a sitting position. "Riley! Get up. You're not done yet. You're going to have to rest later."

She groaned again but still didn't move.

He was going to have to fight a little dirty. Although, he had to admit the thought of this working gave him more hope than anything.

"Wildfire, I need your help. I don't think I'm going to make it without you."

That was true on so many different levels he couldn't even call it a lie, although he could definitely drag himself to the shelter without her help.

But she didn't know that.

"If you can't get us to the shelter, we're both going to die. I'm going to die, Wildfire. I need you to wake up and help me or I'm not going to make it."

She groaned again, but this time those hazel eyes opened.

"Hey, you."

"You've got to get out of the storm," she whispered. "You go. I'll catch up."

Yeah, right. "Come on, get up."

"Can't. You go." Her eyes were already starting to close again.

"I can't make it without you. You have to help me. Please, Wildfire."

With a huge groan she rolled to the side and got up. He knew what a superhuman effort that simple move had taken.

It didn't surprise him for a second that she'd found the strength to do it.

She'd been amazing him from the first day he'd met her. He might be the one who'd gotten famous doing crazy stunts, but she was the one who had the kind of strength that mattered.

"We can't cross the bridge."

He nodded. The lightning was too dangerous, and neither would make it anyway. "Hunter's cabin," he yelled through the rain.

She reached for her medical backpack, but he shooed her hands away. The fact that she didn't argue just proved how weak she was really feeling.

He took off his gloves and put them over her icy hands. They were too wet to help much but were better than nothing.

He grabbed her arm and headed west, in the direction of the shelter, thanking God with every step that he already knew about it. It was only a half mile away, but their pace in these conditions and *their* condition was snaillike.

By the halfway point, he really was afraid he might have to drag her. Her steps were getting slower and less steady with each minute.

Of course, if he was dragging her, who was going to drag him? Because he wasn't sure he was going to make it either.

And this goddamn storm was getting worse. His head was still woozy, his body still weak, and he wasn't sure they were still going in the right direction. The hunter's cabin wasn't meant to be found easily.

Had she somehow managed the superhuman feat of getting him off that rope just for him to lead them to death in the wilderness?

Her small hand slid into his, her grip loose because of her wounds.

"Together." Her voice was too low for him to hear her, but he could read her lips.

She stepped forward again, guiding him.

He moved with her. He trusted her with everything.

Cupping her hand in his, they continued one slow step at a time through the battering rain and winds.

Their speed picked up slightly when they finally saw the shelter, and they stumbled the rest of the way to the door. It couldn't even be called a cabin. It didn't have any furniture, just some very basic supplies.

But compared to the storm raging outside, it was absolute heaven.

They both stumbled through the unlocked door and collapsed onto the ground. He kicked the door shut behind them, and they just lay there. Breathing. Alive.

It wasn't long before he began to regain feeling in his numb limbs.

It wasn't pleasant.

If it was bad for him with his size and muscle mass, Wildfire's body must be feeling it even worse. She needed to get out of those wet clothes immediately. Hypothermia was definitely a possibility. He rolled to the side and forced himself up onto his hands and knees.

The shelter didn't have much in the way of comfort, but it was called a survival shelter for a reason. He crawled over to the corner that held a basic potbelly stove and a pile of dry kindling and wood. In a few minutes he had a good-sized fire going, which added warmth and light to the cramped space.

Girl Riley had gone back to sleep. That wasn't a good sign if they were dealing with hypothermia.

He stripped off his own clothes as he got to his feet and

walked over to her. Being naked actually felt warmer than being in the wet clothes.

"Talk to me, Wildfire. How are you doing?"

No answer at all. Not even a moan. He checked her pulse, reassured when he found it steady and strong.

"I guess you deserve your nap."

He pulled her clothes off, then dragged her by the armpits closer to the fire.

"Never let it be said I'm not romantic." She would've said the exact same thing if she was awake.

He pulled the Mylar emergency blanket from her medical backpack and wrapped it around her, then grabbed the walkie-talkie.

"Base Camp Two, this is Phoenix. Do you copy?"

A few seconds later a voice came from the other end. "Phoenix, this is Zac. Everything okay? Where's Riley?"

"I had some sort of mishap crossing Brickman's Bridge. Felt like some sort of allergic reaction. Riley got me across, but we're stuck now because of the storm."

"Did you make it to the hunter's shelter?"

"Affirmative. We're safe and relatively warm for the time being. Wildfire is conked out. She used all her energy stores helping me."

"Roger that. Stay safe until the worst of this passes. We're getting the rest of the racers to shelters also."

"Will do."

Riley grabbed the large winter coat and a scratchy blanket, both folded in the corner of the shelter. He slipped the coat on himself and wrapped the blanket around both of them. Then he laid himself behind Riley, spooning her close to him. Between him and the stove, her body should be warm on both sides.

With the knowledge that they were safe and Wildfire was in his arms, where she belonged, sleep claimed him.

Chapter 19

Riley didn't wake up any faster the second time than he had the first. Everything was still a little fuzzy.

But this time he didn't want to wake up, not with Wildfire snuggled up beside him. Her fingers were trailing along the edges of the multiple tattoos covering his chest and shoulders.

For just this minute, everything was perfect.

There was no storm still raging outside.

There was no breakup or distance between them.

It was just the two of them lying in a comfortable silence. How many times had they done this on an early morning or late at night? Just lain there, comfortable with each other, not trying to fill the air with unnecessary noise.

She'd turned toward him sometime in the middle of sleeping. Muscle memory, probably. She always fell asleep wanting her own space. Then woke up draped on top of him.

Which suited him fine. Every single time.

The fire was dying down, but between their proximity and the blankets, they were plenty warm.

He held his breath as her fingers skimmed over his left pec. He knew exactly what tattoo she was touching.

The one right over his heart.

He'd waited a long time to get the tattoo there. He'd wanted to make sure the one closest to his heart was absolutely perfect. He'd gotten it a couple of months ago, although he'd known what he'd wanted there for more than a year.

"This is new." It wasn't a question. Girl Riley was intimately aware of every piece of ink on his body. She'd been with him when he'd gotten some of them.

"Yeah. Finally decided what I wanted."

She lifted her head so she could study it in the dim light of the fire. "A globe inside a compass. Simple. I like it. What does the writing say? I can't quite make it out. You're usually one for images, not for words."

That was true. This was the only tattoo of the dozens on his body that included any words. He'd done that on purpose.

"My greatest adventure."

She nodded. "A globe. The world is your greatest adventure. That makes sense. It's a good choice to go over your heart. I get it."

She didn't *get* anything. Couldn't see it all, at least not the details about it that were most important. "Wildfire…"

"If you had to pick one, what would you say was your greatest adventure?"

No, she didn't get it at all.

"BASE jumping from the Grand Canyon?" she continued. "Hiking to Everest base camp? Nah, that's too tame. The X Games? Hell, you have too many gold medals from them for it to be your greatest adventure."

He smiled. He'd definitely done a lot of stuff in his life. "No, the X Games wouldn't even rank in my top five."

The thunder shook the shelter around them.

"Okay." She tapped his chest with her finger. "Hang on, let me see if I can guess. You have to tell me if I'm right."

"I'll tell you if you get one of the top five."

Not that he'd actively sat around ranking the things he'd done in his life. But his top five were the best by such a huge margin it was easy to label them as the greatest.

"Snowboarding in the Alps when you became the only person in the world to complete the quadruple cork with the rotation."

He laughed. She was way more into this guessing game than he would've ever thought she'd be. "That definitely ranks as one of my more memorable experiences, even though I only held the record for less than a month."

"That's not in the top five? I thought for sure that would be number one."

"Nope."

"How about when you were part of the group that got to skydive into Washington DC airspace and land on the White House lawn? That has to rank up there."

"That was good. But nope, not top five."

She smacked him on the chest, and it was so reflective of the playfulness of their relationship that it was almost impossible to believe they weren't still together.

He would do almost anything to keep her with him like this. Surely she'd have to see how good they were together. How naturally they fit.

He'd play the *Guess the Adventure* game until she could see it.

"Come on, Wilde, keep guessing."

"Give me a hint."

"How about I give you one of my top five. A freebie, since you saved my life today and all."

She smacked him again, but this time he caught her

hand and held it against his chest. He started talking before she had a chance to pull away. "Scuba diving two years ago. Great Barrier Reef."

"What? I was with you for that. It was pretty amazing, but I can't believe it falls in your top five."

That's right, sweetheart. You're the smartest person I know. Figure it out. But he just shrugged. "It's definitely top five. I'll even give you another one since your brain is so addled." He smiled at the sound of her laugh.

"Okay, jackass, what?"

"This race three years ago."

She nodded against his chest. He loved her all relaxed like this, even if it was because she was too exhausted to do much else.

"That was a pretty prestigious win. I know the Linear guys were a little surprised. They never expected somebody nonmilitary to win it."

She still didn't get it. Didn't see the top-five pattern.

Didn't see that *she* was the pattern.

She guessed some more, and they talked about other things he'd done and ones they'd done together.

"I'm going to have to think about this longer. I can't believe I can't guess it right off the bat."

Honestly, he couldn't believe it either.

They were silent for long minutes, him rubbing her naked back with the tips of his fingers and listening to the storm outside. They couldn't go anywhere until that passed anyways.

"I let Zac know we were here. He said to wait out the storm."

She nodded against his chest. "Your backpack is at the bottom of the ravine."

"I know. Finn is going to be a little pissed since he let me borrow it. Not to mention it's going to be a bitch going the last two days with no prepackaged food."

"You're not going to quit?"

"Ha. Who are you talking to, woman? There's nothing in the rules that says we have to eat MREs. I'm certainly capable of feeding myself in the wild for two days. I've done it longer than that under much harsher conditions. Not only am I going to finish WAR, I'm going to win."

"Of course you are," she whispered. "That's what you do. Phoenix. You rise from the ashes and go and do and win."

Why did that not sound like a good thing? "Wildfire…"

His lifestyle was crazy. He knew that. In the beginning stages of their relationship, he'd gone out of his way to help her adjust to the travel, the cameras, the people who sometimes surrounded him. He wasn't a movie star, or someone truly famous like Cade Connor, the country music superstar who was dating Riley's best friend, Peyton. But Phoenix's life could get overwhelming.

Yet from the very beginning, Riley had handled it in stride. She was confident in her own abilities as a nurse—which were way more important and impressive than somebody who could jump out of an airplane anyway—and always seemed willing to let him have the limelight when needed for his stunts.

They'd made the crazy life work. Done whatever they'd had to to *make* it work. So what was this emotion weighting her voice now?

Resentment? How could he have missed that for so long?

"Wildfire, if I have been unfair to you these years with how I lived my life, I'm so sorry." He started to sit up so he could look her in the eyes, but she pushed him back down.

"No. Don't apologize for all the amazing things you've done. All the amazing things you're still going to do."

"We can still do them together." Desperation tore at him. There was something in her voice he couldn't quite label, but it was bad. It was the heart of why she'd left him. "Do you want to come on more trips? Fewer? I know you love it here in Oak Creek. I know your job is here. With the new Adventure Channel show, I'll have a lot more flexibility and say in where and when I go."

Maybe now was the time to tell her. The greatest adventure. What the tattoo really meant.

"Listen. I don't know how you and I got so far off our track. And I'm so sorry I didn't recognize there was a problem." The feel of the skin of her back under his fingertips was the only thing keeping him sane. "I want to tell you about the tattoo. About my greatest adventure."

"No! I want to guess."

Her words were emphatic enough that he was sort of stunned into silence. "Okay."

"The wakeboarding tournament you won in Dubai."

"No."

"The race across the volcano in Iceland."

"No."

"Kiteboarding in Nepal. Surfing in Maui. BASE jumping in Brazil." Her voice was becoming more and more frantic. Jesus. What was going on here? Once again, something he didn't understand.

"Riley, stop."

"Freeclimbing the Todra Gorge. Winning the motocr—"

He kissed her. He did it to shock her and get her attention, but her lips fused to his in a way that turned the tables.

She hooked her leg over his hip and swung herself up so she was lying fully on top of him, never taking her mouth from his.

He slid his fingers into her hair at her nape, holding her

in place. Her tongue licked along his bottom lip, and he nipped at it.

She scored her nails across his shoulders and neck in retaliation.

Wildfire had always given as good as she'd gotten.

God yes, he wanted this. He wanted to slow it down, take their time, but when she began kissing her way down his jaw, over his chest, then across his abs, then…

His hips shot off the floor and breath hissed out of his throat when she took him into her mouth. His hands flew down to her head, holding her, guiding her, not that she needed it.

He was alternating between panting and cursing as she licked his length. When her tongue slid over his crown, his head arched back, lifting his shoulders off the ground.

"God, Wildfire."

"I love driving you crazy."

She'd always been able to. But, hell, she drove him crazy when her mouth wasn't even on the same continent as his dick.

She took him deep inside her mouth again and every coherent thought flew from his mind. His fingers were still wrapped in her hair. He loved the feel of it—no matter what color it was—through his fingers as her head moved up and down.

"I'm not going to last another thirty seconds if you keep that up."

She worked him with her hand as she peeked up at him, devil in her eye. "Maybe I don't want you to last."

In all his travels he'd never seen anything as beautiful as her so confident and sexy with her sly smile.

But he knew as soon as this was over, they'd be going back to whatever was broken between them. He didn't want that, or at least he wanted to delay it for as long as possible.

Definitely longer than thirty seconds.

There was one good way he knew to make sure that happened.

The best possible way to make that happen.

She was about to take him in her mouth again, up the score in some sort of game he didn't understand the rules to, when he sat up and grabbed her by the waist.

She squealed as he lay back down on the ground, dragging her up his chest until her thighs were on either side of his head.

"Now let's see how long you can last with the roles reversed, Wildfire."

"Riley, I am—"

Whatever she was going to say was lost as he wrapped his hands around her hips and pulled her down onto his mouth.

God, he loved everything about this woman. Loved her brain, loved the way she laughed, loved her smile, loved her *taste*.

Definitely loved the way she sighed his name over and over as he devoured her.

She tried to pull away as her sounds became more fevered, but there was no way he was going to let her go.

He knew the exact moment she passed the point of reason and got caught up in what her body was feeling. She collapsed forward, catching her weight on her hands, and ground down against his face. He worked his tongue against her clit over and over in the steady motion he knew she wanted, her thigh tensing under his hands as he held her open to him.

He was rewarded a few moments later with her sobs as she jerked, calling his name, then collapsed against him.

He gave them both a moment to catch their breath before he sat up, moving her with him once again, except this time he slid her back until she was straddling his lap.

They both let out a moan as he slid deep inside her wet, slick heat with one hard thrust.

His hand slid back into her hair, bringing her face in for a kiss.

She didn't shy away, but he could see the demons of whatever she was keeping from him clear in her eyes.

"I love you, Wildfire." He punctuated the sentence with a thrust, gripping her more tightly as she ground against him. "I know you still love me too. Say it."

He thrust again, wrapping his hands around her shoulders and keeping her body flush against his.

She shook her head.

Thrust. "Say it."

"Riley—"

"No." Thrust. "Say it."

"I love you."

The words were barely even a whisper, but they were enough. He tilted her body back and thrust over and over until they both gasped and the world burst around them.

He rested his head against her shoulder for a long minute as conscious thought finally reentered his mind. Keeping her pressed safely against him, he lay back down.

She loved him. That was all he needed to know. The rest they could figure out.

He rubbed his hands up and down her back as his eyes began to close.

She loved him. He was not going to let her go.

Not now. Not ever.

But when he woke up again, she was gone.

Chapter 20

She could feel Riley lying beside her, sleeping, as she tried to wrap her head around what had just happened.

Sex had always been good between them but that... That had been almost unfathomable. Not telling him she loved him hadn't even been an option.

And, of course, it had only been the truth.

She was going to have to tell him about the MS. There was no way around it. The most she could hope for now was to tell him after the race. He'd gone through so much to get this far, and he wanted to win. She wasn't going to rip the opportunity for victory from him by dumping this news.

But she wasn't going to stick around here and give him the chance to start wearing down her defenses even more. They were still broken up. Their relationship was still over. That hadn't changed.

Lying here naked was not going to help convince him that she meant it.

She silently slid away from his sleeping form. He hadn't had any more ill effects from whatever had bitten him, but between that and all the excess energy he'd been expending for the race, not to mention the energy he'd just expended a few minutes ago making love to her, his body needed rest. Plus, they needed to go in different directions anyway—her back to the RV, and him forward on to the next base camp.

Him forward, her backward. How apropos.

She slipped on her clothes, which had mostly dried in the warm air of the shelter. She took a calorie-dense nutrition bar out of her bag and set it out for Riley. Since he'd required medical attention, she was allowed to give him that assistance.

She didn't need to worry about him. He'd be awake and on his way toward the new base camp within the next couple of hours. It was about five miles away. He'd be there long before dark. Especially without a backpack. But she left an EpiPen next to the nutrition bar just in case he needed it.

She slid out the door and headed back toward the rope bridge. Her body was stiff and jerky. No doubt a combination of MS-flare-up issues and the extremes she'd put it through—both good and bad—over the past few hours.

When she got to the bridge, she stopped and let out a curse.

It had been hit by lightning some time during the storm. That wasn't really surprising given how crazy the storm had been, but it meant there was no way she could get back over to the RV.

She pulled the walkie-talkie out of her backpack.

"Zac, this is Riley, come in."

A few seconds later the walkie-talkie beeped in her hand. Zac's deep voice came through. "You okay, Riley?"

"Phoenix seems to be recovering without any issues from the anaphylaxis. He'll be leaving the hunter's shelter within the next couple hours, I would think. I came back to get the RV, but the rope bridge was destroyed in the storm.

Zac let out a curse. "Roger that. You're better off turning

184

back around and walking to base camp two. It will be shorter and a more direct walk than trying to circumvent that ravine. I'll send someone from here to pick up the RV and drive it back."

"Will do. Did Anne make it to you all right?"

"Yes. The competitor who was hurt is on his way to Reddington City with her. She'll be back tonight."

"Roger that. I'm running a little slow, so I'll see you in a couple hours."

This area wasn't particularly rough terrain, but her body already wasn't cooperating.

"Roger that. See you then. Be safe."

She didn't waste any time. Boy Riley wasn't going to sleep all day, and she didn't want him to catch up with her. If she could just make it to camp two, she'd be able hold off "the talk" until after the race.

She was about halfway into the five miles she needed to go when she had to accept that the oddness she felt in her body was more than just physical exhaustion, and it was getting worse.

Her doctors had warned her that stress could exacerbate her MS, provoke symptoms and outbreaks.

Today had been way too much. She'd been feeling tingling and numbness in her limbs for a while. She'd kept walking, but when she took a step a mile later and misjudged the distance between her foot and the ground, she knew vertigo and balance issues—both common with MS flare-ups —were coming into play.

But she'd kept moving forward. Slowly, awkwardly, unevenly…but forward.

By the time she was a half mile from the camp, her legs were once again spasming the way they had when she'd fallen into the lake.

She needed a break. Needed to lie down for a few hours

and give her body a chance to recuperate. Hopefully, this wasn't a full-on flare-up, because that would mean leaving the race.

She willed her body to make it. She was so close.

One step at a time. It was taking way longer than she'd told Zac it would.

She finally reached the wooden bridge the competitors crossed less than a quarter of a mile from camp two. Compared to the rope bridge, this was nothing. It was a little shaky, and maybe a little scary if you were afraid of heights, but ultimately, it was pretty harmless. All someone had to do was hold the rails and step across the wooden beams.

For safety's sake, the bridge still offered a means of buckling in via safety line and harness, but most people just chose to walk it. It was wide enough and the boards sturdy enough not to be a real threat.

Unless, of course, just *walking* was a threat, and you might fall over in a minute.

Riley would have to hook herself into the safety line— there was no way she could take the chance of crossing with her legs spasming the way they'd been. She was just about to do so when the walkie-talkie clicked again.

"Riley, you doing okay?" Zac's voice came through.

"Yeah, no problems."

"Good. Hope you're going to arrive soon. Anne's not back yet, and we've got a bunch of little injuries I need you to take a look at. We halted the race for twenty-four hours, but everyone needs to be cleared before tomorrow morning."

A bout of dizziness hit her, and she had to lean against the tree. Shit.

"I'm still about an hour out." She didn't like to lie, especially not when she could almost see the camp from here, but the way she was feeling right now, it might take her every bit of an hour to make it that last quarter of a mile.

"Oh. Okay. I thought you would've been much closer," Zac said. "You sure everything's okay?"

"Yep." Her voice was tight. She was glad he couldn't see her face. "Just a little slow."

"Okay. We'll see you when we see you. Be looking for you in about an hour."

"An hour. Roger that."

She pushed herself up from the tree she was leaning against. She needed to keep making forward progress—an hour would pass quickly, and she wouldn't be able to hold Zac off a second time.

But when she took a step forward and leaned to grab the safety harness lying on the ground next to the bridge, her muscle spasmed—the worst it had done all day. She jerked forward, lost her balance, and fell to her knees.

Shit. This was bad. The annoying, nagging pain that had plagued her since she'd started walking had been bad enough. But it had been manageable.

But her muscles clenching and unclenching like this? That was bad. Very bad.

"You're hurt. Something is wrong, and you didn't tell me." She sucked in her breath at Boy Riley's voice behind her.

This was much worse.

She turned. He stepped out of the tree line just a few feet behind her.

She had to get it together, quick. She forced herself to sit up straighter, like she'd meant to sit down for a little break. "I'm fine. It's nothing. Just clumsy."

"That's bullshit, Wildfire, and we both know it. I was so pissed when I woke up and found you gone."

She didn't want to fight with him. Couldn't afford to fight with him. "In my defense, I thought I was going to get the RV and drive it to camp two. I thought you had to walk since you still wanted to be in the race, so I might as well let you rest. Then the rope bridge was out so I had to turn around."

"I've been watching you for three miles." Those whiskey-brown eyes narrowed at her. "At first I was trying to figure out why you'd left. I thought maybe you just needed some time or something. What happened in the cabin was pretty intense."

She nodded. It was all she could do.

"Jesus, Wildfire, you've never been one to run away. I've always trusted you."

"I've never betrayed your trust. No matter how far apart we've been, there's never been anyone else."

He shook his head. "I know that. For me either. I've never been interested in any other woman but you."

He took a step toward her, and she wished she could scoot away, but unless she wanted to drag herself in the dirt, that wasn't happening. "But I trusted you to tell me when you needed something. To communicate with me. Not run away."

"I always did."

"I would've believed that until today." Another step closer. "I've been watching the pain and stiffness get worse. Dizziness too, right?"

Damn it, he'd always been way too observant. It was what made him such an exceptional athlete.

She had to think of a way to talk herself out of this.

She stretched her leg out in front of her as casually as possible, hoping if it seized or jerked again, it wouldn't be noticeable. "I think we can both agree it's been a crazy day. I might've pushed it a little too far. My body decided that an extra five-mile hike on top of everything I asked it to do today was unreasonable and let me know it."

He tilted his head to the side, studying her. "You know, that's exactly what I told myself. That you had every right to take it as slowly and stiffly as you wanted. That you saved my life today and that I should be *carrying* you if you wanted me to."

She didn't like that he was being so reasonable. Didn't like that he was standing over her, towering over her way down here on the ground. "Why aren't you angry? I left you sleeping without a word."

"Oh, like I said, I was plenty angry. I was going to have it out with you."

"Okay, so let's have it out." She'd been wrong. Fighting was better. She could easily make him mad and get him off topic.

"I'm not going to fight with you, Wildfire."

"And why is that?" She said with a smirk, the furthest actual thing from what she was feeling.

He crouched down so he was more at her level. "Because that's exactly what you want. To distract me with a fight."

Goddammit. "Get over yourself, Harrison. Hell, I'll admit we had some good sex today. But nothing has changed. I still don't want you in my life. We're not right for each other. Never have been, if you think about it."

He tilted his head to the side again. "Do you want to marry me?"

Oh God, her heart was going to break inside her chest. "You're really not good with the concept of a breakup, are you? That's the *opposite* of getting married."

He shifted his weight so he was sitting on the ground near her rather than crouching. "I know we never seriously talked about marriage. Except for when we saw that house. Do you remember that?"

If she could have run away, she would have. "Yes," she choked out. "I remember the house."

She'd lived in Oak Creek all of her life and somehow had never known about the huge old cabin about five miles south of the main section of town. She and Riley had found it almost by accident when they'd seen a realtor's open-house sign as they were driving by the main road last fall.

One look at the place, and she'd fallen in love with it. The wraparound porch. The three fireplaces. The use of native stone for the outer finishes. The creek that ran through the back of the property.

It was like she'd seen her whole future there. Her. Riley. Three kids.

She'd said something of the sort to him, then felt like an idiot. She'd always been the one to belittle the concept of a traditional marriage and family.

She'd seen how ugly marriage could turn out, had been used as a bartering tool between her mother and father for most of her childhood.

She'd wanted to stay as far away from that as possible. He'd known it from the beginning, and it hadn't bothered him.

"I know what I said when we saw the house. It was just hormones or something."

It sure as hell hadn't felt like hormones. It had felt like fate was slapping her in the face, telling her that maybe everything she'd thought she *didn't* want she actually did.

Of course, fate had slapped her again with the MS diagnosis—telling her maybe it didn't matter what she did or didn't want. She was getting MS instead.

"It was the only time you ever talked about the possibility of marriage and a family. I was wondering if maybe you were considering that again now."

She rolled her eyes. "This isn't some elaborate ploy to get you to propose."

He made a choked sound. "Hell, I know that. You don't have an *elaborate ploy* in your body."

Yeah, she'd started thinking about marriage and family

that day. And maybe would've gone down that path eventually.

But when she'd driven by that house a couple weeks later, it had sold. Another family had moved in. It had become the house of *their* dreams.

Probably better in the long run anyway.

"We never talked much about marriage even after that house," he continued, picking at a piece of grass in the ground. "But we always talked about forever. Talked about what we'd be doing when we were seventy. Talked about the places we wanted to travel to, and the types of food we wanted to try, and the things we wanted to do."

She kept her face turned away from him, hiding her mouth in the crook of her elbow so she could hold back her little sob.

"You were always it for me, Wildfire. Marriage license or not. You are still it for me."

"Riley…"

"When you broke up with me, I was angry, sad, confused, then angry again. And that was before we even hung up the phone. Then it just got worse."

"I wasn't trying to hurt you. I was never trying to hurt you."

"Once I could breathe again—and believe me, that took a while—there was an emotion that pushed all the others to the background. Resolve."

She wasn't surprised to hear that at all.

"Resolve isn't something I'm a stranger to. It's part of my career, refusing to turn away even though something is hard or dangerous. I came here resolved to get you back, Wildfire. Or at the very least to get answers and maybe challenge some young, handsome surgeon to a duel if he had tried to steal your heart. I think I could be pretty good with swords if I needed to."

"Riley…" Her voice caught on a sob. She wasn't going to survive this.

"I was *resolved*. I was willing to work out whatever compromise you needed in order to stay in my life. I was willing to fight whoever I needed to—and, you know a surgeon would probably be good with swords, because they're good with scalpels, but I was still willing."

Her laugh was choked. She loved this man so much.

He let out a sigh. "Believe it or not, what I was ready to do in my resolution isn't even my point. My whole emotional gamut—"

Now she turned to him, cutting him off. "Riley, I'm so sorry."

He put a finger over her lips. "I've been sad. I've been angry. I've been resolved. But I haven't been scared. Not until a few minutes ago when I heard Zac say that he needed you in camp to help hurt people, and you told him you were still an hour away."

"I…"

"That's not you. You would never make a hurt person wait. That's when I finally understood there's something so much more going on than just a breakup. The time for hiding is over, Wildfire. Tell me what's really going on."

Chapter 21

Riley had once spent twenty-two minutes trapped under a layer of snow from an avalanche where he and his team had been filming a stunt. He'd only survived because in the first few seconds, when he still had the ability to move, he'd known to create an air pocket around his head.

He'd had a tracker on and known help was coming, but those had still been the longest twenty-two fucking minutes of his life. A frozen tomb. Unable to move. Unable to do anything at all but hope someone would get him out.

And on two separate occasions when he was working with the Linear Tactical guys on a mission, Riley had had a gun held to his head by bad guys who were pretty pissed off that Riley had been working against them. Both of those instances he'd been pretty sure he was about to die. It had only been the Linear Tactical team's decisive actions—a long-distance bullet from Finn, a surprise attack from the ceiling by Wyatt—that had allowed Riley to be alive today.

He did a lot of scary shit on a daily basis.

But nothing, absolutely, completely, and utterly *nothing*

had ever scared him the way hearing Wildfire lie to Zac on that walkie-talkie had.

There was something wrong with his Wildfire.

He'd spent the past few minutes talking to her, trying to get her to a place where she could say it to him. He'd done all he could. Now she had to take the next step. She had to tell him.

"I have multiple sclerosis," she whispered. "I was diagnosed ten days ago."

He only had a vague idea what that was. "Are you dying?" That was the most important thing, right? Everything else was secondary to survival.

"There can be complications that can lead to fatality, but generally speaking, no. MS isn't fatal."

He closed his eyes and let out a breath he hadn't even realized he'd been holding.

She wasn't dying.

It wasn't leukemia or a brain tumor or one of the other hundreds of things that would mean he'd be burying her in the next few months. That had honestly been what he'd been thinking.

"Okay. I don't really know what multiple sclerosis is, but it's not fatal. That's what's important. We'll work through it together. You know I have money. We can find doctors, get whatever medicines you need."

She got up. Slowly. More unsteadily than he'd ever seen her.

He hopped up beside her, arms out to assist. She ignored him.

"MS doesn't work that way. There's no medicine that's going to make all my symptoms go away."

He ran a hand through his hair. "Okay. I'm at a disadvantage because I don't know anything, but we'll figure it out."

She turned and walked a few stiff feet to a nearby tree, not looking at him. "You don't understand. It's going to affect my muscles. My coordination. I won't be able to get around like I am now."

"Right away?"

"I don't know. It's different for every single person. I may be in a wheelchair six months from now."

She was selling him on the worst. He already knew it. "Is that for sure?"

She shook her head. "Nothing is for sure. But—"

He stopped her. "Then we'll figure it out. *Together.*" That was the one thing he was sure of.

"No, we won't." She still wasn't looking at him. "Don't you get it? Our lives were already different enough. And now this? A *wheelchair*, Riley. Not exactly conducive to adventure travel or jumping out of an airplane."

He walked over to her, not sure if he should touch her or not. "We'll work it out."

She laughed, but the sound held no humor at all. She turned around and looked at him. "I knew that's what you would say. I knew you'd be all gung ho about being by my side for whatever happened. But that's just not going to work. We're still broken up. We're still done."

"That's it? You get to just make all the decisions? You keep this from me and then just drop it on me, then refuse to talk about it at all?"

"Honestly, there's not a whole lot to talk about."

Riley struggled to hold on to his temper. Wildfire's spirit and stubbornness were two of the things he most loved about her, but it also meant they sometimes butted heads. "No. You don't get to make yourself relationship judge, jury, and executioner."

"I'm not trying to be that, but the hard fact about MS is

that it's just going to get worse, and our lives are not compatible."

He slammed his fist against a tree, causing water that had collected on the leaves during the storm to rain down on them. "That is complete and utter bullshit. You're scared, I get it. But there's no way—"

The sound of a twig breaking cut Riley off. He turned to find Zac and Wyatt coming in a few yards to the south. They'd obviously made the noise on purpose.

"I'm sorry," Zac said. "I'm truly sorry to be interrupting you, but I thought you'd prefer to know we were nearby."

The other man looked deeply regretful. So did Wyatt.

"How long have you been there?"

"Long enough," Wyatt said.

Wildfire gritted her teeth and gave them a nod. "So now you know. Multiple sclerosis. My body is attacking itself. Blah, blah, blah."

"Annie got back early, and when she found out you were alone and that it was taking you so long to get to camp two, she freaked out. Especially when she found out everything you'd been through today. She was about to come after you, but I talked her into letting Wyatt and me come."

"Annie wouldn't tell us anything, just that you might not be able to make it to camp," Wyatt said.

"I knew she wouldn't tell anyone," Wildfire whispered. "Even if she wasn't a medical professional, I made her promise."

Riley's heart broke a little at the look of defeat that fell over her features. In all the years he'd known her, he'd never seen that look.

Her fearlessness was gone.

"Wildfire…" He stepped closer.

She shook her head. "Don't touch me. I have to go. I can't talk about anything else right now."

She walked toward the bridge, and something akin to panic clutched at his chest. What if she fell? Even with the safety ropes, would she be able to get herself back up?

"I'll help you get across."

She didn't look at him. "I can do it myself."

"No, let me help." He walked around in front of her, taking the safety rope to attach it to the harness. But she snatched it out of his hand.

"I said I can fucking do it myself!"

"Don't be stupid." He took it back from her. "There's no need to—"

She slapped him. The sound of it rang out all around them.

Neither of them had been expecting it. There was probably more shock on her face than there was on his.

"Oh my God." A huge tear rolled down her cheek.

He moved his jaw around a little, not surprised to find the blow had cut the inside of his cheek enough for him to taste blood. "Are you done with your fit now? Are you going to let me help you?"

He almost expected her to slap him again. Wouldn't blame her.

Why was he acting like such an asshole? There were a dozen other ways he could talk to her that would get her to let him help her.

He could joke with her. He could explain that this wasn't about her abilities, but about his own fear.

He could explain that he was reeling because something was hurting her, and he couldn't protect her. Couldn't share in the pain.

He could scream up at the sky and rage at the unfairness of it all that his Wildfire would be struck by something that had *stripped her of her fearlessness*.

He needed a goddamn minute to take all this in and figure out how to breathe again.

But instead he was just being an asshole.

"No, Riley," she said quietly. "I'm not going to let you help me."

She turned away from him, to the bridge, and hooked in the safety line herself.

He was about to reach for her again when she struggled with her balance on the first step, but a hard hand fell on his shoulder.

"You need to let her cross this bridge herself," Wyatt said in a low voice. "The literal one and the figurative one. If you want any chance with her at all, you've got to let her know you believe that she can do this herself."

"But what if she falls?"

"Then she falls," Zac said over his other shoulder. "Right now, you'll have to let that safety line catch her. Because if you try to swoop in and do it, it's going to cause more damage in the long run."

"I want to help her."

He wanted to do so much more than help her. He wanted to carry this for her, make it so she didn't have to go through it at all. He would take it all on himself if he could.

"Sometimes the only thing we can do is stand next to them as they fight their own battles." Zac squeezed his shoulder. "I had to learn that with Annie. Nearly fucking killed me."

"I don't know if I can do it." He watched Wildfire take another tentative step across the bridge. "She needs me."

"She does need you. But right now, she needs to learn how to trust herself. She has to find her new normal. Annie had to do that after what happened to her when she was attacked. I couldn't do it for her."

Riley's fists clenched at his side. He'd never felt so helpless in his entire life. "I—I…" He stopped. He wasn't sure what he was trying to say anyway.

"Believe me," Zac said. "Watching Annie in that hospital was the hardest thing I ever had to do. I couldn't take on the pain or fear for her. All I could do was be there once she was ready to be helped."

"Everybody knows you guys are good together," Wyatt said. "You're meant to be together so much that you even have the same name. It's all going to work out."

A year ago, Riley would have agreed without hesitation. Hell, even a month ago.

Wildfire finally finished crossing the bridge. It had taken her well over double the time it would've normally taken her, even with her dislike of heights. But she had made it. She unhooked her safety line.

She didn't turn to smile at him. Didn't pump her fists in the air or even flip him off. She just kept walking without turning back.

Yeah, today Riley wasn't sure it was all going to work out at all.

Chapter 22

"Mind if I sit down?"

At Anne's soft words, Riley looked up from where he'd been sitting with his head in his hands at the picnic table on the edge of camp two.

It had been a long fucking evening that had turned into a sleepless fucking night.

"Sure, although I hate to even ask what you're doing awake at this ungodly hour." He slid over to make room for her on the wooden table.

"Zac couldn't sleep with you pacing out here. He's worried about you. He was going to come out and talk to you, but I volunteered instead."

"Because he needs his sleep to manage the race?"

Riley could just make out her soft smile in the moonlight. "My husband-to-be can go multiple days without sleep and still function at amazing cognitive and physical capacity. That, I'm sure, was part of his Special Forces training. I plan to put it to good use once we start having babies. He can get up for the three a.m. feedings since he's already wired to withstand that sort of torture anyway."

Riley chuckled. "Smart thinking. I'm surprised you didn't let him come handle this three a.m. feeding." He pointed his thumb at his chest.

"He would've done it, because he cares about you. You may not be from Oak Creek, but he considers you one of the family now. I would've let you both sit out here and grunt it out like manly men do, but I figured I might actually be able to help you a little more. Answer some medical questions about MS."

"I've spent the past two hours cursing the fact that I don't run with any sort of music. If I did, maybe I would've decided that having my phone with me was worth the extra eight ounces in my pack. Then I could've looked up as much as possible about MS."

She shrugged. "Online information about medical conditions isn't always reliable. Plus, if you had brought your phone, it'd be at the bottom of that ravine with the rest of your pack. Not to mention there's not much of a signal out here."

"True on all counts."

The lost pack was part of the reason he was out here right now. All he had left was the emergency blanket and half of one of the meal bars Wildfire had left him in the hunting shelter. Sleeping under those conditions wouldn't have been pretty, but it wasn't lack of comfort that had been keeping him awake.

"I have so many questions I don't even know where to start."

"I am one of Riley's doctors, so I can't talk about her specifically, but I can tell you about MS in general."

"Is she going to die from it? I asked her that. She said no, but now I'm wondering if she lied about that."

"No, MS is not a terminal illness."

"Okay. Good. Okay." That was still the most important thing.

"MS is tricky because it's different for every patient. I couldn't tell you about Riley's particulars even if I was willing to. Most people have what's called relapsing-remitting MS. Basically symptoms will come and go. Some might get worse and become permanent."

"What sort of symptoms?"

"Lack of coordination. Dizziness. Fatigue. Muscle spasms. Maybe even sexual response issues."

He wrapped his hands around his head as if it might keep the information out. He couldn't stand the thought of his Wildfire going through any of this.

"She's afraid, Riley. I say this because of what I've observed as her friend, not as her doctor. She's afraid about the changes in her own health and the lack of control she has over it all."

"Is there anything that can be done?"

"There are some things she can control and regulate—diet, exercise, managing stress—that will help keep the relapses far apart."

"Okay, good." He looked at Anne. "I want to help. I tried to tell her that. I don't mean to be obnoxious, but I have money. I can help get her whatever she needs—medicine, therapy, whatever. I don't understand why she's cutting me out of her life."

Anne studied him in the darkness for a long moment. "Do you know when I first heard of you?"

He shrugged. "No."

"It was when Riley came running into the hospital one day announcing you were about to jump off into that quarry just outside of town. Pike's Peak."

"Yeah, I remember that."

It'd been for an online stunt. He'd gotten more than a

million views, and that video had been what had caught the attention of the Adventure Channel.

"Half the town went out there, Phoenix."

"Yeah, everybody loves the chance to see if the idiot kills himself."

She chuckled. "Maybe that was part of it. But the other part of it was that it was *you*. You're larger than life, not only around here, but all over the world. You're *Phoenix*. You fly and you jump and you make people gasp and shake their heads in wonder."

"That's not who I am, that's just what I do."

"She doesn't want to hold you back. You've got a lot more ahead of you, and she's afraid that being involved with someone with MS will clip your wings."

"But—"

Anne held out a hand to stop him. "Make no mistake about it, Riley's life has changed forever. Her MS is something that will afflict her for the rest of her life. How bad it will get or how quickly, none of us know. But it changes *everything* for her."

"And if we're together, it will change everything for me too, is that what you're saying?"

Anne stood up. "I know you don't want to be the jerk who turns his back on a great woman when something bad happens. But the fact is, you and Riley aren't married. Aren't even engaged."

"I love her."

"You need to take some time. Finish the race and then give yourself a chance to really think about all this. Girl Riley is still reeling from the news, but she's had a couple of weeks to begin processing it all. You need that too."

She patted him on the knee and gave him a smile. "Your Wildfire loves you, Phoenix. She just knows you well enough to know that the first words out of your mouth would be exactly what they were: that you would help, that you would stay, that you would take on this problem as your own."

"Because it's true." Time wasn't going to change that.

"But she also loves you enough that she believes the best thing for both of you is to break up. That your lifestyle—and I get it, it's not who you are, it's what you do, but it's still *what you do*—is not conducive to being permanently attached to someone with MS."

"But—"

"Before you say anything else, consider this. She's not just looking out for *you* when she says that maybe you guys shouldn't be together. She's looking out for herself too. It's important that she do that."

That shut him up. He thought back to what Zac had said the other day when they were looking for the missing puzzle box. That he might be hurting Wildfire without even realizing it.

"I'm not sure what to do."

Anne gave him a crooked grin. "Win the race. I know that's important to you." Her voice dropped to the softest whisper. "And none of us want to see Bo win. What a dick. Let me know if you have any more questions."

"About BoGo being a dick? I think we're all clear on that point."

She smiled and squeezed his hand before walking away. The sun was starting to creep its way over the horizon. He needed to leave before Wildfire came out. He wasn't sure what to say and didn't want her to feel uncomfortable around him. Plus, he didn't have any coffee anyway.

Soon the other participants would be up and awake and excited. It was the last day of the race. Everyone had gotten a break yesterday because of the storm, and now they were ready to go.

Maybe Anne was right. He should concentrate on the

race. Give his mind something else to focus on besides what was happening with Wildfire.

Running the race, *winning* the race, wouldn't change anything about the situation. But it was sure as hell better than sitting here doing nothing and still not changing anything about the situation.

His life was spiraling out of control, but this race, or at least his performance in it, was something he could control.

One last day to push. One last day to win.

It had to make something better.

Because it couldn't get any worse.

Chapter 23

The excitement at the start of the last day of the race was damn near tangible.

Riley and Anne had already done their parts, checking everyone out, making sure they were fit for this final grueling day.

Or mostly Anne had done it yesterday evening while Riley had recuperated in the RV.

"I'm really sorry I didn't do more—"

"Seriously, if you apologize one more time for needing to take a break yesterday, you're not going to have to worry about MS affecting your life because I'm going to kill you." Anne flashed her an angelic smile.

"I know, but…"

"There is no but, isn't that what you say?"

Riley laughed. "There is no *try*. Close enough."

"Plus, you rallied after a couple hours of rest and helped. And honestly, I'm just glad it wasn't a full-on MS exacerbation."

"Me too."

"Not everything bad that happens to you health-wise is

going to be part of your MS. You're still occasionally going to get the flu, or a cold, or just have a shitty day that gives you a headache."

Riley took a sip of her coffee.

Boy Riley had gone without coffee this morning. Another competitor had given him an extra MRE that they'd carried, one of the competitors who'd been doing this race more as a bucket list event than as an actual timed competition. Phoenix had taken it, gratefully, since sharing was allowed between athletes.

Riley herself had avoided him. There was nothing more to say, not now in the middle of the race.

Maybe not ever.

He'd kept his distance this morning too. Hadn't smiled or winked at her. Hadn't cracked a joke in her direction or shown up with any new booboos.

Hadn't shared the sunrise with her.

He was focused on the race and what he needed to do to win. She'd heard the other competitors buzzing about it before they'd left at a sprint about thirty minutes ago.

Good. Let him focus on the race. It was much better than that look of concern he'd given her as she started to cross the bridge yesterday. Like she was an invalid. That look had been what she was most afraid of, had been the very reason she hadn't wanted to tell anyone at all about her MS, especially Boy Riley.

She was glad he was focusing on the race and not her. Glad he had barely even looked in her direction. Glad he was doing exactly what she'd told him to do: move on.

And if it hurt her heart a little bit that he was doing it all so quickly, then she needed to shut the hell up. Because she'd told him to do it. Specifically, she'd told him to set this behind him and go win the race.

Winning was what Phoenix did.

"I never did find any sign of a bite or sting on Phoenix. He should've felt something, or I should've found some sort of inflammation. Honestly, based on what you told me, the whole thing presented itself more like an allergic reaction than a toxin."

"Well, the only thing he's allergic to is penicillin. I don't think that was happening here."

"Whatever it was that bit him, he needs to be aware of it for future hikes and races in this area. Something that life-threatening when he didn't feel a bite or sting? That's scary."

He'd looked ready this morning. Strong. Last night he might've been at a disadvantage from not having a backpack with supplies, but today it would work in his favor. Everyone else would be encumbered by their packs, but not him. He still had forty-five minutes he had to make up in order to take over the lead from Bo, but in a day with this many miles and both a sharpshooting and surprise horseback riding event, he had every chance of doing it.

Riley let out a sigh.

"You doing okay?" Anne asked.

"Yeah. Amazing what some sleep and a full meal can do. I'm going to finish packing up everything in the RV." She took her last sip of coffee. "Everything has been so crazy, I haven't even gotten the files put away from day three. I was in there talking to Amber and everything's been crazy since then."

Anne raised an eyebrow. "That can wait till the race is done. Don't you want to be there to see who wins?"

"No." She turned toward the RV. "I don't need to be there to see Riley win."

Although she had no doubt it was going to happen.

She walked silently back to the RV. Besides updating the files, there really wasn't much to do. She and Anne both preferred a neat and orderly workspace, so they had kept things straightened while they went.

She did an inventory first.

Remarkably, almost everything was accounted for in the log. They weren't too fastidious about every little thing—in a race like this, the number of bandages the medical crew went through was in the hundreds—but things like splints or prescription painkillers were monitored.

Ironically, the only thing missing was a vial of penicillin. Maybe Riley had decided to poison himself with it.

More likely, Anne had used it for a possible infection and had forgotten to log it in. Riley jotted down a sticky note to ask the doc about it.

She got out the files to write down the details of the injuries they'd seen this morning and placed those in the done box. Then she straightened the bandages before going to get a second cup of coffee.

None of it was taking her mind off Riley.

Finally, she moved back to the desk where Riley's and Baby's files still sat. She picked up Baby's and finished writing in the details about the minimal injuries he'd received during the rappelling accident. She picked up Riley's file to do the same.

The papers contained his multiple-injury list. One did not become an extreme sport athlete without breaking some bones and needing a few hundred stitches.

But it had never stopped him. She finished writing about both the bruising to his chest and shoulders from the rappelling accident and the anaphylaxis. She turned the next page to find his allergy reports so she could list Anne's concerns about whatever had bit or stung him.

The paper wasn't there.

She went through the entire file again but didn't see it.

"What the hell?"

She knew for a fact it had been there at the start of the race and it had been there when she'd pulled the file to first write up the rappelling accident.

Anne wouldn't have taken it out. She was notorious for hating paperwork, and the two of them had agreed Riley would handle it.

She unclipped the fasteners at the top of the file, pulling all the papers out.

A tiny section of ripped paper fell onto her lap. The piece that had remained when someone had ripped out Riley's allergy section.

Why would someone do that? *How* would someone do that? Only she and Anne had had access to the file.

Riley's fingers traced across the top of Boy Riley's file, stopping where a tiny water stain still showed. A tearstain.

She frowned, her eyes narrowing, as she grabbed the reports Baby and Riley had given about the rappelling accident.

Riley had been so angry at Bo. Bo had been the last one up at the rigs, alone after Damon had gone down first. He'd definitely had time to sabotage the rappelling gear. And Bo had been the one to say the left rig was the fastest.

Except he hadn't. Amber had been the one to tell Riley that Bo had said the left rig was the fastest. The last one to see him before the accident.

She'd also been the only one to have access to his medical file, just before a vial of penicillin went missing.

Riley looked out the window of the RV and remembered Phoenix sitting out in the rain, the awkward, falling hug Amber had given him.

The perfect time to inject him with penicillin without him realizing it. The anaphylaxis had begun to set in less than an hour later—Phoenix would've been dead if Riley

211

hadn't turned out to see him one last time on that rope bridge.

I want to do something about Felix's death. I'm here to put the past to rights.

Amber blamed Riley for what had happened to Felix.

What if she hadn't entered WAR to honor her brother's memory? What if she'd done it to avenge her brother's death?

And today's section of the race included a shooting range. Way too much opportunity.

Riley ran out the door to find Zac and Wyatt, praying she wasn't too late.

Chapter 24

For the first three miles, Riley pushed himself as hard as possible. In order to win, he was going to have to make up a lot of ground early.

This stage was a particularly brutal ten miles, then the shooting range, and finally ten more miles. It didn't matter who crossed the finish line first *today*, it was the overall combined time that mattered. So, if he wasn't at least forty-five minutes ahead of Bo when he crossed the finish line, Riley wasn't going to win.

Winning was what everyone was telling him to do. Anne when they'd talked. Zac on the way out of camp. Baby had whispered it to him this morning before the start. The mom of four teenagers in her forties who'd given him an MRE so he'd have some energy to burn as he ran.

Hell, even Riley had told him to win yesterday.

That was what he was here to do. Win.

Except...

He'd sprinted another half mile before his brain actually finished the thought.

Except… he *hadn't* come here to win. At least not the race.

That had never been his plan. The race didn't mean anything to him. He'd only decided to try to win because Bo was talking so much shit.

The only winning he'd come to Wyoming to do was winning Wildfire back.

He was running in the wrong direction to do that.

He stopped. For the first time as a professional athlete, Phoenix stopped in a race he could win.

Phoenix was a winner. Phoenix was competitive. Phoenix didn't lose.

But *Riley* didn't give a shit about Phoenix right now. Anything that was causing him to run *away* from the love of his life was something moving him in the wrong direction. Especially right when she needed him most.

She meant more to him than all of it. She wanted to argue that their lives weren't compatible?

Then he would change his life until they were compatible.

Zac and Wyatt had been right yesterday when they'd said she needed to cross that bridge by herself.

And there would be other parts of navigating her MS she would have to do alone. But goddammit, he was going to be with her for every single part she *didn't*. She was going to know that whatever bridge she crossed, he'd be crossing right behind her. Or in front of her. Or beside her.

He wasn't going anywhere. Not without her.

He turned around and headed back toward camp, feeling lighter and happier than he had since he'd started this morning—hell, since Wildfire had broken up with him. He didn't deceive himself into thinking this was going to change her mind, but it at least was going to show her he was serious about his intentions.

She didn't want him to have to change his life.

He didn't want to live without her in his life.

They were going to work that shit out.

And they *would*.

Bo, no surprise, was the first person he passed on his way back. He was probably about twenty minutes behind Riley, slower because of his backpack, and because he was just slower.

Shock slid across Bo's features when he realized it was Riley and that he was moving in the wrong direction.

"Decided you couldn't put in the effort to beat me?"

"Decided my efforts were best spent in a different direction."

Bo rolled his eyes. "What is this, Harrison? Your way of being able to say you didn't try? That I didn't win fair and square?"

Riley wasn't going to get into the concept of fair and square after what Bo had done with both the rappelling equipment and hiding the puzzle clues.

"This race is yours to win or lose on your own, BoGo," Riley finally said. "Either way, I'm out."

"You don't think I'll take the win?"

Riley narrowed his eyes. "I think you were willing to do whatever you had to do to take the win. I've just got more important things to do than to prove I can beat your cheating ass."

"Whatever, *Phoenix*." Bo spat out the word. "I didn't have to cheat to beat you. You beat yourself."

Bo took off without another word.

Riley wasn't even tempted to go after him just to prove who really was the winner.

Riley was already the winner. The prize was just back at base camp.

He passed others on the way. Damon, Baby, Iceland,

some other competitors, they all slowed down to make sure he was okay, but he sent them all on their way. Just told them he'd decided to drop out of the race and would explain the details later.

Maybe one of them could still beat Bo if they pushed.

There was only one person who stopped to talk to him and really find out the details about what was going on.

Amber.

"You're quitting?"

He smiled. "Yeah. There's something I've got to handle, and it can't wait. You go on ahead, and I'll see you at the finish line. We can talk later."

"Actually, I'm in no huge hurry. The first place woman is at least an hour ahead of me in overall time, and then the other women are at least a couple hours behind me."

He nodded. "Second place. That's amazing, Amber. Felix would be really proud, you know."

"I guess I'll never know."

He grimaced. "I'd really like to talk later. About more than just the race. About Felix and your family. About whether there's anything I can do to help." Way too late, but better late than never. "But really, you should get going. There's no need for you to waste time with me. My race is over."

Because he had a much more important one to run now.

Amber gave him a sad smile. "You know, I heard you and Girl Riley broke up. Maybe you and I could go have a drink or something sometime?"

Shit. He wanted to handle this with care. He wasn't interested in the least, but she'd already been through enough. "I'm flattered, Amber. Truly. But Riley and I are trying to work things out."

Or they would be once he sat her down and refused to let

her get back up until she saw reason. He was going to do that, even if it meant literally sitting on top of her.

"That's actually why I'm on my way back to camp, to talk to her."

Amber's face crumbled right in front of him. Without a word she turned and ran off the path farther along the ledge.

Shit.

He ran after her. He couldn't leave her like this. "Amber, please don't be embarrassed. This development with Riley and me getting back together is very new."

She just kept running. Now he was getting concerned about more than just her emotional well-being. If she wasn't careful, she might slip over the ledge.

Just like her brother. Jesus.

"Whoa. Hey, be careful, please. Stop and let's talk."

She stopped so close to the edge, one of her feet actually slid off.

But at least she'd stopped running.

He gestured for her to come back toward him, even though she wasn't looking at him. "Please be careful of that ledge. You're too close."

He stepped closer—could he reach her if she lost her balance and began to fall?

But she didn't lose her balance, she just began to laugh.

"Um, are you okay?" Now she turned to face him. There was no sign of discomfort or embarrassment on her features.

Just full, unadulterated *hatred*.

"No, we wouldn't want me to fall off the ledge, would we now? *You* were the one who was supposed to fall off the ledge. Not get a happily ever after with your girlfriend."

"What are you talking about?"

But he knew. Before she said another word, he knew.

Before he looked down and saw the gun in her hand, he knew.

Amber was behind everything that had happened to him this week.

"Felix idolized you, did you know that? Like, full-on man-crush. All the stupid stuff he did was because of you." She brought the gun up from her side to point directly at him.

Riley kept his hands out low and in front of him, not wanting to give her any reason to pull the trigger. "I didn't know him very well. Not as well as I should have. But Felix knew the risks of what he was doing. Everybody who goes out there knows the risks."

"Someone should have sent him home! *You* should've sent him home. Felix had no business being out on those skis on that kind of slope."

If memory served, they *had* told him to go home, but Felix hadn't been interested in anyone else's opinion. He'd had something to prove, and nobody was going to talk him out of it.

God, in his younger days, Riley had been that person too many times to count. It was common among athletes of their type—ones who stared down danger every chance they got, convinced of their own immortality.

Felix had been one of those too.

But telling that to a grieving sister, especially one with a gun in her hand, probably wasn't the best plan.

He nodded instead. "You're right. Someone should've taken a hard line with Felix. *I* should've taken a hard line with him and told him he wasn't ready."

Riley ran a hand through his hair, then quickly held it out to show her he wasn't doing anything fishy when she jerked the gun in his direction.

She didn't understand the reality of how stunts worked. Didn't understand that, although the finished project may have looked like it was just Riley and a couple of buddies haphazardly filming, in reality, there were sometimes dozens of people involved. Beyond that, there were sometimes fans who came out to try to get in on the action too.

It had been that way on the mountain that day. Riley had known Felix in passing, but not well at all. He'd never had a full conversation with the other man.

But Felix, like so many fans sometimes did, thought he really knew Riley, had built up a pretend connection in his head until he'd convinced himself it was real. That they had a relationship. A friendship.

It was called parasocial interaction, when people felt an attachment and formed an imaginary relationship with celebrities, convinced it was real. He could thank his sister, Quinn, and all her college degrees for providing him with that knowledge.

Not that it was going to make him any less dead if Amber decided to fire that gun.

"And after his accident you should've been there with him. It was your fault he was paralyzed, and then he just gave up. He would've listened to you. He would've tried if you had been there to encourage him. He wouldn't listen to me. Didn't care about anything I said. I wasn't the great Phoenix."

Now *that* he couldn't argue with even if he'd been planning to argue. He should've gone to see Felix, whether he'd known the man well or not. Should've made the time. "You're right. You're right about it all. I should've been more aware and done more after the accident. I should've made Felix a priority."

Her eyes narrowed. "Is that supposed to be enough? Just…you're sorry? You'll do better next time? That's not going to make it right. I came here to make it right."

"What will make it right?"

"It was supposed to have been you on that rappelling rig. I didn't even know Baby was up there."

"Because his stomach was upset." He shook his head, barely able to believe it.

"I knew if I told you Bo said that left rig was fastest that you'd choose it. I had no idea he was already up there."

He needed to keep her talking as long as possible. Give himself time to figure out…something. A way to talk her out of this? A way to get the gun? "It's not too late, Amber. Just put the gun down. Nobody has gotten hurt, and we can still work things out—especially given the circumstances."

"Circumstances such as you murdering my brother?" she sneered. "You're pretty damn lucky, I'll give you that. When I found out how allergic you were to penicillin, I thought my little gift to you yesterday would certainly do the trick."

"That was you?"

"It wasn't as good as you falling, but dead is dead. Except your Florence Nightingale saved you, did she? And now you say the two of you are getting back together?" The gun wavered. "You don't get to have a happy ending! You don't get to ride off into the sunset with the girl when my brother died because of you."

There was definitely going to be no talking her out of this.

She firmed up her hold on the gun. "I want you to fall, Phoenix. I want you to feel what Felix did as he went over that cliff. I want you to know those few seconds of abject terror and knowledge that even if you somehow survive, nothing is ever going to be all right again."

Riley crossed his arms over his chest. He wanted to look still and firmly planted, not about to make any moves. But he kept his weight on the balls of his feet. There wasn't going to be a good time to make a move for that gun. All he could do was choose the least bad time.

She pointed at the ledge with her free hand. "Jump. I want you to dive headfirst over the edge."

"No." He said the word simply. Not adding the insults he'd like to tag on. "I won't do it. I'm sorry about your brother, I really am. Believe me when I say if I could go back and do things differently, I would. But I'm not jumping off that fucking ledge."

"Then I'm going to shoot you in the face."

"You know if you fire that gun, everyone is going to hear it. People will start running in this direction."

She shrugged, unconcerned. "There will be more questions, and I'm afraid poor Bo might be under quite a bit of scrutiny. But let's face it, nobody is going to suspect me. I'm the amazing one, remember? So strong, so noble to do this in my brother's memory."

She took a step closer.

"I am doing the best possible thing for his memory— making sure someone as reckless as you doesn't run around anymore. Maybe after you, I'll make sure Damon and the other members of your team learn an important lesson too."

Jesus, she really was crazy, and even worse, *serious*.

"I've got your attention now, don't I, Phoenix? I can see you measuring the different options in your head. Can you get the gun from me before I kill you with it?"

"Amber…"

In the tree line just over Amber's shoulder, a sound rang out from the woods. To anybody else it would've sounded like some sort of wild bird.

More importantly, to Amber it sounded like some sort of wild bird.

To Riley, it sounded like one of the Linear Tactical signals. He'd been in these very woods enough with these guys to recognize the call.

He had no idea who it was or how they'd known what

was happening, but help was here. He just needed to buy them as much time as possible.

He shrugged, dropping his arms. "You can't blame me for trying to come up with some sort of self-rescue plan."

She tilted her head and gave him a smirk. "I would expect nothing less from the great Phoenix. Too bad you couldn't put that sort of effort into helping my brother."

"I'm not going to jump, Amber." Riley shook his head, keeping her attention on him. "On sheer principle, I'm not going to give you the pleasure of swan diving off of this ledge."

"Oh, you're going off of the ledge. I can shoot you and drag you off, or you can jump and possibly survive."

Wyatt stepped out of the trees about ten yards behind Amber, his weapon trained on the back of her head. He tilted his head and shrugged his shoulders at Riley.

Riley understood. Wyatt could take Amber out and end this right now if Riley wanted him to.

Riley kept his gaze trained on Amber but shook his head slightly.

He was taking a risk. He knew it, but if there was any way to resolve the situation without body bags, Riley wanted to try it. He owed Felix that much.

"How about if I make you a deal, Amber?" Riley actually took a step closer to the ledge. She did what he'd hoped she would do: turned more fully toward the ravine, leaving her back more exposed to the woods. "I'll jump. Like you said, there's at least a possibility I'll survive. But if I do, you let this die with me. You don't hurt Damon, you don't go after Girl Riley. I was the one responsible for that skiing stunt, and I should've made absolutely certain everyone was qualified to be up there. So you let it end with me."

She lowered the gun to her side as Riley deliberately took

another step toward the ledge. Over her shoulder, Zac stepped out of the woods too.

Riley turned back toward the ledge. The best thing he could do now was keep Amber's attention focused on him and believing that he was about to jump.

He was going to have to trust the Linear Tactical guys to do what they did best: save people's lives.

This time it was his.

He held his hands out and open as he took another step closer.

"Promise me you'll get help, Amber. Watching me dive off this ledge isn't going to bring Felix back."

"It'll certainly be a start."

"I hope so. And I hope you'll keep your word that nobody else gets hurt."

She shooed the gun toward him. "Quit stalling."

"On three. One—"

The guys did not wait for three.

One had barely gotten out of his mouth before he heard a thud and moan behind him.

Riley spun, ducking, but he needn't have bothered. Zac already had Amber pinned face down on the ground. Wyatt still had his weapon trained on her as he picked up the gun Amber had dropped.

Riley threw up his hands. "What the hell, you guys? You were supposed to move on *three*. That was when I was going to duck and dive to the side."

Wyatt rolled his eyes. "Everybody knows you don't go on three. I would've chosen two, but we all know Zac here goes off a little early from time to time. Or so I hear from a certain pretty doctor."

Zac glared at them. "She'll be awake in a minute. I can give her the gun back and just let her shoot both of you if you prefer."

"See?" Wyatt shrugged his huge shoulders, the very picture of innocence, dropping his voice to an exaggerated stage whisper. "He's sensitive about it."

"How did you guys even know what was going on?"

Amber was starting to regain consciousness, so Zac zip-tied her hands behind her back. "Wyatt and I had no idea about anything." He turned and pointed toward the woods. "She figured it out."

Wildfire stepped out of the tree line. She'd obviously been running but hadn't gotten there as fast as Wyatt and Zac.

She was staring at him, face pale. "I didn't think we would get to you in time."

Wyatt and Zac helped Amber to her feet as she began to cry. They all ignored her.

"We're going to get her back to base camp. I'll call Sheriff Nelson and explain what's going on so he can officially make an arrest." Zac and Wyatt led Amber away, the woman still crying and starting to proclaim her innocence.

Riley ignored them. Wildfire looked at him with something akin to panic in her eyes.

"I'm okay, Wildfire."

"I've watched you almost die too many times over the past few days. I thought we were going to be too late. You should've been much farther ahead—we never would've caught you. When I figured out it was Amber and that none of this had been a coincidence..." She shook her head and closed her eyes. "I was sure this time we would be too late."

He took a step toward her. "How did you know Amber was trying to kill me?"

"I caught her going through your medical file after the rappelling accident. She stole the page about your allergies. And then when a vial of penicillin came up missing..."

There was nothing he wanted more than to yank her into

his arms. "That's twice you've literally saved my life. You're going to have to start a tab for how many times I owe you."

She let out a shaky breath and a little laugh. "Fine. Next time you can rescue me."

"Deal." He moved in a little closer.

"You still haven't told me why you're this far behind. Are you having some ill effects from yesterday?"

His little nurse. "No, I just realized I was heading the wrong way. Realized that I might cross the finish line first, but there was no winning for me today. At least not in that direction."

He crossed the rest of the way to her and pulled her into his arms. He felt nothing but relief when she didn't pull away. And then nothing but joy when her arms wrapped around him to keep him clutched to her.

"I thought we were too late."

"You can't get rid of me that easily, Wildfire. Not in any possible way. I was coming back for you. I was coming back because you mean more to me than any race, any jump, any stunt, and anything else in my life."

"Riley—"

He pulled back and placed a finger over her mouth. "Let me finish, okay?" She nodded, but he didn't move his hand away from her face. He needed to touch her skin, see her hazel eyes. "Not only do you mean more to me than any of those things, you mean more to me than all of them *combined*. I refuse to accept that we can't find a way to navigate your MS together. I know it's something you have to live with, but I love you, and I'm going to be by your side as you do."

"What about your career?"

"We'll figure it out. Let's face it, the half-life of an extreme sport athlete isn't that long anyway. I'm almost thirty-one years old. A ten-year run is not bad. It's time for me to do the stunts I want to do. And right now, for however long it takes, the stunts I want to do are here in Oak Creek."

"I might need hospital stays. In-home care."

He leaned his forehead against hers. "Then I'll get to be your nurse for once. How many days have you nursed me through sprains and dislocations? Hell, remember that time you had to babysit me when I broke my ankle? How cranky I was after being stuck in bed for three weeks? You threatened to sit on my face if I didn't shut up."

He loved the little smile that floated onto her lips. "I remember the sitting-on-your-face part."

"Give us a chance to work this out. Together. I know it means so many changes for both of us, but we're worth it. We are worth finding a way to make it work."

She pulled back a little. "I'm probably going to end up in a wheelchair at some point. It might be twenty years away, but it might be twenty months."

That didn't scare him a bit. "Either way, it doesn't matter. You're still going to be my Riley. My Wildfire. You'll just come with a set of wheels."

Chapter 25

"So if I hadn't had recurring diarrhea that required me to be sitting in the Wyoming wilderness, wiping my rear end with a leaf and cursing my brother and his friends for creating such a sadistic race, I'd be dead at the bottom of the ditch now."

Baby raised his beer as everyone around him in the locals' favorite bar, The Eagle's Nest, chuckled.

"You may be wondering what diarrhea has to do with a wedding toast. But then again, it is the wedding of Cade Connor, notoriously known for having his head stuck very far up his—"

"Uncle Baby!" little Jess's voice rang out. No one was surprised the five-year-old had figured out what Baby was going to say before he said it. Riley had known Jess since before she was born. The kid had an IQ higher than most of the adults in the room.

Combined.

Baby winked at the little girl. "Head stuck so far up his turtleneck is what I was going to say, sweet Jess."

Jess just raised an eyebrow and shot him a "don't give me that four-year-old stuff, I'm five" look. She had her glass of juice in her hand, standing next to Finn's son Ethan, as usual, ready to toast her mom and dad.

"Anyway." Baby held his beer bottle up once more. "To the bride and groom. You tried to sneak a wedding past us, but you should have known better. We're glad to celebrate you. I know of no one who deserves happiness more than you two. Love favors those who never give up believing in its power."

Cries of agreement rang out as everyone sipped their drinks.

As far as wedding receptions went, this one was a little unusual. But the entire wedding had been a little unusual—a private ceremony with a judge turned full celebration.

Riley was just glad Peyton and Jess were both alive and safe. She looked over at Boy Riley, who was now harassing Baby about his speech.

He was safe too.

Between what had almost happened to Boy Riley because of Amber and what had nearly happened to Peyton and Jess in the last ten days since the race…they were all due for a little downtime here in Oak Creek.

If this town was the setting for a romantic suspense movie, the suspense part would be over, and it would be time for the romance.

That suited Riley just fine.

She took a sip of her Electric Smurf, the blue concoction that had started more than one relationship here in town. She watched her best friend, Peyton, kiss her new husband.

Baby was right, love did smile on those who believed in its power.

She smiled when Phoenix winked at her from across the room as he took little Thomas from Finn's arms.

Something melted in her heart to see him nuzzle and

sniff the top of the infant's head as he cradled him so safely against his shoulder.

This was what she wanted. She'd always been afraid of marriage and family since it had ended so badly for so many of her immediate relatives. But her Linear family had taught her there was a different way, that forever love did exist.

Her MS diagnosis had changed her perception on everything too. She didn't have time to be afraid of marriage anymore. She had real things to be afraid of.

Boy Riley had been right by her side since the moment they'd rescued him from Amber.

Once it'd been determined that Amber had in fact deliberately manipulated different sets of equipment in the race, Zac had deemed the race canceled for this year with no winner. Bo, in a giant surprise to nobody, had thrown a fit.

Until, upon questioning, it became evident that Amber hadn't had any connection to Riley's missing puzzle box in the navigation section of the course. Nobody could prove Bo was the one who had moved it, but neither had Bo continued demanding someone declare a winner once it became evident he was the prime suspect.

Riley had no doubt Bo would be back next year.

And maybe Phoenix would too. By then, they might know more about how her MS was going to present itself. They were learning together. Riley had already rescheduled some of his events, putting the Adventure Channel show plans on hold temporarily.

They were taking it day by day, figuring it out.

After his words to her that last day of the race about giving them a chance *together,* she knew she couldn't keep him out anymore. Had no desire to keep him out at all.

His words had changed everything.

He was right. If something had happened to him, some sort of accident limiting his physical abilities, she would still love him and want to be with him. To suggest he didn't feel the same about her curtailed their love.

My Wildfire. You'll just come with a set of wheels.

There hadn't been a hint of trepidation in his words when she'd mentioned a wheelchair. Not a flinch or even a brave face.

He was ready. Whatever this condition threw at her—at *them*—Riley would be by her side helping in all the ways he could.

She'd been such a fool not to include him from the beginning. He knew her so well, knew what she needed, sometimes even before she did.

Like the dawn a few days ago when he'd taken her back out into the wilderness, far away from everything and everyone... and just let her scream.

Let her scream and rail and sob.

Let her take a branch and beat trees and boulders and the ground.

Because it was just all so goddamned unfair. She didn't want this. She didn't want to lose her abilities and independence. She was so terrified of what she might become.

He'd caught her when her energy had finally run out, lowering them both to the forest floor.

"You're not alone," he'd whispered into her ear, hand grasping the hair at the back of her neck and pulling her forehead until it rested against his. "Never again do you try to face this alone."

Finally—*finally*—in that moment, she'd begun to heal. Now that all the fear and bitterness and rage and pain had been screamed out for the wilderness to help hear and carry.

For Boy Riley to help hear and carry.

Not her alone. Never again.

The MS diagnosis hadn't changed, but she was ready to move forward.

She walked over to Riley, hugging and talking to people as she went. When she got to him, instead of kissing him, she bent and kissed little Thomas's cheek.

"Come on now, don't make me be jealous of a newborn," Riley said.

She rolled her eyes but tilted her face back so he could kiss her lips.

Except, instead of the little peck she'd expected, he caught her bottom lip between his teeth and tugged before shifting Thomas to the side so he could deepen the kiss.

"Gross, get a room!" Baby said.

"Yeah, I still have my badge. I'd hate to have to arrest you for unlawful PDA," Gavin joked.

They broke apart at the heckles around them, but both of them felt the heat coursing through their veins. It might be time to leave the party soon.

"I'll save you from certain jail time." She pulled back and winked at Riley. "I've got to run out to the car and grab my present for the bride and groom anyway."

It wasn't much, just a coupon she'd made for free nights babysitting so Cade and Peyton could have some alone time whenever they wanted it. It was the novelty wrapping paper she really wanted to show off—it was meant for business or office gifts, wrapping paper designed to look like contracts. And the primary words visible were *nondisclosure agreement.*

Most of the people in the room wouldn't understand, but Cade and Peyton, given their history, would get a kick out of it.

"Do you want me to go get the present?" Riley was carefully neutral in how he phrased the question, and she appreciated it. It was one of the big things they were having to figure out, balancing his need to protect and care for her with her need to be independent. It was going to be a continual give-and-take that would change as her MS progressed.

But they would work it out.

"No, you've got your hands full. I'll be back in a minute."

He bent down and kissed her on the nose, then moved his lips to her ear. "Hurry, so we can find a coat closet, and I can give you a couple of hickeys where no one will see them but us."

She pulled back and her eyes flew to his. "You really are going to get us arrested."

He winked at her.

Her heart turned to goo. God, she loved this man. She'd been so damn stupid to think she could live without him.

Outside, the late November air was cold and brisk. She made a beeline for her car, grabbing the present from the front seat.

She closed the door and turned back to The Eagle's Nest, jumping a little when a limousine pulled up and a very handsome man of Middle Eastern descent got out of the back seat. His suit had to cost more than what she made in a month.

This had to be one of the groom's friends or business partners. Word must be getting out about the nuptials.

The man gave her a smile as he tapped on the hood of the limo and it pulled forward, leaving him here.

"Pardon me, this is The Eagle's Nest?"

"Yeah." Riley smiled. "Don't tell me, you're a friend of Cade's?"

"No, I know Riley Harrison. Actually, I should say Riley came to my home in Egypt to ride motocross bikes on my personal course."

"Yeah, that sounds exactly like Phoenix." She shouldn't be surprised he'd made friends as far as Egypt. Riley had fans wherever he went.

The man gave her a charming smile. "Yes, it was a great honor to have the world-renowned Phoenix in my home. Accepting my hospitality and goodwill. And now I am in his own backyard as he was in mine, as they say."

His phrasing and terminology were stilted. Odd. But one thing traveling around the world with Riley had taught her was that communication had different rhythms in different cultures. Sometimes communication wasn't possible at all, so when it was, even when it was stiff, it was to be appreciated.

She smiled again. "You should come inside. I'm sure Riley will want to say hello to you. There's a celebration going on, but there's always room for one more."

"I've come a long way to personally deliver a message to Phoenix."

"Okay, I'll help you find him."

The man took a step closer. "Actually, I need you to help me deliver the message."

"Really, you should just tell him yourself. I'm—"

"The message is 'You took something that belonged to me. I have returned the favor.'"

She felt a sting on the back of her neck and spun in time to see the limo driver step back from where he'd snuck up behind her.

"What the hell?"

Everything began to blur. She stumbled toward the door of The Eagle's Nest.

"No one steals from Sayed El Kadi without retribution. It's time for your Phoenix to learn some manners."

She mentally clawed to hold on to consciousness, knowing this was her only chance to get away, but she couldn't stop the world around her from spinning and fading to black.

Chapter 26

"Sorry, buddy," Phoenix cooed into Thomas's tiny ear. "I'm going to have to give you back to your mom or dad soon. I'm not sure what's taking your beautiful aunt Wildfire so long, but I need to do some things to her when she gets back that you won't appreciate until you're much older."

Baby walked over to him and gestured to Thomas. "You next? Is a kid in the cards for you and Girl Riley?"

It had been one of the things he'd been researching on his own. If MS meant Riley couldn't safely get pregnant, that was fine. They could adopt, or it could just be the two of them.

One of the things he was trying to help Wildfire focus on was that she didn't necessarily have to assume the worst-case scenario for everything involving MS. She liked to be prepared for the worst, but that didn't mean it was going to happen.

Riley shrugged. "Kids are definitely possible, no reason why we can't. But we'll see if it's in the cards. I've got to talk her into marrying me first."

Baby smiled. "The great Phoenix wants to settle down

and get married and raise little Phoenixes. Never thought I'd see the day."

"Believe me, the great Phoenix would've settled down roughly two point five weeks after meeting Girl Riley if he could've talked her into it."

Baby took a sip of his beer. "Really? She always made it seem like you weren't interested in marriage either. We all know how she feels about marriage."

He shrugged. "I tried to play it cool. Maybe I played it too cool. But all that is about to change. Full-court press. I've got a ring and everything."

He was biding his time because he knew Wildfire was still afraid he was just in this out of a sense of duty. But he had proof that marriage had been on his mind before MS was even on the radar. When the time was right, he was going to show it to her.

Baby slapped him on the shoulder. "That's good to hear."

"How about you? So many ladies around here, and I haven't seen you really talking to anyone. Quite unusual for you."

"Uh. Listen." Baby shifted on his feet, uncharacteristically awkward. "I might need to discuss something with you."

"Oh yeah? What?"

"A few days ago, right after the race, I… Shit. Look. Nobody knows this, but I've been taking some community college classes for the last couple of years. Almost five actually."

Why would that make Baby uncomfortable? "That's great, man. I might be following in your footsteps soon. What are you studying?"

"Engineering. Maybe. It's a long story. But that's not what I wanted to talk to you about." He ran a hand through his dark hair. "Look. It was your sister's birthday a week and a half ago…"

Oh shit. "With the crazy going on with Amber and the race, I totally forgot. I didn't call Quinn or anything."

"I know."

"Damn it. She always remembers mine. I can't believe I did this again. I— Wait. How did you know it was my sister's birthday?"

"Well, that's what I wanted—"

He was cut off as everyone cheered when Violet and Aiden walked in with huge boxes labeled *Fancy Pants Bakery*. It looked like the wedding cake—or multiple wedding pastries in the form of whatever Violet had at her shop for this last-minute event—had arrived.

But Riley wanted to know more about how Baby knew he'd missed Quinn's birthday.

And why the other man was looking decidedly uncomfortable about it.

"Bollinger, what the hell is going on?"

Riley was cut off again by the bride's surprise laugh and yell. "I know this wrapping paper is from Girl Riley. Phoenix, where are you hiding her? I've got to get a picture of us with it before I open it."

Riley turned away from Baby, his concern about his sister forgotten.

Where was Wildfire? She'd gone out to get the present almost twenty minutes ago.

"She's around here somewhere," he called out. "She brought in the present."

A small blond woman he hadn't met shook her head. "Actually, I brought that in. It was sitting right outside the door with Peyton and Cade's names on it."

Now Riley started really looking around. Had she had some sort of MS flare-up? Fallen and hurt herself?

"There was a note next to the present," the blond woman said. "I didn't read it. Maybe it's from her?"

Peyton reached beside the box to the piece of paper. Riley knew as soon as she unfolded it that it wasn't good. All the color drained from her face as she handed it to her new husband.

Cade read it. "'Phoenix, you took something from me. Now I've taken something from you.'"

All the air had been sucked out of the room. The silence was deafening.

"Who is it from?"

"It's hard to make out the signature," Cade said. "Sayed something."

The entire Linear Tactical team went on alert.

The party was over.

Riley didn't even wait for Cade to finish. He dashed out the door, most of the Linear team on his heels.

There was no sign of Wildfire anywhere in the parking lot or around the building. No sign of Sayed.

He heard curses behind him, but he was too numb with terror to come up with any curses himself.

"Sayed El Kadi. He's the Egyptian we infiltrated two weeks ago, right?" Zac asked. He didn't do much active field-work anymore, but that didn't mean he didn't keep abreast of all the Linear Tactical mission happenings.

Riley looked at Wyatt, then Gavin. They were the ones who had been there. "Would Sayed do this? I know we didn't leave any trace of me being involved."

"We always do our best never to leave any trail back to you. But in this situation the timing was a little too convenient for him to ignore," Wyatt said. "That rescue cost him a lot of money, and more than that, it may have cost him respect. That would be a true insult. One he would take personally."

"He may have already killed her." Riley could barely get the words out.

"No," Gavin said immediately. "That wouldn't make sense. If he had wanted to kill her, he would've just done it here and left the body out in public for you to find."

Now all the air had been sucked out of the universe.

Kendrick Foster, the Linear computer guru, pointed up at the convenience store across the street. "You guys, there are some cameras around here I should be able to access from my computer. We just need to get back to my house."

"We don't have to do that." This from the blond who'd brought in the present.

"Who the hell are you?" He should be gentle, polite. But he had neither gentle nor polite in him. Not while Wildfire was being held by a terrorist known for his brutality.

"This is Neo," Zac said. "She's helped us out more than once."

"I have my laptop here. I never go anywhere without it." She raised an eyebrow at Kendrick as if to ask why he didn't do the same. "Mine's faster than his anyway."

Kendrick looked like he was going to argue, but Wyatt held out a hand. "Get it. We need any intel we can get."

She had it out and on the hood of a car in less than a minute. She and Kendrick were bickering about the best computer nerd stuff to get access to the cameras they needed.

With every word, Riley came closer and closer to losing his shit. Every second these two spent half flirting, half fighting was a second Riley might be in pain.

A hand fell on his shoulder, stopping the ugly words that were about to spew out of his mouth.

"They work better this way. One-upping each other moves them faster. Let them work their way." Baby's whispered words made Riley swallow his biting comments, but only barely. He understood what Baby was saying. How many times had he and his team used inappropriate humor during dangerous stunts? It was a coping mechanism.

He nodded.

Neo had the footage up just a couple minutes later. "Here, and for the record, faster than Blazing Saddles over here could've done it. This is the best picture we're going to get."

She brought up a grainy image that was obviously a reflection of some type.

It was Sayed talking to Wildfire.

"Oh fuck," Wyatt said. "He's here himself."

"What does that mean?"

Wyatt looked over at Gavin, then back to Riley. "Honestly, probably means he came here to kill you. He felt personally slighted by you and wanted to do it himself. But then saw an eye-for-an-eye opportunity with Girl Riley and took it."

Neo and Kendrick were already bickering about something else.

Riley was just trying to keep from screaming. He wasn't sure how much longer he could keep it in.

The thought of all the things Sayed could do to her... might have already done to her...

It was Wyatt who got right in front of Riley's face and cupped his cheeks. "You can't go there, Phoenix. If you have to deal with that later, then we'll find a way, but right now you've got to stay functional. You don't do her any good sitting here playing *what if*. You only do her good if you are firing on all cylinders."

He took a steadying breath and nodded. Wyatt was right and had worked enough of Linear's hostage and kidnap cases to know what he was talking about. He had even lived through tragedy himself.

"I don't know if I can live without her," Riley whispered.

Wyatt shook his head. "You're not going to have to live without her. We're going to get her back. Say it."

"We're going to fucking get her back."

Wyatt patted Riley's cheeks, then reached over and kissed him on the forehead. And there wasn't a single thing weird about it. "That's right. We're fucking going to get her back."

"I've already got an APB out on that limo," Gavin announced. "We can't have cops stopping every single limo on the road, but it at least makes them aware there could be one with a problem."

"It's going toward Reddington City International," Kendrick and Neo said at the same time, still looking at her laptop on the car hood.

"We've logged into the DMV's cams, and unless he's planning to take a vacation in Utah, he's headed to the airport." Kendrick pointed at a map on the screen.

Zac started barking orders to the Linear Tactical guys, falling back to the days when he had been team leader. Everybody headed toward different cars.

Riley was about to get into his when Wyatt grabbed his arm and pulled him to another vehicle. "Get in. I'm driving. No argument."

Riley gritted his teeth and nodded. He wouldn't attempt a stunt in this frame of mind; he shouldn't get behind the wheel either.

Aiden and Baby piled into the back seat. Riley knew others would be right behind them.

There was nothing safe about the speed at which Wyatt pulled out of the parking lot, but it made Riley feel better. Of all the Linear guys, Wyatt spent the least amount of time here in Wyoming and the most time on life or death missions.

And that was very definitely what this was.

"He's trying to get her out of the country," Wyatt said. "I studied Sayed before we went in to rescue Andre and Josh. Sayed is one of the richest men in Egypt and is also one of the most powerful. He's got government ties, business ties. He probably wants to get back to where he has home field advantage."

"Also probably means that Girl Riley is alive," Aiden added. "He wants to toy with you, Phoenix."

Sayed could toy with him all he wanted; Riley just wanted Wildfire safe.

"We've got to stop him from getting her out of the country," Baby said. "Once he's out of the country, our options become a lot more limited."

Every mile felt like a hundred. Baby was providing updates from info he was getting via text.

"Gavin's trying to get Reddington International to refuse to let Sayed's plane take off, but Sayed has diplomatic ties, so they can't get involved. Kendrick and Neo are trying to work some sort of voodoo also, see if they can create a problem with the flight plan—anything to keep them on the ground."

Riley had never felt more helpless in his life.

They were ten miles from the airport when Aiden reached under the seat and pulled out two Glock 26s. He handed one to Wyatt and inspected the other one for himself. "These are the not-so-legal concealed weapons. The legal ones are in the glove box."

Riley opened it and handed one back to Baby. He didn't have to look at his friend to know that he was comfortable with the Glock resting in his hand. He may not have ever been a soldier like his brother, but that didn't mean he didn't know how to fight.

"If Kendrick and Neo can't get the plane grounded electronically, what's our plan?" Aiden asked.

"We can't let that plane take off," Riley bit out, surprised his voice sounded anywhere near normal.

Everyone agreed, but they all knew there was no good way to handle this. It was going to call for desperate measures.

"I know Reddington International isn't a huge airport, but they're not going to let us come running through the terminal, weapons hot." Wyatt didn't take his eyes from the road as he spoke.

Wyatt was right. Ditching the car and going through the terminal wasn't an option. That would require minutes they didn't have.

"Sayed's plane is already on the runway," Baby said. "We don't have that kind of time."

Riley shook his head, gripping the dashboard. "I'll stop and you guys can get out in a second. The only option is going to be to halt all takeoff traffic on the runway. A car driving out there all crazy should do that."

All three men voiced their objections. They didn't want to get out.

Riley held up a hand to stop them. "Look, we're talking about jail time here. There is no way law enforcement is just going to let this slide."

"And there's no way I'm stopping this vehicle while there's any chance we might get Riley off that plane while it's still on the ground." Wyatt's eyes were glued to the road as he tried to milk even more speed out of the vehicle. "I'll slow down if somebody wants to dive out, but I'm not stopping."

"Besides," Aiden continued, "you're going to need man- and firepower to go up against Sayed's jet. The chaos will only keep them grounded so long."

"I—I..." He wasn't sure exactly what to say. These guys were risking a lot for him.

"You guys are family, Phoenix. You and Girl Riley both," Baby said.

"Not to mention all the times you've helped Linear out," Wyatt added. "Hell, you're in this to begin with because of Linear's mission. We don't leave our people behind."

Riley just nodded. For the first time since realizing Wildfire had been taken, he felt hope. Yes, there may be repercussions from them driving onto the runway, but the most important thing was that they were going to get her out of that plane and home safe.

His relief was short-lived.

They were a half mile from the airport, coming up a side road that would lead them directly to the runway rather than the terminal, when Baby received a text from Kendrick.

"Fuck. We're too late. The plane just took off."

Riley gripped the dashboard and looked out the windshield. Sure enough, a small luxury jet was climbing into the sky.

Taking his entire life with it.

Chapter 27

Terror threatened to overwhelm him. Sitting in that car less than a mile from the airport, knowing they'd been so close and were now so far, was eating Riley alive by the second.

Communication was going on all around him. All three of his friends were talking to different people. Riley didn't know who, couldn't even bring himself to form coherent sentences. Every single breath hurt. Finally, he couldn't stand it anymore, he ripped off his seatbelt and stumbled out the car door.

There wasn't any more air outside than there had been inside the car. He gulped in oxygen like he was running a sprint and even then, it wasn't enough.

"Riley. Riley!"

Baby was in his face.

"Keep it together. Falling apart isn't going to help her. This changes the plan but doesn't put us out of the game."

He nodded. Riley had learned long ago that no matter how hopeless the first round looked, that didn't mean the game was lost. But that was a hell of a lot easier to say when it wasn't the life of the woman he loved at stake. Still, he nodded.

"Riley is strong," Baby said.

That, Riley had no doubt about.

"Finn and Zac are on their way. Wyatt and Gavin are already putting together a plan since they've studied Sayed the most. You're going to get her back."

The second vehicle with more of the Linear guys pulled up a few minutes later. They were all talking on the phone also. Riley racked his brain, trying to figure out who he knew in Egypt who could do something…anything.

"Kendrick says the flight plan for that jet was Cairo." Zac ended the call and turned to Riley. "That's probably good news."

But the tightness of the other man's mouth told them all it wasn't *that* good of news.

"I'll keep it together." He was going to have to. If he wanted to be a part of this rescue mission, he was going to have to lock down his fear. "Tell me what you're thinking."

Zac shrugged. "He hasn't killed her outright. Maybe because he wants to torture her and toy with you. Maybe he hopes to make some sort of trade, you for her, or maybe some sick combination of both. The fact she's alive is what we're going to concentrate on."

"What about going public?" Gavin asked. "We've got proof he was in Oak Creek. We could get Andre and his cousin to talk about the fact that they were held by Sayed. It could shift tide in our favor."

Wyatt shook his head. "I think all that would do is force Sayed to kill Riley and get rid of the body. We should only go public as a last resort."

"We have to do something. I can't just wait and do nothing." Riley's whisper was hoarse.

Zac nodded. "You are going to do something. You're

going to use what you have to your advantage, something Sayed doesn't know about: us."

Riley shook his head. "Unless you have some jet pack that can get me onto that plane, I'm not sure Linear Tactical is going to do much good."

"Sayed thinks you're alone, and that, at best, it will take you a while to get anything organized. Finn is on his way with the gear and weapons we'll need to infiltrate. Dorian should be here soon too."

"Gavin and I are already familiar with Sayed's compound," Wyatt added. "I'm sure Kendrick and Neo will stop fighting long enough to give us other pertinent information."

"What about transportation?" Riley looked toward the airport. "I have finances to charter a flight, but it'll take a while to get it organized. Time we don't have."

Baby held up his phone. "Cade just offered his assistance in any way we needed—including the jet he had waiting to take him and Peyton on their honeymoon."

Riley shook his head. "I hardly even know Cade. Why would he do that?"

Baby shrugged. "His wife and your woman are best friends. Like I said, family."

～

LESS THAN AN HOUR LATER, they were in the air on their way to Egypt. Looking around him, it was easy to see why the guys of Linear Tactical had been so effective as Special Forces soldiers.

They were like a well-oiled machine.

Zac, Gavin, and Wyatt pored over the electronic plans Kendrick had sent, discussing different infiltration points and their pros and cons.

Dorian, who Riley hadn't seen in more than a year, had arrived with a petite woman in tow, ready to help. Dorian introduced her as his wife, Ray.

Riley hadn't even known Ghost had a wife.

Ray and Dorian were in the back with Finn, sorting out weapons and gear.

The help didn't stop there. Back in Oak Creek, Baby was making calls on behalf of Linear Tactical, reaching out to military and government contacts they had. Linear had done a lot of favors for a lot of people over the years, and if they had to cash them all in now, they would.

Lyn, Gavin's sister, and her fiancé, Heath, were busy translating anything and everything Kendrick and Neo could provide concerning Sayed, since they were both fluent in Arabic and Lyn was an expert in Egyptian culture.

Riley just wished he had a job, something to keep his mind off Wildfire.

When his phone buzzed in his pocket a few minutes later, it almost startled him. It was an unknown number.

Zac looked up. "Kendrick worked his magic so you can receive calls on your phone."

"It's an unknown number."

"It could be Sayed," Gavin said. "It would be about the right amount of time. You've got to play it cool, Phoenix. Our biggest advantage is that he doesn't know you're so close behind him."

Riley nodded. He hit the receive button. "Hello. Who is this?"

"It's Sayed. I thought you'd be expecting my call."

Riley swallowed the string of curses he wanted to throw in Sayed's direction. Everybody on the Linear Tactical team had a job. He did too. It was time to do it. "Sorry, Sayed. I don't have time to talk about motocross racing right now. My girlfriend is missing."

Wyatt and Zac both nodded.

Silence rang out from the other end of the line and Riley was worried for a moment he'd played it the wrong way. "Did you not receive my note?" Sayed said.

"We got a note, but it was hard to make out the signature and a drink got spilled on it. That was you? What the hell, Sayed? What's going on?"

"You took from me. And now I take from you. It's that simple."

"Dude. Are you pissed because you lost that race? Jesus, man. I thought better of you."

"I know what you did." Sayed's voice was cold. "You were a front. You distracted me so that others could slip in and take what was mine."

"I have no idea what you're talking ab—"

A sob rang out on the other end. Wildfire's sob.

"Your woman seems so strong. It's a shame you care so little about her well-being. She bleeds such a pretty red."

"Goddammit, Sayed!"

Wyatt got right up in Riley's face, mouthing for him to stay calm.

Staying calm while someone hurt Wildfire might be beyond what he was capable of.

"Do you still want to say you had nothing to do with the departure of my previous guests?" Sayed asked.

"No. Fine. Whatever. I admit it. Somebody paid me some money to distract you. But I didn't know they were stealing from you. And she has nothing to do with it. If you've got a problem with me, take it out on me."

"See? Now we are talking like reasonable men. I will trade Miss Wilde for you."

Riley didn't hesitate. "Done. Name the time and place, and I'll be there. Is she still in Wyoming? Are you in Wyoming? I'll drive wherever you want."

The Linear guys were nodding. Wyatt circled his finger in the air, telling him to continue that line of conversation.

"Riley—no!" Wildfire's voice called out. "He's going to kill you. We're already on a plane—"

The sickening sound of flesh hitting flesh filled the cabin before Wildfire cried out once again.

"Don't you touch her, Sayed! I've agreed to meet you. Leave her alone."

Wildfire, be quiet, baby. Don't be your brave self.

"Like I said, she's strong. And she's right, we are no longer in your beautiful Wyoming mountains."

"Fine. I'll get on a plane and come to you. Just tell me where."

"No, I think I'll send my jet to get you, the one you were so adamant about not utilizing last time. And I don't want to give you a chance to pull any of your famous Phoenix stunts. You will come to me the way I insist, and Miss Wilde can go free."

Wyatt made an exaggerated *what the hell* face, obviously wanting Riley to pretend to be skeptical of the plan.

"How do I know I can trust you? How do I know you'll let her go?"

"Unlike you, I'm a man of honor. I do not arrive at a home under the guise of accepting hospitality and then steal from others."

Riley rolled his eyes. Yeah, Sayed was a prince among men.

"Subterfuge is not my way," Sayed continued. "If I'm going to shoot you, you will know it is me. That is true power, looking your enemy in the eye as he dies."

The man obviously meant every word, Riley had to give him that.

"Fine. You're a man of your word. You trade her for me."

"My jet will be there to get you in twenty hours. Be ready. If you're not at the Reddington airport, I'll assume you've decided Miss Wilde should die slowly and painfully."

"I'll be there."

"I'll assume the same if I get word of any law enforcement or government intervention in my direction. No tricks this time, Phoenix."

"Just don't hurt her."

The phone went dead.

There was silence all around him as he stared at the phone.

Zac broke it. "Okay, people. Phoenix bought us a few hours. Let's not waste them."

"Ray and I will inventory exactly what weapons we have," Dorian said. His hand hadn't moved far from his wife's the entire time they'd been on the plane. Riley had never seen any two people so in sync with each other.

"I'll help them." Finn jerked his thumb toward the back, face tight. "Let us know what the plan is, and we'll be ready."

It couldn't be easy for Finn, not after what had happened to his wife Charlie when she'd been kidnapped last year.

"Our best bet is to infiltrate as soon as possible," Gavin said.

Good. *As soon as possible* Riley liked. It meant less time Wildfire was in that bastard's clutches.

Wyatt placed the electronic tablet on the small table between the four chairs facing each other. "Sayed's security is pretty much impossible to get around from the outside. It's why we used Phoenix in the first place to get the kids out a couple of weeks ago. We needed to get inside."

Gavin nodded and pointed to an area on the screen. "The one weakness is near the southwest corner. It's hard to guard with manpower, ironically because of Sayed's motocross course. But to make up for that, he's bulked that area up with electronic security. Security that can only be accessed from inside. Cutting the feed and alarm from the inside is our best bet."

"Okay." Riley nodded. "How do we get inside?"

Wyatt and Gavin shot each other a look. That wasn't good.

Wyatt shrugged, then ran a hand through his black hair. "Probably paying someone off. Someone local. I can already tell you it's not going to be easy—people around there are pretty terrified of Sayed. We weren't successful when we tried before."

Gavin sat down in one of the seats and turned the screen toward Zac and Riley. "The next best option would be to sneak in as workers ourselves. But Sayed will be on alert for something like that, and it won't be as fast as we need it to be. He isn't going to allow any unknown entities inside right now."

Zac picked up the tablet. "Okay, he's highly fortified. What are our outside-the-box options?"

Both men were silent for long minutes. Riley stood and started to pace, biting his tongue to stop demanding a plan. Everybody here was working toward the same goal.

"Single parachute in the dead of night," Wyatt finally said. "We considered it very briefly, but then decided it was too risky. It's not much more than a suicide mission."

Riley stopped pacing. "Would it work?"

Wyatt shrugged, shaking his head. "Possibly. But we eliminated it because the level of expertise required in skydiving was beyond us. Even with the hours we logged in the army."

Riley leaned against the table and looked at the guys. "It's not beyond me."

Every stunt he'd ever completed, the hours of work preparing and practicing and bleeding, not just in skydiving but in it *all*, was coming down to this. "I'm one of the top ten skydivers in the world. If it's doable, I can do it."

Gavin shook his head. "That's just it. We don't know for sure that it's doable."

Fuck that. "If it will save Riley, I'll make sure it's doable. The slimmest of chances is better than no chance at all."

Zac nodded. "Okay, then unless we come up with another plan in the next hour, we go with this. Wyatt, Gavin, get us all up to speed on what's going to happen once Riley successfully parachutes into Sayed's property and cuts off that security feed. Let's figure out what we need."

Riley nodded, glad Zac was treating it like a foregone conclusion that he would be successful.

Because he would be.

Chapter 28

Riley applied pressure to the knife wound on her arm. One of Sayed's men had thrown a cloth napkin at her and yelled something in Arabic, which she assumed meant to stop bleeding all over the place.

The cut could probably use a few stitches, but it wasn't going to kill her. This Sayed guy really had a hard-on for jerking Boy Riley's chain. She was just the most convenient tool for doing that.

The one good thing that had happened since she'd woken up on a plane surrounded by people who wanted to kill her? It definitely put her MS in perspective.

Sitting here in this plane with this psychopath, she could die any minute.

She wanted to live, MS or not.

She peeked out from under her hair at Sayed to where he sat across from her on his luxury jet that was all champagne wishes and caviar dreams. Seriously. There was gold-plated stuff everywhere. Sayed might as well take out a billboard with his picture and the words *Hey, I'm rich*.

She didn't talk to Sayed, hadn't said anything since he'd

backhanded her in the mouth when she'd tried to warn Riley he was in trouble. She needed to be smart. Stay alive for… however long it took Riley to get to her.

It was just a matter of time before that happened. She knew about the undercover work he'd done with Linear Tactical, and that he loved it. They would get her out. Plus, he owed her one, right? They'd agreed she'd saved his life twice, and he owed her.

Looked like he'd be paying that debt sooner than expected.

Her job was to stay alive until he arrived. Pretend to be passive. Weak. Lie. She'd certainly had enough practice over the past week doing that—but lying to the wrong person.

No more lying to Riley, no more hiding.

As long as she got out of this alive.

"Nothing more to say?" Sayed raised a dark eyebrow at her. "American women always have something to say."

She had a role to play in her own rescue. Convincing Sayed that she was weak and terrified and useless didn't make her weak and terrified and useless; it made her smart. Yelling to try to get information to Riley had been a mistake. She needed to be careful not to make another one.

So she didn't respond to Sayed's question, just kept her head down and wounded arm pressed against her chest.

"I'm going to teach Phoenix how to be more polite. Not to ignore, how do they say it, cultural norms. I'm going to teach him respect."

She had to bite her tongue to keep from asking him why he didn't just ask Phoenix out on a date. Sayed was obviously obsessed with him.

She whimpered, shying away as he reached for her, fighting every instinct to use the multiple self-defense moves she knew. She could break Sayed's arm and then probably his nose in under ten seconds.

But that wasn't going to get her off this plane.

Save it.

"Phoenix will do anything for you, won't he?"

"He'll give you money if that's what you want." She purposely made her voice shaky. "But he's not rich. Not rich enough to afford a plane like this."

"I don't need money. I'm not interested in his money at all. I am interested in teaching a young, brash American what happens when he disrespects someone of importance in my culture. Do you know anything about my culture, Miss Wilde?"

She really should've listened to her friend Lyn more closely when the woman had rambled on about ancient Egyptian ideas and languages, her dissertation topic. The most Riley really knew about Egyptian culture came from an online quiz she'd found that determined how many camels someone was worth.

That probably wasn't what Sayed was talking about.

Terrified. Passive. She shook her head. "No."

"So many nowadays think we should be more progressive, but I believe the great Egyptian culture should go back to its basics. There are reasons we are one of the oldest cultures in the world. Because of our strengths. Some would call it barbaric what used to be done to those who did not respect our ways."

He touched her shoulder, and she couldn't stop her flinch.

"I've done nothing the past two weeks but think about the ways I could make your Phoenix understand the true price of insulting someone the way he has insulted me."

Sayed removed his hand and settled into the chair beside her. "In your culture, everyone is so quick to forgive after an apology and charming smile. In my culture, in the *real* Egypt, such a thing is unforgivable. It is paid for with one's life."

Sincerity and belief fairly dripped from Sayed's words. He was absolutely committed to what he was saying. He planned to teach Riley this "lesson" in the most painful way possible.

"If hands were cut off for stealing a loaf of bread, how much worse should it be for someone who enters a home under the guise of friendship and then commits robbery?"

She shook her head, keeping her gaze lowered.

"Undoubtedly your Phoenix thinks he can talk his way out of this, charm me with his American wit, and a wink as he has to so many of his YouTube followers. Not this time. Not again." He stretched out his legs in front of him. "The myth of the Phoenix was of a creature that burned, and then rose from the ashes. This time, Phoenix will only burn."

Riley glanced over at Sayed to find him smiling with authentic joy.

Suddenly, passive and terrified didn't require any acting at all.

PHOENIX WAS ABOUT to make the jump of his life and there wasn't a single camera anywhere in sight to capture it. No doubt the sheer risk alone would have garnered millions of hits.

Riley had learned early in his career that nothing brought out viewers like the possibility of serious hurt.

In this case, he might get seriously dead.

So many things could go wrong with this jump. The wind was already too high to be considered safe. The pilot was nervous and a little sketchy.

Then, once Riley jumped, he had to land with precision. The rooftop he had to land on was roughly the size of a postage stamp. And all it would take was one person of the dozens and dozens Sayed had on his property to look up into the beautiful Egyptian sky and it would be all over for Riley. Gavin hadn't been kidding when he'd said this jump was just short of a suicide mission.

This was not the type of jump he'd normally be willing to risk no matter how many views it got him.

But he was willing to try anything for Wildfire.

Any jump. *Every* jump.

He double-checked his parachuting rig again. It was just him and the pilot on the plane. The rest of the team was on their way into Sayed's compound by land, ready to rendezvous once Riley had interrupted the alarm in the security room.

According to the heat signature scan information Kendrick and Neo had provided—Riley didn't know how they'd gotten that information because it meant hacking a military satellite, but he was damn glad they had—it looked like Sayed was keeping someone in the same holding cell where he'd kept his kidnap victims last time. Wyatt and Gavin had both agreed that Sayed would like that sort of symmetry, and that it was very possible that's where he was keeping Wildfire. It would be the first place they would check, and then they'd go from there based on what they found.

But everything hinged on Riley being able to shut down that security feed and alarm in the southwest corner.

Then the plan was what it always tended to be when he worked with Linear Tactical: get in and get out before anyone was aware.

As much as he'd like to stick around and kick Sayed's ass, all that mattered was getting Wildfire out.

But if Sayed had hurt her... If she was dead...

Riley couldn't even let himself think about it.

But if the worst had happened, that motherfucker was going down.

He had to focus, had to believe that Riley was going to be okay, and he was about to get her out of here.

He touched the long-range comm unit in his ear. Everyone on the team had one.

"Cyclone, my flight should be in range in about five minutes. I'll be going hands-free."

He would need both his hands to successfully land on the roof. His comm unit would run the whole time.

"Roger that, Phoenix," Zac said. "Everyone will maintain mission-critical communication only. We'll all be hands-free."

"Roger that." Riley swallowed. "Zac, if I don't make it… If something happens…"

"We'll get her out, Phoenix. Nobody's leaving here without her. Count on it."

He heard the grunts of agreement all around.

"Thank you. I know you're taking considerable risks, and you all have families of your own."

"We have family inside that compound too," Wyatt said. "The Rileys are part of our family. Thanks for not having to make us say two different names. Makes heartfelt speeches a lot shorter."

Everyone chuckled.

"Not to mention, Charlie will kick my ass if I come home without Riley." The laughter grew at Finn's comment. "Seriously, you guys. We've got a new baby in the house, and if you think Charlie is scary on a good day, you should see her when she hasn't slept in four nights."

There was real fear in Finn's voice, which was hilarious, considering he was well over six foot and his tiny blond wife was barely pushing five. "So, for me, Phoenix, please don't die."

He loved these people. And Wyatt was right. They were family.

He chuckled. "Roger that, Eagle. Everyone will get in and out safely just so you don't get an ass whooping at home."

"All right, let's cut the chatter," Zac said. "Phoenix, we'll see you on the ground."

"Roger that."

Two minutes later, the pilot signaled and said something in Arabic. Riley assumed that meant it was time. He slid open the door, making out the lights of Sayed's house and grounds far below them. The plan was for the plane to be high enough that it wouldn't draw any attention. Riley would free-fall for as long as possible, then pull his chute at the last moment.

"I'm jumping in five, four, three, two, one."

He let himself fall out of the airplane.

He wished he weren't making this jump now, but he was never going to get tired of this feeling. That free-fall lurch, the wind flowing by him at speeds that made talking or even thinking almost impossible. All he could do was feel.

The house and grounds came up quickly. At the very last minute, way later than what would be considered a recommended safe distance, Riley pulled the parachute cord, saying a small prayer of thanks when the thing actually opened correctly.

He fought the winds to steer himself to where he needed to be. He hit the roof hard but ignored the jarring impact, unbuckled himself, and turned to yank at his black parachute. Once it was in his arms, he stuffed it into the sack and dumped it near the corner of the roof.

"Landed."

"Roger that. We're in position."

He wasn't sure exactly who'd said that and didn't stop to figure it out. Every second counted.

Navigating off the second-story roof took a little bit of gymnastic coordination. Using his core strength, he lowered himself over the side and onto the open portico below.

He pulled the tranq gun from one of his holsters and kept it pointed in front of him. They wouldn't make this a bloodbath if they didn't have to. And some of the people who worked here were regular household employees, not soldiers who would try to kill them.

But Riley also had a second weapon in a back holster if tranquilizers weren't an option.

Keeping to the shadows, he made his way down the hall until he was outside the security office's door. This place wasn't well guarded. Sayed had concentrated his manpower on the outer walls, trusting no one could get inside. Riley opened the unlocked door and walked inside. A single man sat watching the camera feeds.

The man never even turned around at the sound of the door opening.

He was in the middle of saying something in Arabic as Riley squeezed the trigger, the tranq dart shooting out and hitting the man in the neck.

The guy made an irritated sound, slapping at his neck before slumping over to the side, unconscious in his chair.

Riley left him where he was and began typing in the code Kendrick had given him. Moments later the system rebooted. The cameras facing the southwest corner flickered to static, and the light on the console that had been red turned green.

"Cyclone, the southwest perimeter systems are shut down. You can move in undetected."

"Roger that," Zac said. "We've got a lot of extra manpower around here. Sayed might not be expecting us yet, but he's not just sitting on his ass either. It's going to take us a little extra time to get there."

Riley wasn't going to wait. "I'll meet you at the holding cell. If Girl Riley isn't in there, we're going to need to know that sooner rather than later."

"Roger that."

He moved silently out of the security room back down the hall the way he'd come.

There weren't very many of Sayed's men around. Like Zac said, they were busy protecting the perimeter.

Keeping his back to the wall, he made his way as quickly as possible toward the place he hoped they were holding Wildfire. The tranq gun had bought them a couple hours at most. A room-by-room search of this entire compound was going to take longer than that.

When he finally got down the hallway and saw the two guards posted outside the door, he knew he'd found her.

"*Salām 'alaykum*," Riley said as he walked down the hall, still in the shadows, using the Egyptian greeting Sayed himself had said to him.

Again, not expecting trouble, the men responded likewise.

Riley pulled up his gun and shot them with the tranquilizer before they could even realize something was wrong. He found the key to the door in one of the men's pockets and immediately opened it, wincing when the door creaked way too loudly.

His heart shattered into a million pieces at the sound of sobbing coming from over in the corner. Oh God.

"Wildfire?" He ran over to her.

"Riley?"

He could make out the tear tracks and the bruising on her face in the dim light. Her arm was wrapped in some sort of bandage, blood seeping through it. And those were only the wounds he could see. God only knew what had happened to her.

"Oh God, baby, don't cry. It's going to be okay. I'm going to get you out of here." He wanted to pull her into his arms but stopped himself. He had to consider the fact that the unthinkable might've happened to her and she might not want to be touched by him or any man.

"You got here a lot faster than I thought you would."

He was amazed at how even her voiced sounded. "Are you okay? Oh God—"

She reached out and cupped his cheeks. "I'm fine. I swear. Just this cut on my arm and a little bruising on my face."

"But you were crying so hard…"

"Part of my plan. Make them think I'm scared and weak and useless as possible." Her smile lit up her face.

Lit up his *world*.

"You are the most amazing woman I have ever known or will ever know." He reached in and kissed her gently on the lips. "Let's get out of here."

He helped her stand and led her back toward the door, but when she grabbed his arm and tugged, he stopped. "I want to get married."

So much for his planned proposal. "Yes. A thousand times yes. Every day for the rest of my life yes."

She reached up on her tiptoes and kissed him. "Now let's get out of here."

"Congrats," Wyatt said in the barest of whispers through the comm unit. "We're still pinned down."

He'd forgotten everyone could hear what he was saying.

"Roger that. I've got Girl Riley. We're coming to you." He pointed to the comm unit in his ear so she would know who he was talking to. He grabbed her hand and they made their way forward.

She stayed right on his heels as they crept back down the hall and then outside. They ducked around sections of the motocross course, headed for the hole he'd made in security. Maybe they'd make it out of this without needing the team at all.

Riley had no idea what Sayed would do when he discovered Riley had somehow tricked him again. But that would have to be a problem for another day.

He spotted the low section of wall, and they were about to make a dash for it when suddenly all the lights from the motocross course turned on. It was nearly blinding after the dimness.

Sayed and a dozen of his men surrounded them, weapons pointed directly at them.

"Drop the gun right now, or you both die this second."

Shit.

Riley looked around. There was nowhere to run. Nowhere to send Wildfire running while Riley fought them off.

Sayed stepped out of the shadows, head tilted, eyebrows raised as he looked at Riley's gun. Riley eased his finger off the trigger, then set it on the ground. One of Sayed's men came and took Riley's other weapon out of its holster and stepped back.

"So, we meet again, Phoenix. Once again on the motocross course. I think this time perhaps I will be the winner."

There was no sound from his comm unit. Riley didn't know what that meant, perhaps that the team was too close to be able to talk safely.

But it could also mean that the team had been silently taken out.

"This was never personal for me, Sayed. Just a job. Business. You understand that, right?" He slid an arm around

Wildfire and pushed her behind his back. It wouldn't do much good, there were guys behind them too, but if Sayed decided to shoot him, he didn't want the bullet to hit her.

"You got here much more quickly than I expected. You're a tricky one. And, once I discovered you had links to these men from the company called Linear Tactical, I wasn't expecting you to come alone. But skydiving was smart. Except, how did you plan to escape?"

"I was just taking it one step at a time, honestly. I figured I'd get us off your property first, then worry about the rest."

Sayed had no idea Riley's friends were here.

Sayed nodded, obviously trying to understand Riley's plan. "You might have made it to Cairo, but that would be as far as you could go. I have eyes and ears everywhere in Cairo. That's how I learned a plane had taken off from Quwaisna Airport with a single white man who wanted to skydive in the middle of the night. Sounded like someone I was familiar with."

"Sayed, listen, I know you took it as a personal insult when I helped break out the people you were holding. But it was business."

"Business or not, you insulted me and my household and my hospitality. That must be answered for. Not only you, but all those you work with. How does it feel knowing that you have unleashed the wrath of old? Not only on you, but on your associates and their families."

He held up a file in his hand. "Zac McKay. Looks like he has a fiancée named Anne Griffin? Finn Bollinger. What a shame the death of his wife and children will be."

"Goddammit, Sayed. This is between you and me. This medieval-revenge bullshit is out of control."

"No, not medieval. Much, much earlier than medieval. *Ancient* revenge." Sayed's smile was pure evil. "You chose the wrong person to slight, to steal from. It is a matter of honor.

Something you and your young country know nothing about. It is time for you to learn these actions will not be tolerated any longer."

"Buy us two minutes," Wyatt's voice whispered in his ear. Riley had never been so happy to hear a voice.

But two minutes was an eternity in a situation like this.

"Sayed, be reasonable." Riley held his hands out in front of him. He could feel Wildfire plastered against his back. "You're talking about killing innocent women and children. They have nothing to do with anything that has happened here."

"Oh, I know all too well that innocent women and children are sometimes collateral damage."

Oh shit. This was way more than just spouting ancient-end-of-days bullshit. This was personal for Sayed.

And when Sayed lowered the file in his hands and raised a gun, Riley wasn't even sure they had the last few seconds the team needed to get into place.

"Don't worry, they will die quickly, which is more than my wife and children were given."

"Sayed, look, man, I'm really sorry about your family." He reached out and tucked Riley more firmly behind him. "I've got an idea. You and I can work together. Take revenge on the people who did this to your family. I have connections all over the world."

Riley was just making shit up as he went, praying he was giving the team enough time.

Sayed gestured with his head, and two of his men began walking toward him and Riley.

"No. The loss of my family was a gift. It showed me that the modern way holds no honor, only the ancient way. Yes, I like my motocross course and the internet. But when it comes to what is inside a man"—Sayed tapped himself on the chest with his gun—"modern is useless. Your friends will die. Their families will die. Because I have learned the laws of the ancient. Mercy is for the weak."

"It doesn't need to be this way."

"These men around me, they do what I tell them to because they know what will happen to their families if they do not. What I do to your friends and their families will just reinforce that in their minds."

Sayed's man ripped Wildfire from his grip.

There was nothing Riley could do. All he could do was trust that his friends—his *family*—would take care of them.

"Kill her. Shoot him in the knees and take him back to the cell."

"No!" Girl Riley began to struggle against the man holding her.

This was it. They were out of time. The team was either about to make their move or they were going to be too late.

Riley turned his back on Sayed. "Wildfire, look at me."

Those beautiful hazel eyes, wide and full of fear, turned to him. He didn't want her to see what was about to happen. He yanked her from the man, into his arms, holding her face against his chest. "I love you. Should we go back to Bali for our honeymoon?"

A single shot rang out in the night, but Sayed and all of his men fell to the ground, including the ones closest to him and Wildfire.

Riley didn't hesitate; he knew what had happened.

Sayed had signed his own death warrant as soon as he had mentioned harming the families of the Linear Tactical team. He didn't know which one of them had made the kill shot, but it didn't matter. Any of them could have, and would have, done it.

The rest of the men were merely unconscious, shot with tranquilizers. Whatever hold Sayed had had on them would be gone once they woke up.

He grabbed Riley's hand and they ran for the closest section of the wall.

Chaos and shouting went up behind them, but they didn't look back.

One by one the rest of the Linear team joined them, and they disappeared into the night.

It was time to go home.

Chapter 29

"I love you. You know that, right?"

Riley was perched on the countertop, watching the world-famous Phoenix load the dishwasher.

They'd been home from their very short stint in Egypt for a week and had barely gotten out of bed the entire time.

He shot her a look from the corner of his eye. "I'm already doing the dishes; you don't have to butter me up."

Her hands were stiff, and she was a little tired. MS stuff. Instead of making a big deal about it, he'd just set her up on the countertop and done the dishes himself.

And she did love him. To distraction. But there was something she needed to say.

"That stuff I said about getting married when we were in Egypt? We don't have to do it. We were both under a shit ton of stress at Sayed's compound."

She was glad Sayed was dead—she wasn't going to lie. They'd found out later his family had died pretty horrifically, and she was sorry for that, but he had been half insane. He never would have stopped coming after Riley or her or the people at Linear Tactical. So no, she wasn't sad.

Phoenix turned slowly and deliberately away from the dishwasher, grabbing a towel, and dried his hands. "Do you not want to get married anymore?"

She stretched her hands out in front of her, easing their stiffness. "I do. Just…you haven't mentioned it again since we've gotten home. So I thought maybe you'd just gotten caught up in the moment while we were there."

"I wanted to marry you day four after meeting you."

She rolled her eyes. There was no way he'd wanted to marry her for that long and never really mentioned it. "Look. I just want you to feel like you have options. I don't want MS to be the reason you tie your life to mine."

He pushed back from the sink and walked over to her, stripping off his shirt as he went.

Good Lord, would the sight of his naked chest ever not affect her? "Are you trying to distract me with sex, Harrison? If so, it's working."

He reached down and took her hand and placed it on his heart. "I want you to look at this tattoo again."

She trailed her fingers along the words. "My greatest adventure. You still never told me what that is."

He took her hand down from the ink. "Look at it closer."

She had no idea what point he was trying to make. There were the words around the outside of the globe. What more was there to see?

He flexed his pecs just a little—*show off*—and she saw the upper edge of the globe wasn't made of a solid line at all.

"They're numbers." She looked closer at them and realized they were…"Coordinates? For where?"

"Yup. Ready to go geocaching? Grab your coat and pocket tracker. No cheating."

She jumped down from the counter. They both enjoyed geocaching, even though it wasn't so trendy anymore. She could cheat and google the coordinates, but what would be the fun in that?

"All right, you're on. But what does geocaching have to do with us getting or not getting married?"

He moved in closer, his arms resting on either side of the counter around her. "You think this idea of marriage is new to me. It's not. MS, no MS, crazy Egyptians kidnapping you, it doesn't matter. You have always been it for me, Wildfire. I just want to prove it to you so there is no remaining doubt."

Not that she had much doubt anyway.

He'd basically moved in over the past week. She'd sat with him as he'd had numerous video conference meetings with both the Adventure Channel and his YouTube video team.

For the foreseeable future, Phoenix would be doing much less international traveling. There would still be stunts, but they'd be in proximity to Oak Creek.

She'd watched closely to make sure he didn't feel resentful of these changes, but if anything, he'd seemed happier. When she'd pressed, he'd just kissed her and told her Phoenix wasn't who he was, it was just what he *did*.

She loved who he was. What he *did* didn't matter to her as long as he was happy.

But what this geocaching location had to do with marriage or proving his love, she had no idea.

Twenty minutes later, they were on the outskirts of Oak Creek. As they turned down the side road, she realized where they were headed.

That house. The cabin she'd loved so much.

"I know where we're going," she told him. "We can stop. Somebody else already bought it. There's a family living there. I checked months ago."

She'd cried that day. It had been a sign that she and

Riley weren't meant to get married. Which was stupid. Who made a decision about that based on a house?

He kept driving until they were able to see it, then stopped the car.

"I bought it."

"What?"

He reached into the glove box and pulled out the top sheet of a deed of sale, sure enough, for that very house.

"I don't understand. There's a family living in it now."

"The Williamses. They needed a one-year lease, and you weren't anywhere near ready to get married, so win-win."

"You bought this house? When? Why? I don't understand."

"When? The day after we drove by and you fell in love with it. Why? Because you looked at me and said you could picture our future here. Three kids, and sitting in rocking chairs by the fireplaces. That was enough for me. Just the *chance* that you'd share that with me was enough for me to buy the house. Marry me, Wildfire."

This man, this Phoenix who could burn and rise and do *anything*, wanted to live a life with her.

She was done questioning it. She was just going to spend the rest of her life enjoying him.

"Yes. I'll marry you. I love you."

He reached for her hand and put it on his heart once more. "Ask me again."

She knew what he meant. "What's your greatest adventure?"

"You, Wildfire. You and whatever future we have together. You are my greatest adventure."

Bonus Epilogue

Two and a Half Years Later

ZAC MACKAY HELD a hammer in his hand and looked out at the newest addition to the Linear Tactical facility.

Not just the newest. The most important. Perhaps the greatest teaching tool that would ever be utilized here.

This was truly the way of the future. And it was finished. All the Linear Tactical guys had banded together to make sure this facility became operational today. The need for it was crucial.

There was no one else he'd rather have standing with him at this monumental moment than the men with him here now.

Finn. Aiden. Gavin. Wyatt. Dorian. The original group who'd served with him in the Special Forces and had been with him as the dream of Linear Tactical became a reality nearly eight years ago now.

His brothers-in-arms.

His *brothers*.

Dorian and Ray had been showing up in Oak Creek more and more over the past year, Ray's features less pinched and tortured. Zac even heard the small woman laughing earlier today. Everyone had stopped for a second at the sound, then immediately went back to work not wanting to draw attention to it.

Nobody had needed to say what they'd all been thinking: how beautiful that sound was.

Of course, Ray had multiple reasons to laugh now, didn't she? Or at least two very distinct ones. Nobody had seen that coming. But they'd all been thrilled when it did.

There were others here Zac hadn't served in the military with but who were just as important to him.

Gabriel Collingwood, the Navy SEAL who'd stormed into Oak Creek following his sister and then had stayed and made himself Jordan Reiss's personal guardian angel.

Jordan Reiss *Collingwood*. The two had gotten married on a beach in Maui almost two years ago now. Zac had been honored to be there watching them officially declare their love for and commitment to each other.

Zac's life would always be tied to Jordan's in tragedy, but the young woman deserved the happiness Gabriel was determined to give her.

Cade Conner was here too. The music superstar had been a huge financial part of Linear Tactical at its onset. His money hadn't been needed to fund this latest addition to the facility, but he'd still been here in support.

His wife Peyton, and daughters Jess and newborn Ella had been touring with him the past two months. Jess was currently glued to Ethan's side, where she'd been since the minute she got home, the two of them inseparable as always, even as they got older.

Zac had laughed watching Finn nearly kill his pre-teen this summer. Ethan had never been one for moping, but had seemed a little lost without Jess. Charlie had put him to work babysitting his younger siblings Thomas, a toddler into everything, and Derek almost six months old and just starting to scoot around. That had kept the kid busy.

Boy and Girl Riley were both here, although neither of them really had a stake in or use for this new facility. Phoenix was surprisingly terrible with tools, given his talents at so many other physical endeavors. But he'd still been there, lending support.

And been by Girl Riley's side for every step in her MS journey. It had been a learning process for her as an individual, them as a couple, and all of them as extended family who'd wanted to help however they could.

Riley had learned to prevent her MS flare-ups as much as possible by figuring out her triggers and avoiding them when she could. An ever-changing blend of the correct amount of exercise, diet, rest, and medicine.

She'd gotten herself a t-shirt they all loved: *Multiple sclerosis...an autoimmune disease. Because the only thing strong enough to kick my ass is me.*

Girl Riley had taken an extended leave of absence from her job as an ER nurse last year so she could travel around with Phoenix while he filmed the first season of *Phoenix Rises*. She'd gotten quite a bit of screen time too. The Adventure Channel had expanded the program to include her MS struggles. She'd become a voice for millions of people suffering with similar autoimmune diseases: lupus, celiac, rheumatoid arthritis, and the many, many others that afflicted so many.

Phoenix had had to share the spotlight with another Phoenix rising.

Which he'd obviously been more than happy to do. Those Rileys were going to be just fine.

"There's really only one word for this piece of beauty:

strategery." Baby flipped a wrench around in his hand—catching it in a way that spoke of years of familiarity. He also wouldn't be affected much by this newest Linear Tactical facility, but he'd not only helped build it, he and Kendrick had designed the damned thing.

Finn rolled his eyes. "I know your Ivy League wife doesn't let you get away with those sort of made-up words."

Baby grinned. "My gorgeous bride has no problem with whatever words I use as long as when we're in bed I—"

Finn popped a hand over his brother's mouth. "Please. I do not want to hear about your sex life."

Baby chuckled behind his brother's hand.

Gavin crossed his arms over his chest, just as proud as Zac. "Think of the skills that will be learned here. Leadership. Situational awareness. Agility. Downright survival."

Dorian reached down at his feet and grabbed a water bottle. "I never would've believed Linear would expand to include something like this."

Zac clapped his friend on the shoulder. "And here you are about to be the one to get the most use of it, Ghost."

"I thought I'd gotten my miracle the day I discovered Ray was alive." Dorian glanced over his shoulder at where Ray was over talking to the other wives. Their thirteen-year-old son and eleven-year-old daughter were with her, running around with Ethan and Jess. "But those two…they completed me in a way I didn't even know was missing."

"Your family's story is not a traditional one, that's for sure." Gavin rubbed some grease off his hands. "But it's damned beautiful."

Dorian grinned and bumped fists with Kendrick who was standing next to him. The most dire of circumstances had caused the two of them to become even closer friends in the last year. "You got that right."

Considering three out of the four of Dorian's family

were legally dead in the eyes of the government, it was definitely untraditional.

But the unadulterated love shining out of Dorian's eyes? Beautiful.

"Be a while before you'll be using this, Zac," Gavin said. "Me too, I guess."

Zac looked over at his own bride, holding their six-month old daughter in a sling against her slender frame, talking to some of the other women.

Annie had known terror. First, when they'd gotten together four years ago, and then again with the almost-tragedy on their wedding day eighteen months ago. It was still hard for Zac to let her out of his sight.

But through it all, Annie had never lost the quiet, gentle smile everyone loved about her.

Zac glanced over at Noah Dempsey, also former-military and Gavin's cousin, and gave the man a nod. If it wasn't for him and his wife Marilyn, Zac's world might've been crushed on his wedding day. Noah may be Gavin's family by blood, but he was Zac's family in every other way possible.

Zac was glad he and Marilyn and their two kids were here today. Glad all his extended family were here today for this important event.

"Alright, guys, I think this is as complete as it's ever going to be," Zac announced. "It's time we opened this thing for business. I'm ready to see if it can live up to the hype."

"Hear, hear," Finn said. "Let a new generation of tactical awareness training begin."

"LOOK at our big alpha men over there." Charlie laughed from where she was getting out food at the picnic tables with the wives and girlfriends.

The women all knew the men didn't expect them to just stay over here for "women's work." But none of them were dumb enough to get in the guys' way when they were in full tactical mode. All the women had known they were falling in love with warriors from the beginning.

Not that they could've stopped themselves from falling even if they'd wanted to.

Violet reached over and grabbed baby Derek so Charlie could move more easily. "I know. Standing around congratulating themselves like they just created some sort of huge training facility rather than a playground."

Ray began opening bags of chips and laying them on the table. "You know they've been planning that thing down to the last detail. It's all Dorian has been talking about for weeks. He and Theo met with Baby about the design more than once."

Ray was glowing.

Annie was honestly thrilled to have her here talking—to just have her here at all interacting with people would've been enough. But Ray was so much more than talking. She was smiling and laughing. She'd come so far from those heartbreaking, noise-reducing headphones she'd worn over her ears for so long.

Ray's life hadn't been easy or traditional. No one should be surprised that her journey into motherhood had been unique too.

She'd been thrust into it—sink or swim.

She'd swum. Amazingly well, she'd swum.

Theo and Savannah were her children—it was obvious in every glance and touch. Maybe not by blood, but in every way that mattered. The kids adored her and Dorian also.

A family of survivors all willing to protect each other no matter what.

The results of Ray's medical tests in a file on her desk at

the hospital weighed heavily on Annie's mind. Ray had been through enough, and Annie hated to have to give her difficult news.

Annie had hard news for both Ray and Baby's new wife.

The talks were going to be hard. Requiring life-changing decisions from both women and their husbands. The knowledge of it weighed on Annie.

But this wasn't the place or time to discuss it. This was a time for celebration and laughter.

Case in point, all the kids running and cheering towards the new playground now that the men had deemed it ready. Ethan and Jess ran with Theo and Savannah, slowing to let two-year-old Thomas run with them. Noah and Marilyn's kids, Sam and Missy, were right there in the fray too, always welcome when they were in town.

Annie kissed the top of Becky's head in the sling at her chest. She hated the choices her friends were going to have to make but was selfishly thankful she didn't have to make them herself.

Becky shifted and opened her big blue eyes. Zac's eyes. "Hi, baby girl," Annie whispered.

"Are you really going to make me wait until next week to come into your office and talk about the test results?" Girl Riley walked over, then reached down and kissed the soft fuzz on Becky's head before knocking Annie's hips with her own.

"It's nothing bad, I promise." The least of the concerning news she needed to give.

"Then tell me now. Is it a new MS breakthrough somewhere? I promise I won't get my hopes up just because you tell me there's a new type of medicine. I know not every MS medical breakthrough will benefit me."

Annie smiled at her friend. Riley had been doing so well with her day-to-day health challenges. It hadn't been easy, but Mrs. Riley Harrison was a trooper, especially with Mr. Riley Harrison right beside her every step of the way.

"Just come in next week. We don't need to get into it here."

Riley's eyes narrowed. "Now you've really got my attention. What's going on?"

Annie shook her head. "Seriously, it's not—"

"Look, just spit it out. I can take it. Was it something with my latest MRI?"

Riley was bracing herself for bad news. Damn it, this wasn't what Annie had been trying to do.

"No, not at all. I promise." She touched Riley's arm. "We'll talk about it in the office on Monday."

"It's MS related. Damn it, I knew it. Knew things had been going too good lately. I knew if—"

"You're pregnant, Riley."

"—I changed my meds I…" Riley's eyes widened, and words trailed off. "What?"

"You're going to have a baby," Annie whispered. Nobody was really listening to their conversation, but Annie didn't want to announce it.

Riley shook her head and backed up, stumbling a bit and stretching her hand back to catch herself on the nearby picnic table.

"Wildfire!" Boy Riley yelled, as always, aware of what was going on with his wife. "Clumsy or medical?"

Annie knew that was their code, one Girl Riley responded very well to. She didn't want every mishap she had to automatically be lumped under MS. Boy Riley always asked—knew that fighting her own battles was important to her.

Girl Riley turned to look at her husband, then back at Annie. "Are you sure?"

Annie reached over and squeezed her hand. "Yes. And

before you ask, no, there shouldn't be any complications related to MS. As a matter of fact, many women report fewer flare-ups while being pregnant."

"Wildfire?" Boy Riley was jogging over to them now. "You've got me a little worried. Clumsy or medical, sweetheart?"

Girl Riley turned towards him. "Neither. Pregnant."

Now it was the great Phoenix's turn to stumble just a little. "*Pregnant?*"

Girl Riley nodded.

He turned to Annie. "For real? Is it safe? Okay?"

"Yes. It's absolutely safe and okay. No more risk than any other pregnancy."

Annie stepped out of the way as Phoenix went and knelt in front of his wife and tenderly kissed her still-flat belly. "We're going to have a baby, Wildfire."

She trailed her fingers through his hair. "Just like that vision I had in our house."

He stood up and turned back to the guys. "We're going to have a baby!" He picked Riley up and spun her around. "I'm going to be a dad."

"Please don't name the kid Riley," Kendrick yelled. "Your names are confusing enough as it is."

Everyone laughed and soon hugs were being shared all around. The kids enjoyed the new playground and the parents got out the rest of the food and drinks to make the most of this gorgeous Wyoming summer night.

"You okay?"

Annie leaned backwards as Zac's strong, familiar arms came around her and Becky, pulling them both against him.

"Yes. I didn't mean to tell Riley about being pregnant. But she was worried it was something bad."

"Definitely not bad. The best. They're going to be a family."

She looked around at this crazy crowd—everyone passing around babies and food, laughing and talking all over each other. "We're already a family. It's just going to grow a little more."

She thought once more of the other news she still had to break. Riley had definitely been the easiest of the three. What was coming wouldn't be as easy. But this family would get through it the way they did everything.

Together.

About the Author

"Passion that leaps right off the page." - Romantic Times Book Reviews

USA TODAY bestselling author Janie Crouch writes what she loves to read: passionate romantic suspense. She is a winner and/or finalist of multiple romance literary awards including the Golden Quill Award for Best Romantic Suspense, the National Reader's Choice Award, and the RITA© Award by the Romance Writers of America.

Janie has lived in Germany (due to her husband's job as support for the U.S. Military) for the past five years, with her hubby and four teenagers. When she's not listening to the voices in her head—and even when she is—she enjoys engaging in all sorts of crazy adventures (200-mile relay races; Ironman Triathlons, treks to Mt. Everest Base Camp) traveling, and movies of all kinds.

Her favorite quote: "Life is a daring adventure or nothing." ~ Helen Keller.

facebook.com/janiecrouch

amazon.com/author/janiecrouch

instagram.com/janiecrouch

bookbub.com/authors/janie-crouch

Printed in the USA
CPSIA information can be obtained
at www.ICGtesting.com
LVHW091604070224
771186LV00065B/1882